PUFFIN BOOKS

Also by Robin Stevens:

MURDER MOST UNLADYLIKE

ARSENIC FOR TEA

FIRST CLASS MURDER

MISTLETOE AND MURDER

Available online:

THE CASE OF THE BLUE VIOLET

THE CASE OF THE DEEPDEAN VAMPIRE

Tuck-box-sized mysteries starring Daisy Wells and Hazel Wong

Coming soon:

CREAM BUNS AND CRIME

Tricks, tips and tales from the Detective Society

JOLLY FOUL PLAY

A MURDER MOST UNLADYLIKE MYSTERY

ROBIN STEVENS

PUFFIN

PUFFIN BOOKS

UK | USA | Canada | Ireland | Australia
India | New Zealand | South Africa

Puffin Books is part of the Penguin Random House group of companies
whose addresses can be found at global.penguinrandomhouse.com.

www.penguin.co.uk
www.puffin.co.uk
www.ladybird.co.uk

First published 2016

005

Text copyright © Robin Stevens, 2016
Cover, map and illustrations copyright © Nina Tara, 2016

The moral right of the author and illustrator has been asserted.

Set in ITC New Baskerville

Printed in Great Britain by Clays Ltd, St Ives plc

A CIP catalogue record for this book is available from the British Library.

ISBN: 978–0–141–36969–3

All correspondence to:
Puffin Books
Penguin Random House Children's
80 Strand, London WC2R 0RL

To my parents.
Everything I write is really for you –
this book especially so.

JOLLY FOUL PLAY

Being an account of

The Case of the Murder of Elizabeth Hurst,
an investigation by the Wells and Wong Detective Society.

Written by Hazel Wong
(Detective Society Vice-President and Secretary), aged 14.

Begun Wednesday 6th November 1935.

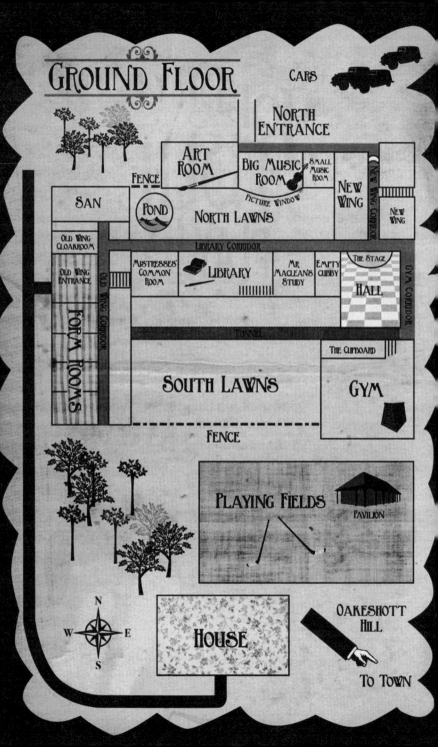

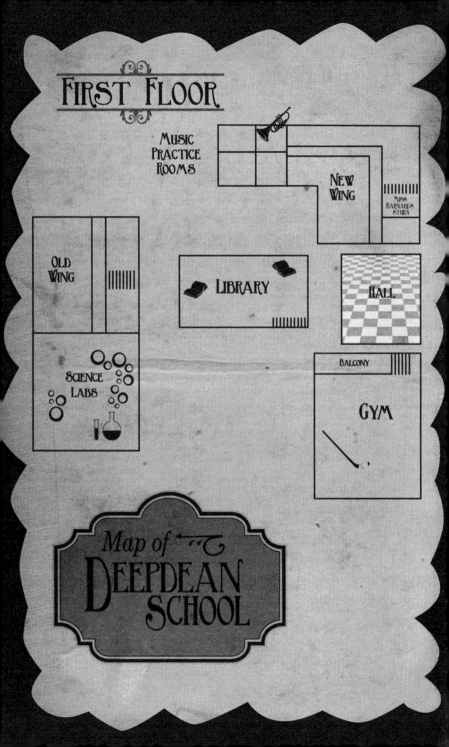

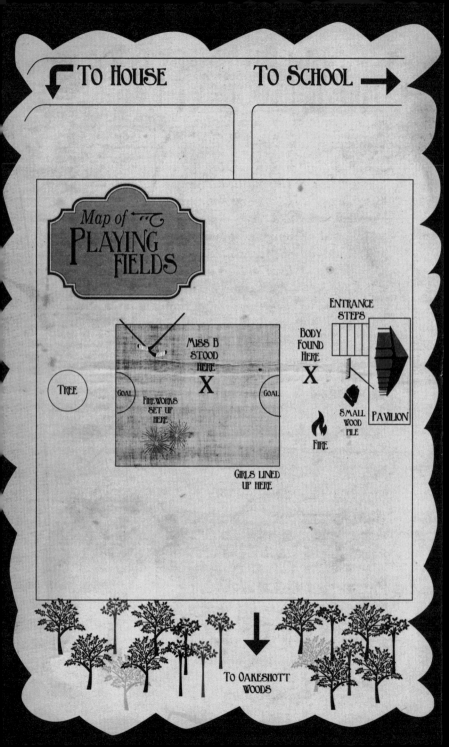

DEEPDEAN SCHOOL

THE STAFF

Miss Barnard – *Headmistress*
Miss Lappet – *History and Latin mistress*
Mr MacLean – *Reverend*
Mademoiselle Renauld, 'Mamzelle' – *French mistress*
Miss Runcible – *Science mistress*
Miss Morris – *Music and Art mistress*
Miss Dodgson – *English mistress*
Miss Talent – *Games mistress*
Mrs Minn, 'Minny' – *Nurse*
Mr Jones – *Handyman*
Matron – *Matron*

THE GIRLS

Daisy Wells – *Fourth Former and President of the Wells &
Wong Detective Society*
Hazel Wong – *Fourth Former and Vice-President and
Secretary of the Wells & Wong Detective Society*

HEAD GIRL

Elizabeth Hurst

PREFECTS

Florence Hamersley
Lettice Prestwich
Una Dichmann
Enid Gaines
Margaret Dolliswood

BIG GIRLS

Pippa Daventry
Alice Murgatroyd
Astrid Frith
Heather Montefiore
Emmeline Moss
Jennifer Stone
Elsie Drew-Peters

FOURTH FORMERS

Lavinia Temple – *Assistant and Friend of the Detective Society*
Rebecca 'Beanie' Martineau – *Assistant and Friend of the Detective Society*
Kitty Freebody – *Assistant and Friend of the Detective Society*

Clementine Delacroix
Sophie Croke-Finchley
Rose Pritchett
Jose Pritchett

THIRD FORMERS

Binny Freebody
Martha Grey
Alma Collingwood
The Marys

SECOND FORMER

Betsy North

FIRST FORMERS

Emily Dow
Charlotte Waiting

PART ONE

SPARKS WILL FLY

1

We were all looking up, and so we missed the murder.

I have never seen Daisy so furious. She has been grinding her teeth (so hard that *my* teeth ache in sympathy) and saying, 'Oh, Hazel! How could we not notice it? We were *on the spot*!'

You see, Daisy needs to know things, and see everything, and get in everywhere. Being reminded that despite all the measures she puts in place (having informants in the younger years, ingratiating herself with the older girls and Jones the handyman and the mistresses), there are still things going on at Deepdean that she does not understand – well, that has put her in an even worse mood than the one she has been in lately.

And, if I am honest, I feel strangely ashamed. The Detective Society has solved three real murder mysteries so far, and yet we still missed a murder taking place under our noses, in our very own Deepdean School for Girls – the place where we began our detective careers one year ago.

It really is funny to think about that. It seems in a way as though we have not moved at all – or as though we have made a circle, and come all the way back to the beginning again. I suppose I still *look* almost exactly like the Hazel I was when I ran into the Gym and found Miss Bell, our Science mistress, lying on the floor last October. I am not much taller, anyway. When I measured myself last week, I found I have hardly grown at all – or at least, not upwards. My hair is still straight and dark brown, my face is still round, and I still have the spot on my nose (I suppose it must be a different spot, but it does not look that way). Inside, though, I feel quite different. All the things that have happened the past year have made me quite a new shape, I think – one who has faced up to the murderer at Daisy's home, Fallingford, and defied my father to solve the Orient Express case. On the other hand, sometimes I think that even though Daisy keeps on shooting upwards, and becoming blonder and lovelier than ever, she has stayed the same inside. She bounces back from things, like a rubber ball – not even what happened at Fallingford could truly alter her.

Before the fifth of November, I had not been enjoying Deepdean much this term. Just like the changes that have taken place in me, the school has felt different from last year, and not at all in a good way. It has felt as though something awful were rushing towards us all term. Last night was dreadful, but now it has happened I feel almost relieved. It is like the difference between waiting to go in to the dentist and sitting in his chair.

And now that there is a murder to solve, Daisy and I can be the Detective Society again. It is sometimes difficult being Daisy's best friend, but being her Vice-President and Secretary is much more simple. This case, though, will not be simple at all.

You see, the person who has died – who we think has been murdered – is our new Head Girl.

2

This case began yesterday, on Tuesday the fifth of November, but all the same, to explain it properly I must wind backwards, all the way to the end of summer term.

That was when Daisy and I were preoccupied with our upcoming holiday on the Orient Express, but although we were not paying much attention to them at the time, extremely important things were happening with Miss Barnard and the Big Girls.

For the purposes of this new casebook, I must mention who Miss Barnard is. You see, after the case of Miss Bell was over, there were almost no mistresses left at Deepdean. This means that everyone except red-haired, dramatic Mamzelle, old Mr MacLean, and Miss Lappet with her big bosom, is entirely new since last December. Miss Barnard is our new Headmistress. She is slender and tall, and I think quite young – at least, there is still brown in her hair. She is also calm, and kind, and sensible, and she has a way of making you feel safe – something Deepdean badly needs, after last year. But sometimes kindness is not the best thing. As Daisy always says, it is no good being nice if the people you are being nice to are not nice themselves.

Now Miss Griffin, our last Headmistress, always chose the next Head Girl at the end of each school year. She knew every girl's character, and judged it carefully before she made her choice. But Miss Barnard did not know any of the Big Girls really well by the time it came to make her selection last summer term, and so instead of choosing, she let it go to a vote. And that was quite disastrous, for it meant that Elizabeth Hurst could bend the vote her way, and have herself elected Head Girl.

The outside of Elizabeth Hurst was not particularly remarkable. She was tall and broad-shouldered, with a pale face and sandy hair, just like most of the girls at Deepdean. The only clue as to what was inside her was the smile at one side of her mouth. It never went away, and it was not a very nice smile. It looked as though she was remembering something nasty about you, and deciding whether or not to say it aloud. That smile was the truth about her, for Elizabeth was in the business of secrets.

That makes her sound somewhat like Daisy – but while Daisy likes to know things just for the pleasure of it, to make things fit in her head, Elizabeth *used* the things she knew. Just like a cat snatching little birds out of their nests, she took all the information she could find about each girl at Deepdean, and kept it. And she didn't simply use the information she gathered – or at least, not immediately. Instead, she would store it up like a present for the day when it would become useful to her. And when it did – well, then you would be ruined.

There had been one girl, Nina Lamont, generally thought to be the front runner for the Head Girl position – until Elizabeth was seen paying Miss Barnard a visit one morning, looking very grave. Later that day it came out that Nina had stolen from the Benefactors' Fund. And after that no one could vote for her at all. She did not even come back to Deepdean this year. Apparently, she had been sent to prison – although Daisy said that this was not true, and that it was only to a school in France.

Elizabeth led a group of five girls, the oddest and angriest and most hateful in their year. They were Elizabeth's helpers, like a bruising, bullying version of Daisy's little informants, and they went about prising facts out of all us younger years and feeding them back to Elizabeth. We called them the Five, and we hated them.

So you can see why everyone at Deepdean was quite terrified of Elizabeth, and why we all got the most horrible thrill when we heard that she had indeed been elected Head Girl – and, as was tradition, had chosen five other Big Girls to be her prefects. Of course, she chose her helpers – and so when we came back to Deepdean this year, Elizabeth and the Five were running the school.

3

We had been afraid of Elizabeth and the Five, but all the same, I do not think we quite understood how dreadful the new year would be until we were a few weeks into it. At first, the autumn term felt as clean and full of possibility as ever – new timetables, new pencils and inkwells, and exercise books with none of their pages torn out to pass notes. We were fourth formers, closer than ever to being Big Girls, and we undid our top buttons daringly in celebration. Kitty even tried to leave her hair down, although Miss Lappet told her off at once. Clementine had a new contraband bracelet, and Beanie had a dormouse which she hid in her tuck box (it was called Chutney, and all it did was sleep). It seemed as though this term might be better than the last – the shadow of Fallingford had finally lifted, for The Trial was over and the murderer in prison.

But then the Five began their punishments.

Elizabeth was absolutely in control of the school's discipline, and behind everything that happened, but the genius of her was that *she* never carried out any of the punishments. It was only ever the Five who came after us, and they did it quite dreadfully.

Red-headed, fierce, athletic Florence Hamersley, captain of the hockey team and in training for the hurdles at next summer's Olympics, was a stickler for laziness. If you were late to breakfast or dinner, or slow at toothbrushes in the evening, her hand would come down on your shoulder and the next thing you knew you were running ten laps around House in the cold and the rain. If you did it slowly, you had to run twenty.

Dark-haired Lettice Prestwich was even nastier. She ought to have been pretty – she would have been, if she were not so thin. With her, we lived on shifting sand, waiting for the catastrophe. Any flaw in your uniform at all – a missing button, an undone tie – and she would pounce on you, shrieking. She made the shrimps cry almost every day. Once she marched into our dorm and, hearing squeaks from Beanie's tuck box, discovered Chutney the dormouse. She took him to Matron at once, who put him outside – Beanie sobbed, of course, and we were all furious. Beanie, our friend and dorm mate, is very small, and not at all good at schoolwork – but she is *good*, and that counts for quite a lot. But there was nothing to be done. Chutney was gone.

Una Dichmann is from Germany, where her father has a most important position in the Nazi Party, and she is blonde and pretty as a fairy-tale princess – but if you failed to treat her, or any of the rest of the Five, with the respect you ought, she would have you carrying her books between lessons and shouting at you if you did not move quickly enough.

Enid Gaines does not look as threatening as the others, at first. She is a swot, Deepdean's great hope for a Classics place at Oxford next year, and her nose is always in a book. She is small – almost as short as I am – and has a dull, forgettable face. But if you laughed in the corridors, or whispered in Prayers, she would turn on you, and you would find yourself writing lines – *I must obey my elders and betters* – a hundred times at lunch break.

The last member of the Five is Margaret Dolliswood. She is large and angry – unhappiness radiates off her in waves. Fail to get out of her way, or draw attention to yourself at meals and bunbreaks, and you would find your food snatched out of your hands and your wrists pinched. I have gone hungry many times because of her – which I think the worst cruelty of all.

The Five's punishments were dreadful, and there was no escape from them. When we went up to House, one would always be taking our Prep, and another supervising the common room, and they all sat at the end of our tables at dinner. We were under siege, and the worst thing was that none of the mistresses or Matron noticed. Grown-ups never do see this sort of thing – to them, any harm children do to each other does not really matter.

It felt as though we were rabbits waiting for the fox to pounce. Elizabeth and her five prefects patrolled the school, and their viciousness spread down, until we were all at each other's throats. They made us all so miserable that even the nicest girls began to argue and snipe at each other horribly. Under the force of the Big Girls' nastiness, we all became nastier too – the fifth form-ers to the fourth, us to the third, the third to the second and so on. All the old alliances broke down under the pressure of it. Deepdean itself was changed, so much so that although its black-and-white corridors and wide windows and chalk smell was no different, I could barely recognize it.

Daisy, of course, was furious. There are certain places that, in her own mind, belong to her. Deepdean is one of them, and the fact that it had gone wrong sent her into an absolute rage. I had decided that this year would simply have to be endured, like any other unpleasant thing, but Daisy does not endure. She cannot bear not to try to solve any problem that she comes up against, and Elizabeth and the Five became the most fascinating of problems, all the more so because the truth was that

13

there was nothing she could do about them. She did not even have her old confidant King Henry to give her prestige among the Big Girls – for, of course, King Henry was no longer our Head Girl. She was far away at Cambridge, where Daisy could not use her.

'I'm watching them,' Daisy told me, over and over again. 'I'm watching *her*. Elizabeth can't think she'll get away with it. She can't be allowed.'

It seemed to me that she could – and that she was. Elizabeth had committed no crime apart from nastiness. Her blackmail was so subtle that there was nothing we could pin on her, nothing we could detect. In fact the Detective Society had no cases at all this term, apart from the strange case of Violet Darby which Daisy solved in a day in September. (Daisy is rather proud of that case.)

'I'd like to squash Elizabeth's head,' said Lavinia furiously as Beanie sobbed over her fifth detention in two weeks (for misspelling the word 'privilege' in the essay she wrote for her fourth detention. This was not fair at all. Beanie struggles with making her words the right shape, and her numbers add up properly on the page). 'I'd like to squash her into pulp.'

We all agreed with her, but all the same we (except Daisy) understood how hopeless it was to expect anything to change.

That is, until what happened on Guy Fawkes Night.

4

The fireworks display on the fifth of November was Miss Runcible's idea at first. Miss Runcible is our new Science mistress. She is very cheerful and excited about life – which is odd, after cold Miss Bell. Her Science lessons are always very full of strong smells and explosions (which make them excellent for pranks – in the third week Kitty tricked Clementine into getting too close to one of Miss Runcible's experiments, then there was a *pop!* and Clementine's eyebrows burned away to nothing), so I suppose it was not at all surprising that she should want to hold a proper Guy Fawkes Night celebration, even though such a thing had never happened at Deepdean before.

Miss Barnard announced it in Prayers towards the end of October.

'Girls,' she said, standing very calm and collected at the lectern. 'On the fifth of November, Guy Fawkes

Night, you are to go up to House for dinner and then march back down to the sports field for a bonfire and a fireworks display. The prefects and Head Girl will be supervising, as well as Miss Runcible and myself, and you are all to have an excellent time.'

We all went rather tense. I remember thinking how very optimistic Miss Barnard could be, and how concerning this plan of hers was. It was yet another opportunity for the younger girls to be bullied by Elizabeth and the Five – and this time we would be shivering on a cold sports pitch while it happened.

Then I looked over at Daisy. As I knew she would be, she was staring not at Miss Barnard, but at Elizabeth and the Five. I saw the familiar crinkle appearing at the top of her nose. I knew that expression, and I felt rather apprehensive. I knew that Daisy was still looking for a way in to Elizabeth and the Five – but I could not see how a Bonfire Night celebration would be any help with that at all. I almost opened my mouth to tell her to leave it, but I knew it would only make her more determined. So I began to think about something quite different: the letter that would almost certainly be waiting for me when we got up to House for lunch that day.

You see, this term I have a secret. I have been writing to someone, and they have been writing back to me. The Hazel of a year ago would never have dared to keep such a thing hidden from Daisy – but I am not the Hazel

16

of a year ago. I am still not a heroine, but I think I am a little braver.

There is now quite a pile of papers at the bottom of my tuck box. Every time I slip another letter on top of it the fizzing in my chest grows stronger. It is lovely, but all the same it turns me jumpy. The two of us send each other logic puzzles, and funny things that we notice at school, and little cases – nothing at all, really, but I know that if Daisy were to find out, she would be terribly cross. She does not like me detecting with anyone else, you see – in her mind, I am *her* detective friend, and although we have assistants, no one else can truly be a part of that.

I was still thinking about the letters, and what Daisy would say if she knew, on the evening of the murder.

Our dorm walked down to the sports field together on Tuesday night after dinner, wrapped up in our hats and scarves and shivering. No one was feeling cheerful. We were having one of those strange not-arguments that happen so much this term, where everyone simply complains at each other and you are left feeling worn out and cross.

'Beanie's still upset about that fifth former taking her pudding last night, even though I've told her not to be,' said our dorm mate Lavinia, shaking back her heavy dark hair. 'After all, I got her one of the shrimps', didn't I? I don't see what the fuss is.'

'You can't take other people's things!' said our other dorm mate, Kitty, self-righteously. Kitty has brown hair and freckles, and loves to gossip. 'It's not nice, Lavinia. You wouldn't have done it last year.'

'Yes I would,' said Lavinia. 'Don't be po-faced, Kitty.'

Kitty scowled. 'Well, *you* might have done, but you still oughtn't.'

'Everyone's so nasty this year,' said Beanie sadly.

'It's Elizabeth Hurst,' I said, stepping in without meaning to, and then wincing. I knew what must come next, and sure enough—

'Exactly!' said Daisy triumphantly. 'I've been saying this all term, Hazel. Elizabeth Hurst and the Five are the problem, and we must solve it.'

'It isn't a problem we can solve!' I said. 'Oh, do give over, Daisy.'

I suddenly felt the difference between us. All of Daisy's head was obsessed with Elizabeth Hurst, focused on her like a spotlight, while all of mine was wrapped around the newest letter that had been waiting for me that afternoon, as I'd hoped. It was all I could see, overlaying the dark line of girls in front of us, the pavilion and the flare of the lit bonfire beyond.

5

Apart from the brightness of the bonfire, the field was dark, little tendrils of fog drifting through the crowd. I could only dimly make out the shadow of the pavilion behind the fire, and the girls crowding in front of it looked like scribbles on a page. I could not even see the trees on the far edge of the pitch that led into Oakeshott Woods, although I knew they were there. I breathed out and my breath misted in front of me. I shuddered. I do not like English winter nights at all.

Through the gates we walked, and there was Miss Barnard, calmly greeting all of the girls as they went by. Next to her was Elizabeth Hurst. She was smiling as usual, but her smile looked hard and fake. For once the Five were not behind her, but ranged away to the side, with a gap between her and them. They were not smiling at all. I would like to say that I wondered about this, and that I caught how Margaret was clenching her fists, and how Florence, wrapped in her scarf, was pale, and Una flushed, and Enid was poison-faced and Lettice was shaking, her thin form looking unusually bulky in her big Deepdean coat – but I did not. I was distracted.

We milled about a bit, once we were on the field, jostling against other groups of girls from other years. We were supposed to be in form group sets, but of course that started to go wrong in the darkness and the excitement. Then Jones, Deepdean's handyman, came forward with the Guy. As he tossed it onto the bonfire, which had been set up near the pavilion (though not too near), sparks flared out and it blazed up fiercely. Everyone surged towards it. All of us fourth formers were swept up in the confusion – I bumped against Lavinia and she said 'Hey!' but good-naturedly.

Jones bellowed at us all indignantly to keep away. Only Elizabeth and the Five were allowed to go near the fire – Elizabeth was supervising the Five on bonfire duty. They were bringing armfuls of wood from the pile near the pavilion to throw onto the blaze. They worked in shifts, walking back and forward from the pavilion to make sure that the fire was never left untended.

My eyes were on the Guy, a hot dark shape at the middle of the blaze. Guys always give me an eerie shiver down the back of my neck, although I know that they are not real – they look so like a body that I cannot quite bear it. It makes me feel as though I am in the sort of dream where something is wrong, and I am the only one to know it.

I was brought back to myself when Daisy nudged me and pointed. There was Margaret Dolliswood, a load of wood in her arms. She was not taking it to the fire, though, but standing by Elizabeth Hurst. She looked as though she wished she could have hurled the wood at her, but Elizabeth did not seem intimidated. Instead, she leaned forward, a swagger in her shoulders, as though she owned the sports field and everything in it. I could not see her face, or hear what she said, for we were too far away, but the fight went out of Margaret's pose, and Elizabeth seemed to stand taller. Then Margaret turned, walked stiltedly over to the Big Girl Astrid Frith and snapped something at her. Astrid burst into tears, and Margaret spun round and stormed back to the bonfire. She hurled her armload onto the flames, and they flared up, with a crackle and burst of redness.

'Now, what was *that*?' Daisy asked me, without turning round. 'What did Margaret say to Astrid? And why?'

'It was only Elizabeth making the Five be horrid, as usual,' I said, not wanting to encourage her. 'Look, it's time to light the sparklers.'

Miss Runcible, Enid and Lettice were handing out sparklers. Miss Runcible gave one to me, looking as excited as the shrimps. There were yells and whoops as the sparklers blazed up, spitting fire in long trails. Lavinia lunged out with hers as though it was a sword, and even Beanie was laughing and swirling hers in circles, quite happy again. Mine hissed in my hand, and it lifted my heart. I turned to Daisy at exactly the same time as she looked at me, and caught an expression I had not seen in her face for a long time. I drew a fiery W in the air, and so did she – we were Wells & Wong, and for a moment I forgot all my worries.

But only for a moment.

6

Everyone was so excited, playing with their sparklers, that at first they barely noticed Miss Barnard standing in the middle of the hockey pitch and shouting for quiet. She had to wave her hands, a torch in each, as though she was signalling in semaphore, and at last the sparklers fizzed out into darkness and quiet went rippling through the crowd. We all turned towards where she was standing, away from the bonfire and the Guy.

'Girls,' said Miss Barnard then, speaking in the way she has that is not loud, but makes you lean forward to hear what she wants to say. 'Thank you all for coming. I hope you are enjoying the evening – we must give credit to Miss Runcible for suggesting it, and to Mr Jones for helping to bring her vision to life. And of course to our wonderful Head Girl, Elizabeth Hurst, who has been so helpful and responsible, as always.'

I felt a flash of annoyance. Why could Miss Barnard not see the truth of what Elizabeth was?

'I am sure that this night will be just the first of many, and that our Guy Fawkes celebrations will become part of the proud traditions of Deepdean.'

I heard what she was not saying – that after what had happened last year, Deepdean needed new traditions, new things to be proud of. Miss Barnard is trying to make everything new for us this year, as though she can erase Miss Bell and what happened to her. But all she is really doing is painting over it, again and again. In the end, it will still show through.

I had a rather horrid moment's realization, then. Elizabeth and the Five would go on being nasty, and we would go on bearing it, until their year sat their university entrance exams in the summer term and left us alone.

My stomach sank. It had not been a good term, not even with my letters lighting up certain days like struck matches. A year of Elizabeth was going to be awful.

'Now, girls!' said Miss Barnard. 'You have got yourselves in rather a muddle. Line up in your form groups again, please. Prefects, help them. No pushing! Once you have done so we can move on to the real event: the fireworks!'

We all grumbled and shoved (and were shoved by some of the Five, who came away from the bonfire for a moment to corral us at Elizabeth's shouted command) and struggled back into our regimented form-group lines. The youngest shrimps were at the front, closest to Miss Barnard, and the rest of us were ranged behind them, with the Big Girls closest to the bonfire, which was at all our backs (that was the trick, you see, that the youngest ones should be cold and the oldest have all the warmth. Elizabeth, of course, was next to the heat of the fire, between it and the pavilion, with her prefects near her).

Miss Barnard looked at us all, and gave a nod, and then Miss Runcible, ever eager, jumped forward. She went and busied herself further out in the darkness, lighting the fireworks at almost the other end of the pitch, and Jones went to help her. The Five all went back to their places by the bonfire. For a moment we were all hushed, waiting. And then the first rocket went off with a scream, and burst above us in a shower of green and yellow.

It was as though the night had come to life, the whole sky rattling and soaring with sound and light. I gasped as the noise of it went all through me. Daisy leaned against me, and I turned and saw her face all lit up royally in purple and red. Kitty, Beanie and Lavinia were beside her, and everyone's faces were bright, but I only saw that for a moment, because I wanted so much to look up at the display. It was like gazing up into the Hong Kong New Year's sky, and it gave me a little ache of joy. Sunbursts of orange and gold, a spray of blue, a shock of red again, all fountaining above us. I am sure I forgot to breathe.

And then it was over. The last green light faded from the sky, and the whole field rang with quiet. It was hard to bring my head back down to earth. But there was Daisy next to me, and Beanie beaming and clapping, and all the other girls around us murmuring and laughing and slowly beginning to move away from their lines. I turned and saw a dark shape moving in front of the bonfire – one of the Five was still on bonfire duty. Then I turned back again to hear what Lavinia was saying to me.

The first shout came a few minutes later.

It was only a sort of yelp of surprise. Daisy says she remembers the girl, a little first-form shrimp, call, 'Miss Barnard! I think someone's fallen over!' We both remember the louder shriek she gave then, though, and then the scream the girl next to her let out.

At that noise I spun round to look at Daisy – of course, she was already turning to me. Her eyes were blazing, as though there were still fireworks in them. It is funny, because I tell myself after every case that I do not really want another investigation, and I believe it – but then I hear a scream like that and my pulse beats in my hands and feet and I know that there is nothing in the world so wonderful as being on a case. At that moment, that was what I felt – pure rightness, for the first time in months.

I knew what to do.

7

Daisy and I ran towards the noise, beyond the bonfire –
and so did everyone else, so that there was a scrum
around the screamer, and for a while I could not see
anything except half-darkness and confusion and spinning flashes from torches, of people's hands and grey
school coats and hats and worried faces.

Then Miss Barnard shouted, 'STAND BACK!' and
everyone was shocked into pulling away a little – everyone except Daisy, and, because she had hooked her
fingers around my wrist, me. I peeled away her hand
and looked down, and there on the ground, lit up by
the beam of torches, was Elizabeth Hurst.

She was lying with her face up to the sky, her arms at
her sides and her eyes open. She was not moving at all,
and it was not hard to see why. Along the length of her
body was a rake, one of the old, battered ones that Jones
uses. Its pronged base was under the back of her feet,

27

and the top of its handle, beside her head, was covered with blood. I could tell from the rather ill feeling I got when I looked at Elizabeth's head that there would be blood on the ground beneath it too.

Miss Runcible was kneeling next to her, feeling for a pulse, and I remembered, in a sort of all-over gulp, Miss Bell in the Gym last year with blood on *her* head. It felt *the same*, and in that moment I knew that I was reminded of Miss Bell because this body, just like that one, had something unnatural about it.

Miss Barnard was shouting now, for Jones. 'Bring a stretcher!' she cried. 'There's been an accident! A girl has trodden on a rake.'

I knew those words were not true. It was not an accident. It might look like one, but *something was wrong*.

Jones was already hurrying over with Miss Runcible, a greatcoat hanging between them as a makeshift stretcher. 'Make way!' he bellowed at the shrimps. 'Make way!'

Beanie burst into tears. 'Oh!' she wailed. 'Not AGAIN!'

'Quiet!' hissed Daisy. 'Don't draw attention!' and I knew it was not only me who had thought back to last October.

Judging by the sobs all around us, the whole school was as horrified and frightened as Beanie. 'Prefects!'

shouted Miss Barnard. 'Prefects! Take Elizabeth's things back to House, and get the girls back as well! Hurry, now!'

'Who put that rake there?' Jones asked furiously. 'I left it propped up against the pavilion before the girls arrived!'

'I shall be asking you about that later, Jones,' said Miss Barnard. 'For now, take Elizabeth down to San as quickly as you can. Go!'

I noticed, with a start, that the Five had gathered around Elizabeth's body. Or, at least, four of them had. I could not see Lettice – I thought she must be lost in the crowd. They were all still and silent, but then Florence spoke, words that sent a little shock through my body.

'*Is* she dead?' she asked. 'Is she really?'

It was not so much an odd thing to say as an odd *way* to say it – hungry and breathless. My detective sense tingled again.

Could my suspicions really be right? After all, if this *was* something more than an accident, it would be the Detective Society's *fourth* case. But then again, I know that for Daisy and me, unusual things happen all the time – just like the White Queen's six impossible things before breakfast.

'She is hurt very badly,' said Miss Barnard. 'We must get her help immediately.'

I stared around at the prefects again. They were all rigid with shock, pale and gasping – but all the same their expressions held something that was not just horror. They all looked rather – *relieved*.

I swallowed. We had all thought that Elizabeth was dreadful and dangerous. But now it seemed that she had turned out to be not the criminal, but the victim.

8

'Prefects!' cried Miss Barnard again, more forcefully this time. 'Hurry up. Take the girls back up to House! Quickly, please, while Miss Runcible and Jones take Elizabeth to San.' She was pale and drawn in the light of the bonfire, but she did not break down for a moment.

The prefects could not ignore her any more. They began to herd us away, and as they did so I looked back too, at Miss Runcible brushing tears off her cheeks and shaking her head while she and Jones lifted Elizabeth up between them. But by now we could all see that Elizabeth would not get better, no matter what Miss Barnard said. Whatever Mrs Minn the San nurse tried, it would be hopeless. Elizabeth was already dead.

As we walked back up to House, running feet and sobs echoed all around us, and torches danced hysterically on the path. Everyone was talking, and I could hear the same words: Elizabeth! Hurt – dead – awful – accident – never! – Miss Bell – *murder.*

And there it was. *Murder.* It really was not just me who wondered whether this was truly an accident. But . . . I thought about it. If this *was* murder, there was one very important way in which this was different to the murder of Miss Bell. The only mistresses on the field had been Miss Barnard and Miss Runcible, and they had been standing in front of us with Jones all the time the fireworks were going off. I remembered that I had heard Elizabeth shouting at the Five to get us all back into line after Miss Barnard's speech – she must have been alive then, and neither Miss Runcible, Miss Barnard nor Jones had moved past us to the bonfire after that. They were ruled out immediately.

Which meant – *one of the girls.* If someone had killed Elizabeth, it was another Deepdean girl. But could that really be true? And if it was – who?

9

Up at House, the shrimps squealed in the corridors, and everyone else clustered on the front stairs, talking, talking, talking. The prefects were trying to get everyone's attention – but, and this was most odd to see, they were ignored. For once, we were all more frightened of what had just happened than of the Five, and any punishment they could inflict on us paled next to what had just happened to Elizabeth.

'You nasty little things!' Una cried, throwing up her hands, her crown of golden hair catching the lights in the House hallway. She stormed over to stand next to Florence. I could see that she was upset, although she did her best to seem only angry.

Florence, I could tell, was upset as well, but she showed it in a different way. Arms crossed like a vice in front of her, she narrowed her eyes and turned to stare at Una. The look that flew between them, cautious and assessing, made me wonder all over again. What did they think of what they had just seen? Was murder in their heads as well?

'Half an hour,' Florence shouted, turning away from Una with a start. 'All of you into bed by then, you little ones! Or else!' But the shrimps ignored her.

I noticed something else, then: one of the Five was still missing. No matter how hard I looked, I could not see Lettice at all, until I turned to spot her standing next to the front door of House. Her hair was wild, there was a leaf clinging to one sock, and she was patting herself down with trembling, distracted fingers. How long had she been standing there?

Just then, though, Daisy made a dash for the stairs – and the gossip – and we all had to follow. As we climbed into the heart of the chatter, I kept on hearing Elizabeth's death bounced back to me, slightly wrong, like echoes in a cave: her head had been quite broken open; she was hardly marked at all; the killer was a mystery; last year's killer was back (I shuddered at that, although of course I knew it was not true at all – I had heard from Inspector Priestley himself that they were locked away safely in prison, and Inspector Priestley is the most truthful person I know); a man had been seen running away towards Oakeshott Woods just before the fireworks began.

That last made Daisy prick up her ears. She turned sharply on the teller, a third former called Martha Grey, and said, 'Nonsense!'

Martha turned pink and opened her mouth shyly. Being spoken to by the glamorous Daisy Wells was daunting. 'It—' she said. 'It – isn't—'

'What she means is that it isn't nonsense!' said Binny Freebody, stepping in. Binny is a third former who happens to be Kitty's younger sister. She is dreadfully forward and bold, and we are careful not to seem to take her seriously, even though she did give us very useful help during our first case, last year. I think Daisy is still cross about that.

'Of course it is,' said Daisy severely. 'You never saw a man, did you, Martha?'

Martha squirmed. 'Not *exactly*,' she said.

Daisy raised her eyebrow at Binny. 'This is your doing, isn't it?' she asked. 'You're a fearful liar, Binny Freebody, and you're making your friends lie as well.'

'I am not lying! But don't believe us if you like. We don't mind, we just shan't talk to you any more,' said Binny. 'Serve you right! Come on, Martha.'

She stalked away up the stairs, and Martha trailed after her, still blushing.

'She really is dreadful,' said Kitty. 'I'm sure she must be adopted. I know she didn't see anything, and neither did Martha.'

'Are you sure?' I asked. 'What if it's a—?'

Daisy shot me a glance, and I bit down on the word *clue*. 'I'm sure it's not,' she said. 'Idiots like Binny simply want to be involved in anything exciting. They never really *know* anything.'

'So there wasn't a man?' asked Beanie. 'Oh, I hope there wasn't! I don't want it to be murder again!'

'Hah,' said Lavinia ghoulishly. 'But it *is* murder.' She nodded at me and Daisy knowingly. 'That's what you think. Don't look like that, I saw you staring at each other just now. You think this is just like Miss Bell, last year. I'm not stupid.'

'Of course not!' said Daisy. 'Two murders, in one school? It simply doesn't happen.'

She was trying to cover up our suspicions, to keep the Detective Society secret and to leave Lavinia out. It was what we had done last year, after all. Then, the secret of the Detective Society had been mine and Daisy's. But things had changed. Beanie and Kitty had helped us at Fallingford, and on the Orient Express we had been helped by Alexander, as well as by Daisy's maid, Hetty. Why should Lavinia not be part of this case, and Kitty and Beanie as well?

I felt a flush all up my body, and I said, 'Yes. We think it is murder.'

Beanie looked as though she wanted to weep.

'Hazel!' cried Daisy. 'Be quiet!'

I knew that Daisy wanted to keep the Detective Society hidden, and treat this case as though we were still the Daisy and Hazel we had been last year – but we had to include the others now, and I knew how to make her do it. Daisy likes secrets, but she loves her own cleverness even more.

'Well, I suppose there isn't any way to be sure,' I said. 'After all, Elizabeth might very well have stepped on that rake, just the way Miss Barnard said.'

'She did *not*!' Daisy said hotly. 'That's the trouble with ordinary people: they look but they don't *notice*. The rake was lying *next* to her, and that's quite wrong. If she'd stepped sideways onto the rake, it would have hit the *side* of her head, and we'd all have been able to see the wound. But we couldn't, and that means she was hit on the *back* of her head. The rake shouldn't have fallen like that afterwards – it wouldn't have, if it really had been an accident. And that means it wasn't. Someone hit her and *then* put the rake next to her, after she had already fallen. Oh, bother you, Hazel, you've made me say it now! I taught you that trick, it really isn't fair.'

I shrugged. 'You have to let Kitty and Beanie and Lavinia help us detect,' I said. 'You know Beanie and Kitty already know about the Society, anyway.'

'What Society?' asked Lavinia. 'Is this that stupid thing—'

'Stop!' said Daisy. 'Don't say anything else!'

I knew she was annoyed with me, but I also knew I was right. Although Daisy has a nose for investigating murder – a talent for it, the way other people can simply sit down at a piano and see the music, or get onto a sports pitch and understand how to put the ball into the goal – even she cannot detect quite on her own.

We all climbed the stairs, past the Marys, third-form friends who adored Daisy, who were huddled together comforting each other. I stepped aside to avoid them, and caught myself staring at the worn patch on the tenth stair up. I saw how frayed the edges of it were, and how the railing next to it was dented and scarred from hundreds of fingernails picking away at its varnish. When I am on a case I suddenly become utterly noticing, as though I am even more in my skin than usual. I could feel myself gathering up all my detective skills once more. We had solved three cases – we could do it again.

10

I had plenty of opportunity to watch the uproar that House was in as we got ready for bed. No one was keeping to their proper routine – the shrimps were all still awake, when they should be asleep by now, and some of the older girls were getting ready for bed early, just so they could talk without fear of the Five overhearing.

At toothbrushes there was an absolute scrum, and we had to squeeze all five of us around one sink. Beanie was wriggling like a nervous, excited puppy next to me (Kitty elbowed her, and she squeaked but did not stop), Kitty was winking at us all in the mirror, and Lavinia, next to me on the other side, breathed hotly on my neck and stared at Daisy curiously. Daisy herself was ignoring us. She was flexing the fingers of her free hand as though trying to pluck the problem straight out of the air, and I knew that she was preparing to investigate – and also to leave Kitty, Beanie and Lavinia out, despite what I had said to her. But I knew she could not be allowed to do that. I had to make her let the other three in, so that we could all work together. I scrubbed away at my teeth furiously and thought. Then I put my hand on the letter in my pyjama pocket and felt it crumple reassuringly. It reminded me that although Daisy might be the President, the Detective Society was larger than she was. I could overrule her for the good of the case.

Florence came into the bathroom then. I caught a flash of her red hair in the mirror. 'Fourth formers, you ought to have been back in dorms by now!' she snapped, but her tone did not quite have the usual bite to it. She was still rattled.

Lavinia spat into the sink, quite deliberately. It was a rudeness, and it made Beanie nervous. As we went past Florence, she stumbled sideways and bumped against her. It was exactly the provocation Florence needed – something concrete that she could punish.

'MARTINEAU!' Florence cried, rounding on us. 'You did that on purpose! Out into the corridor, now!'

Out into the corridor we went, to see Margaret waiting there. My heart sank.

'Margaret,' said Florence, looking pale with rage. 'This fourth former has been insolent. She thinks that because Elizabeth is— *isn't here*, she can do whatever she likes. Show her she's wrong, if you would.'

At the mention of Elizabeth, Margaret flinched. She opened her mouth and then squeezed it shut again. A moment later, she was back in control of herself. She narrowed her eyes at us. 'Up on one leg, Martineau,' she said. 'Stand until we give the word.'

'Let *me* do it,' said Lavinia at once. 'I tripped her.'

'You filthy liar, Temple,' said Florence. She exchanged a glance with Margaret. 'But all right, if you're so keen to. On one leg, now.'

We all had a shock at that. We have an unspoken rule that Lavinia tries to take most of our punishments, and I try to take the rest. Beanie is too liable to cry, and Kitty to talk back, and no one ever punishes Daisy, but Lavinia and I can bear it. Usually, though, the Five squash that idea immediately. That they were allowing us to share out the punishment now – to work together, against what they had said – was yet another strange thing about the evening.

But we were not about to argue. With a wobble, Lavinia raised one leg up off the ground. We all watched her sway slightly from side to side, her face going purple with concentration, until Margaret shrugged and said, 'Stop. All right, that's enough. Get in your dorm. And not another word, or I'll have you all copying her.'

Lavinia stood straight again, and quick as anything Daisy clapped her on the back. 'Good show,' she said. 'Jolly well done.' Lavinia shook back her tangled hair and looked crossly pleased, the way she always does when someone praises her.

Margaret turned away from us hurriedly, as though she could not wait to be rid of us, and she and Florence moved off together.

'Elizabeth—' I heard Margaret begin, but Florence replied swiftly, 'Wait. Upstairs, come on.'

Daisy's head was angled after them, and I could tell she had heard as well. I wanted to follow them, and so did she, but of course neither of us could. Despite the new state of affairs, we were still powerless against the rules of House. We were not old enough to follow prefects to the upper floor, no matter what had happened to the Head Girl.

We had no other choice but to go to our dorm. The door closed behind us, and Kitty and Beanie looked at Daisy expectantly. I knew what they were waiting for: a Detective Society meeting.

11

I could tell that Daisy still did not want to dilute the Detective Society.

'Stop looking at me like that!' she said to Kitty and Beanie.

'We're waiting for orders,' said Beanie rapturously.

'What orders?' asked Daisy.

I could not bear her pretending to be ignorant any longer. 'Daisy,' I said, 'tell them properly! You've got to. You promised earlier, and Beanie and Kitty know already, anyway.'

Daisy groaned. 'Didn't I say there would be medieval tortures if you ever revealed the Society?' she asked Beanie.

'Oh, I forgot!' gasped Beanie.

'If you're going to be detectives again, we want to be a part of it as well,' said Kitty. 'It isn't fair otherwise.'

'Look,' said Lavinia, 'if it's me you're worried about, you needn't. I already know that you've got a stupid secret society that you won't tell me about.'

Lavinia is, if anything, even less tactful than Kitty.

Daisy looked furious. 'Who's been talking?' she asked. 'Who?'

'*Huh*,' said Lavinia expressively. 'No one's been talking. But I'm not *entirely* stupid. You've got another secret society, a detective one, and what happened last Easter was part of it.'

'It really is too bad of you to have found out,' said Daisy. 'It's supposed to be a *secret*. But – bother!' She stood beside her bed, her arms folded, and glared around at us all. 'All right, all right! Yes, there is a Detective Society, Lavinia. We detect murders, and I believe that what happened tonight may be the beginning of a new case. If so, you may assist us, along with Kitty and Beanie – but you'll have to prove yourself worthy. A place in the Detective Society has to be *earned*.'

Lavinia glared. 'That's stupid,' she said. 'Like your—'

'Oh, do say you'll join!' said Beanie. 'It's terribly fun, even though it's awful as well. Although – oh dear. I don't want there to have been another murder.'

'Before we say anything further, Lavinia has to take the pledge,' said Daisy. 'And promise not to mention the case to anyone else. In fact, you all must. It is most

44

important that the Society does not keep on *expanding* like this.'

'I promise!' said Beanie eagerly.

'I promise,' said Kitty, rolling her eyes.

Daisy looked at me.

'All right, I promise,' I agreed. But I felt a pulse of uncertainty as I said it.

'And now you have to take the pledge,' said Daisy to Lavinia. 'Listen to me, and say *I do* afterwards: *Do you swear to be a good and clever member of the Detective Society, and to logically detect the crimes presented to you using all the cleverness you have, not placing reliance on grown-ups, especially the police? Do you solemnly swear never to conceal a vital clue from your Detective Society President and Vice-President, and to do exactly what they say? Do you promise never to mention this to another soul, living or dead, on pain of medieval tortures?'*

Lavinia snorted, but all the same, she said *I do* in the right places. I think, secretly, she was quite pleased to be inside our secret at last – and I could tell she relished the medieval tortures idea.

'All right,' said Daisy, in a way that I could tell meant that she had not quite forgiven me. 'Now that that's agreed, let's assume that this is a case – that Elizabeth's death was a murder. If so, then we must investigate. Detective Society, it's time for a meeting. Hazel, take notes.'

I nodded. I had a brand-new casebook waiting in my tuck box, on top of this year's supply of moon cakes, ready for a new case. I dug it out now gladly. I turned to the clean front page and wrote: *The Murder of Elizabeth Hurst. Meeting of the Detective Society. Present: Daisy Wells, Detective Society President; Hazel Wong, Detective Society Vice-President and Secretary; Kitty Freebody, Beanie Martineau and Lavinia Temple, Detective Society Assistants.*

'All right,' said Daisy, 'what do we know?'

12

'We know that Elizabeth's dead,' said Lavinia. 'There, the case is solved. This is easy!'

'It is *not* solved,' said Daisy, bristling. 'And if you are insolent I shall have to ask you to be quiet.'

Lavinia and Daisy glared at each other. I bit back a smile. I thought that it was quite good for Daisy to be challenged from time to time.

Victim, I wrote. *Elizabeth Hurst.*

'And she died on the sports field,' said Kitty. 'Hit on the head by that rake. Do you really think it was on purpose?'

I nodded. 'Daisy's right about the position of it. It doesn't make sense that Elizabeth stepped on it by accident. The position of her injury is all wrong!'

'And we all know that Jones would never leave something like that lying about,' Daisy butted in. 'He's a very careful person, and very tidy. He gets frightfully cross when anyone tracks mud into the corridors, and he never leaves a tool out of place. We heard him say that the rake was leaning up against the pavilion the last time he saw it, and I'm sure that's true. Someone else must have taken it from where Jones left it and hit Elizabeth with it.'

'But how can we be *sure*?' Kitty persisted. Kitty, as she had at Fallingford, was proving herself a rather smart detective.

'Well,' said Daisy, scowling. 'We *can't*, yet. We can only guess. We must put it in our plan of action, to prove that the rake was moved deliberately. Now, time of death.'

'Time of death,' I said, scribbling. 'I remember hearing Elizabeth shouting at us all to get back into line just before the fireworks, so she must have died *during* the fireworks display.'

'Exactly,' agreed Daisy. 'And of course, it would have been the perfect time – when everything was loud, and we were all looking up and away from the bonfire.'

'That was ten minutes,' said Lavinia unexpectedly. 'I was looking at my wristwatch. I got bored. It began at 7.40 and it was over by 7.50. And no, before you ask, I didn't see anything. I was looking away from the fire too.'

'So were we all!' said Beanie, wrinkling her forehead. 'We were all in our form rows, and Miss Barnard and

Miss Runcible were in front of us, with Jones. How could any girl have been able to get out of line and hurt Elizabeth without the other members of her form noticing?'

'No!' I said. 'Not all of us were in rows.' I looked up to see Daisy nodding.

'Watson is quite right,' she said to the others. 'We *were* all lined up – apart from the Five. They were behind us, next to the fire and the pavilion, and next to Elizabeth. One of them was supposed to be always tending the bonfire, but they were changing over all the time. Anyone not on duty would have had the perfect opportunity to do it.'

'But they were her friends!' gasped Beanie. 'That's dreadful!'

'Not everyone likes their friends as much as you do, Beans,' said Kitty, nudging her.

'It's true,' said Lavinia. 'I don't like *any* of you.'

'Shut it, Lavinia,' said Kitty.

'They weren't her friends!' said Daisy. 'They all disliked her as much as the rest of us. I've been watching – she was dreadful to them, just the way she was to us. She made them do everything she told them to, after all! I can imagine that any one of them might want to murder her.'

It was exactly what I had been thinking, but hearing it explained that way made me realize, suddenly, how familiar *she made them do everything she told them to* sounded. I – we – were subject to Daisy's whims, after all. In Daisy's mind she is quite different to Elizabeth, and all the things she asks us to do are sensible and good, but is that entirely true? The world is not as black and white as Daisy expects it to be, although she can never see that.

'We saw Margaret and Elizabeth arguing beside the bonfire,' I said. 'Perhaps that's important?'

'Absolutely!' said Daisy. 'And all the others, they were behaving oddly as well. They all seemed upset, even *before* Elizabeth died.'

'So,' I said, 'we really think that one of the Five did it?'

'Yes!' said Daisy. 'Now we have to discover exactly *why*, and from that, *who.*'

'How are we supposed to do that?' asked Lavinia scornfully. I could tell that she was not quite believing in the Detective Society yet.

'Ooh, we have to hunt for motives, and evidence, and alibis!' said Beanie eagerly.

Daisy nodded. 'Exactly. At school tomorrow we need to gather information from the other girls. Anyone may have seen something important. Remember what we say?'

'Yes!' said Beanie. '*Constant vigilance.* Oh, hooray!'

PLAN OF ACTION

1. Prove that the rake was moved on purpose, and that this really is murder.
2. Gather evidence about our five suspects — discover their motives, and find out whether they had alibis for the ten minutes of the display.
3. Look for clues.

SUSPECT LIST

1. *Una Dichmann.* Was near the bonfire when Elizabeth was killed.
2. *Florence Hamersley.* Was near the bonfire when Elizabeth was killed.
3. *Lettice Prestwich.* Was near the bonfire when Elizabeth was killed.
4. *Enid Gaines.* Was near the bonfire when Elizabeth was killed.
5. *Margaret Dolliswood.* Was near the bonfire when Elizabeth was killed. Was seen arguing with Elizabeth before the fireworks display by Daisy Wells and Hazel Wong.

13

We all climbed into bed, and Lavinia put out the light. I could hear Matron calling for quiet as all the other dorms whispered and guessed and wondered about Elizabeth's death. The ordinary House noises were amplified – everything really had become strange this evening.

I listened to the noises in our own dorm too, as Beanie went creeping into Kitty's bed, and they began to talk together in soft voices. Lavinia was snoring defiantly, to show that she did not care about being left out by them. Daisy was quite silent, and I could tell that she was going over and over the events of the evening. But there was one more thing I wanted to do, and that had nothing to do with Daisy. It was time to read my letter.

I rolled over onto my stomach and pulled the covers over my head. In the warm, close, blanket-smelling air I could at last unfold my letter. I slipped my little torch from under my pillow, careful not to let any light leak out, and held it as close as I could to the paper. The message on the front was very dull indeed.

Dear Cousin,
I hope this finds you well. I am well also. We have eaten semolina pudding all week, and written an essay on the French revolution. Georgina sends her regards. How is Daisy?
Yours sincerely,
Alexandra

But the message on the front was not what I was looking for. I turned the piece of paper over and felt myself smiling. A torch, even a small one, gives out a surprising amount of heat, and on the once-clean back of the letter had appeared a spider of brownish words.

elloHay, azelHay! oringBay eekway. eWay olvedsay

It looked like nonsense, but of course I knew the trick of it. It was written in Pig Latin, which is simply English with the first letter of each word moved to its end and the letters 'ay' added. Translated, it read:

Hello, Hazel!

Boring week. We solved the Mystery of the Missing Ferret (it was in Jenkins's tuck box, quite happy), and Hendricks Minor ate three puddings in a row and was ill. I worked out the answer to the latest puzzle you sent, it's 42. Have you found anything proper to detect? If not, here's a puzzle. Sophie's mother has four children. The first is called April, the second is called May and the third is June. What is the fourth child's name? George says hello too, he's the one who came up with that. How is Daisy?

Alexander

I read, my heart jumping and my fingers fizzy with excitement – until I reached that last line, and felt a twinge of unhappiness. *How is Daisy?* I reminded myself that Alexander was a very polite and nice person. It was only natural for him to ask after Daisy as well as me. Alexander and Daisy had met at the same time he and I had, on the Orient Express this past summer. The three of us had worked together to solve a most unpleasant murder – and that is the sort of experience that you do not forget.

I liked to think of Alexander and his best friend George, the other member of his detective society, the Junior Pinkertons (I had never met George, but I imagined him as looking very much like Alexander, although more bossy), at their school. I saw it like Deepdean, only full of boys instead of girls, eating the same heavy food and running about on the same sort of sports fields as we did. Before I met Alexander, I used to think that boys must be entirely different to girls inside, like another species, but now I see that this is not true.

I so wanted to tell Alexander about what had just happened, but I remembered Daisy making me swear not to talk about the case. She would be fearfully angry if I disobeyed her, I knew, but I wanted to. Alexander had helped before, and he might be able to help again. I turned the question over and over in my mind, the pen frozen in my hand – and finally, with a guilty leap in my stomach, I made a decision. It had nothing to do with *her*, who else I was friends with. I could make decisions for myself, I thought, and if I wanted to bring in another detective society, there was nothing she could do to stop me.

I turned to a new page of this casebook, and took out my secret pen, the one filled with lemon juice. I would write the letter now, and post it very first thing tomorrow.

Deepdean School, Tuesday 5th November

Dear Alexander,

You'll never guess what happened — or perhaps you
will, because I think it really is true what you said once,
that mystery follows us around. There's been another
murder at our school. Or at least, someone has died.

The facts in the case are these. The new Head
Girl — the horrid one I've told you about — was found
after our Bonfire Night fireworks display near the
bonfire, her head bashed in and a rake lying next to her.
It looked like an accident — but all the same, we think that
it wasn't an accident at all. The grown-ups are sure that
Jones the handyman simply left the rake lying about, and
Elizabeth stepped on it by mistake, but we don't believe
that. We think someone hit her on purpose. You see,
everyone hated Elizabeth — so anyone at Deepdean
would have a motive to kill her.

But here is the interesting thing: almost none of us,
or any of the mistresses, could possibly have done it. All
the girls were lined up on the sports field in year order,
facing the fireworks, and the mistresses and Jones were
standing in front of us, where we could all see them. No
one could have moved from their rows without being

noticed. The only people – the only girls – who weren't standing where they could be seen were the five prefects. They were all behind us, near Elizabeth. They were supposed to be stoking the bonfire, and watching us, but any of them could have slipped over to where Elizabeth was (it was quite dark, apart from the light from the bonfire), and killed her. It's dreadful, because the Five were supposed to be her best friends – but now that Elizabeth is dead, none of them are acting as though they are sad about it at all. In fact, they are all behaving terribly suspiciously.

Do you see why I think we may have a new mystery to investigate? The other girls in our dorm – Kitty, Beanie and Lavinia – will help me and Daisy, but ~~twisk~~ it would be useful to have the Junior Pinkertons on the case as well. Will you and George help?

Ask any questions and I will try to answer.

Hazel
P.S. It's Sophie, of course.

The words faded away as soon as I had put them down, so I could not see what I had written. But despite that, I felt better than I had all evening. Just like that, I had thought my way into the case. Telling it to Alexander had truly made it like one of our logic puzzles. I imagined him frowning as he read, tugging his too-short sleeves down over his wrists, and I could feel myself smiling.

I clicked off my torch and lay there, my cheek against the paper of Alexander's message.

PART TWO

CONSTANT VIGILANCE

1

When the wake-up bell went the next morning, I blinked my eyes open and for a moment forgot what had happened the night before. The familiar sick feeling settled in my chest – and then I remembered, and it lifted again, to be replaced by something else. Elizabeth was *gone*. Elizabeth was *dead*. And it might be murder.

We went down to breakfast, and I saw Beanie blush. I could tell that she felt nervous about detecting. Daisy caught her eye, and Beanie went even redder and dropped her gaze.

At breakfast, of course, whispers about Elizabeth's death were flying about the room. At first the murmurings were kept under cover as the Five glared about terribly from their places at the heads of each table, trying to regain the control they had lost the night before. I think we were all so used to being quiet and afraid that we could hardly believe that things had changed. But then someone laughed, quite brazenly. We all froze, waiting for the punishment to descend – but nothing happened. There was another laugh, a testing one, and again nothing happened.

I looked more closely at the Five, and I saw that however they might be trying to hide it, their fear and confusion from yesterday were still there, worse than ever. Florence, at the head of the third-form table, drummed her fingers on the table top. Una was buffing her nails so hard I thought they would wear down to nothing. I could see Margaret pinching her thigh so hard that it surely must leave a bruise, and Enid, although she was head-down over a textbook, never turned a page. Lettice, at the head of our own table, was pale and tense as a string pulled tight, shredding a tiny bit of toast on her plate into smaller and smaller pieces. I never saw her take a bite, and usually, she at least pretends. The Five were changed, and the other girls could feel it. They became bolder and bolder, and the talk rose until it was nearly a roar.

I looked over at Daisy and caught her eye. She winked, very carefully, and I smiled at her. Across the table, Rose and Jose Pritchett from the other dorm were whispering with Clementine. 'She'll never, now! You're quite safe!' hissed Clementine. I knew she meant Jose, who had been due to take her punishment from Una this lunch time, for not remembering to fetch Una's coat for her last week. Una would be too distracted to care now – in a moment, last night's events had changed the whole school.

As well as the excitement of seeing the Five lose their power, the prospect of a new case beginning made me tingle brightly all over. As we walked down to school together I felt the same focus I'd had the night before. I could see everything: all the whispering groups, all the glances they cast at the Five. The whole world seemed to be fizzing with nervous energy, and the whole school seemed dizzy, as though today was a secret holiday. Lavinia kicked up leaves into Kitty's face, and Kitty squealed like a shrimp, wheeling about and dashing a bundle of them into Lavinia's face (most of them missed, and showered Beanie). I posted my letter, as slyly as I could, and I think I got away with it, for Daisy was watching Kitty, Beanie and Lavinia.

We stepped through Old Wing entrance and found it ringing with shrieks and laughter. But the excitement came with an edge. Elizabeth was not there to quell us, because Elizabeth was *dead*. I could tell that everyone was wondering who was responsible this time, and whether danger might be lurking down the next corridor, or even in their own dorm. Miss Lappet came past, and a group of third formers shrank back, and when Miss Runcible came rushing into our form room to take the register, even I felt a moment's fluttering heart. It was hard to remember that, this time, the mistresses were not our enemies. In this case, none of them could have done it, and none of them had a motive.

To the grown-ups, Elizabeth had been a good Head Girl. Only we knew the truth. No, this time the murderer was a Big Girl – it was the Five we had to watch.

2

In Prayers, Miss Barnard stood up to speak, even though it was not her day for it. 'Girls,' she said, and everyone went very still, as though the whole hall had sucked in a breath and was waiting to let it out again. 'Girls, I am afraid to tell you that following last night's unfortunate accident, efforts to revive Elizabeth Hurst were unsuccessful. She has passed away. Now, I know you are all very upset by this – please, quiet, girls, let me speak – but I want to reassure you that this *was* nothing more than a very unfortunate accident, unlike . . . well. You must not be alarmed. You are all quite safe. A memorial service will be held for Elizabeth in due course, and I must ask that you are sensitive to the feelings of those close to her.'

Of course, that was an invitation for everyone to look at the Five again. They all stared straight ahead, and Una and Lettice even dabbed their eyes with their handkerchiefs. They were working hard to pretend – to a grown-up they might seem every inch the good prefects they ought to be – but I could see that those eyes were dry, and I could feel quite other emotions bubbling up behind their solemnity, like laughter that they could not quite hold down. Daisy gave a small scornful snort, concealed as a sneeze behind her hand, at their deception, and I nudged her with my shoe.

'Out of respect to Elizabeth, the sports field will be closed until further notice. Now, over the next few days, I expect you to conduct yourselves as good Deepdean girls should,' Miss Barnard went on. 'Carry on as you would normally, be obedient to your mistresses and prefects, and help us keep the spirit of Deepdean alive and well. I do not expect to hear idle rumours in the next few days; rest assured that the only person responsible for what happened to Elizabeth will be disciplined immediately, and that no other action will be taken. I hope I have made myself clear.'

My heart clenched. What did she mean, *the only person responsible*? That could mean only one man – Jones. I glanced over at Daisy, and saw the wrinkle at the top of her nose. Daisy had thought exactly what I had, and she did not like it either.

Then the organ, played by Reverend MacLean, rumbled into life, and we all gathered up our hymn books rather haphazardly and began to sing.

'Stop wriggling,' said Daisy to Beanie. 'You'll give us away!'

'But what did Miss Barnard mean?' whispered Beanie. 'It wasn't an accident, it was mur—'

'Shh!' gasped Daisy. 'I know! But we've been over this – *she* doesn't know that. She could never imagine that the Head Girl might be murdered by another pupil.'

Daisy, as usual, was quite right. It was all part of what I had noticed before – that grown-ups never see the truth of what goes on among us. They have forgotten quite how difficult it is to be young.

'You think . . . she's going to blame Jones?' I asked, the blare of the organ drowning out my voice. '*Walk upon England's mountains green*, I mean.'

'Humph!' said Daisy. 'Just let her! Why – that's injustice! And the Detective Society does not stand by and allow injustice . . . *laaaaaaamb of God, on England's—* Oh, Elizabeth still manages to poison everything, even from beyond the grave. I – we – simply must work out what happened to her, so we can save Jones.'

'But what if we can't?' said Kitty. 'Miss Barnard's a grown-up. She can do what she likes – *pleasant pastures seeeeeeen.*'

'Detectives,' said Daisy, and her eyes were very blue as she stared at us. 'This is not an acceptable attitude. *Bring me my spear!* Hazel and I have solved *three* murder cases, which is exactly three more than most grown-ups ever manage. We can do anything we put our minds to.'

'*Bring me my chariot of fire!* I'm only being practical,' Kitty said.

'So am I,' said Daisy darkly. '*Nor shall my sword sleep in my hand!* We have to go and speak to Jones immediately. This is crucial!'

'All right,' I said. 'We're with you! *England's green and pleasant laaaaaaand.*'

'Hm,' said Daisy, and I felt her gaze on me, as though I was a wriggling little animal under a microscope in Science. 'Are you sure, Hazel?'

'Of course I'm sure!' I said. 'Straight after Prayers! All of us!'

'All of us!' said Beanie.

'All of us,' sighed Kitty.

'I suppose,' grumbled Lavinia, and the hymn ended.

3

As soon as Prayers was over, and the lines of us were streaming out of the Hall, we ducked and dodged from form to form, Daisy in the lead, on our way to find Jones. We were heading towards the North Lawn, but we did not have to go so far – we came upon him in Library corridor. He had on his usual stained old overalls, but the scowl on his wrinkled face was unusually heavy, and his lazy right eye was more off-true than I had ever seen it. There was a bag on his back, and a rolled-up bit of canvas in his arms, and he was wearing his hat indoors.

Daisy blinked at him. 'Jones!' she cried. 'Where are you going?'

'I'm leaving, Miss Daisy,' said Jones, his shoulders hunched, and his lazy eye shifted uncomfortably. 'Headmistress's orders.'

'But . . . you can't!' said Daisy shrilly, not worried about being overheard, although we were in the middle of a stream of girls, and speaking to the handyman so familiarly is a terrible breach of Deepdean etiquette. 'It wasn't your fault that the rake was there!'

'I'm afraid it was,' said Jones.

Beanie gasped, and I felt upset, as though a rug had been pulled from under me. Was Jones admitting it had been his mistake after all? *Had* Elizabeth's death been an accident, and had we merely been imagining the murder?

'I don't remember leaving that rake there,' Jones went on sorrowfully. 'I used it to sweep up some leaves on the field yesterday afternoon, before I built the bonfire, and I could have sworn I left it leaning against the pavilion before you all arrived. But then, there it was, next to Miss Elizabeth. I must be going cracked, and there's no use for a cracked handyman at Deepdean, is there? Like Miss B says, perhaps I oughtn't to be around you all. So I've agreed to go quietly. No hard feelings.'

'No hard feelings!' Daisy cried. 'But . . . Jones—'

'Now, Miss Daisy, don't fret,' said Jones. 'You won't even notice I'm gone. It's kind of you to pretend, but I must be getting on. Miss Daisy. Girls. Er.' He tipped his hat at Daisy, nodded at Kitty, Beanie and Lavinia, and stared awkwardly at my ear, and then he carried on down the corridor, towards Old Wing and the way out of Deepdean.

Daisy was left gasping in shock. For once she was not even pretending. Jones matters to her, both as part of Deepdean and (I know, although she has never said it) in his own right.

'This is dreadful!' she burst out. 'This – it isn't right! It wasn't his fault – how can he be punished for it?'

'Daisy, *do* you have a heart after all?' asked Kitty.

'I have a conscience, and so should you,' said Daisy.

'But if he didn't move that rake,' I said, because I could not stop myself, 'and he really did leave it propped up against the pavilion, then—'

'It was the murderer who took it!' Daisy finished triumphantly. 'Again, it all points to one of the Five! They were going between the pavilion, where the firewood was, and the fire, all the way through the evening, to stoke it. Any one of them could have picked up the rake along with a stack of firewood and hit Elizabeth with it. No one else could have been carrying that rake about without attracting notice, and we know that no one *did* notice, because no one's mentioned seeing it in an odd place before it was found next to Elizabeth. It fits! It has to be one of them!' We grinned at each other. 'But – oh, how horrid. By using the rake, instead of just a bit of wood, the murderer must have known that Jones would be blamed. They did it on purpose – to frame him!'

'Oh no!' said Beanie in horror. 'Would they really?'

'They did murder someone, Beans,' said Kitty. '*Framing* someone isn't even half as bad.'

But it was, I thought. Why, Jones might have been sent to jail for it. It was a horrid thing to do. This murderer, whoever it was, truly was dreadful. We had to catch them – it was our duty.

'Now—' Daisy began again.

Una came down the corridor suddenly, at the end of a trail of first-form shrimps. 'You lot!' she snapped. 'Fourth formers! Why are you out of your lines? Get back in at once, or you'll be punished!'

All of us flinched automatically. But then Lavinia shook back her hair and glared at Una. 'No we won't,' she said.

This time it was Kitty who gasped.

'Lavinia!' said Daisy, scandalized.

Una went scarlet. 'How dare you!' she said. 'Why, haven't you any respect?'

'Haven't you?' asked Lavinia boldly. 'Elizabeth Hurst is dead. You can't punish us. You're supposed to be in mourning for her.'

For a moment I thought that Una might slap her. She stepped backwards, her whole face flushed and her mouth open. 'I—' she said. 'I— Get to your form room at once! Get out! Go!'

We five turned and – not ran, because that would be against Deepdean rules, but walked, as quickly as we could, away from Una. I was shaking all over, and Beanie was making little whimpering noises.

'Lavinia!' gasped Kitty, once we were a safe distance away. 'Whatever came over you?'

'Well, why *should* we do what they say any more?' asked Lavinia, sticking her chin out. 'Whether or not I believe that one of them murdered Elizabeth, everything's changed. Can't you feel it?'

I knew what she meant. Things *had* changed at Deepdean. All the rules had bent, and the power had moved. Elizabeth Hurst's reign was over, and none of us knew what would happen next.

'Well, it was very bold of you,' said Daisy, frowning. 'But listen, the important thing is Jones. You saw him just now. He won't fight for himself, and that means that we need to fight for him. We have to!'

'We will!' I said, to comfort her, for she looked truly upset. 'We're the Detective Society. That's what we do.'

4

At bunbreak (slices of Madeira cake, which was lovely), gossip about Jones was all over the lawn.

'Jones has left!' said Clementine as we stood in a shivering huddle on North Lawn, peering up at the heavy grey sky.

'We know,' said Daisy shortly.

'It's because he was the one who caused the accident,' said Clementine, full of her news. 'You heard Miss Barnard. He was the one who left out the rake, that Elizabeth stepped on.'

My heart chilled. It was true. Poor Jones really was being framed.

Daisy's hands were clenched against her skirt. For once, she was struggling to control herself. 'It's not right!' she said at last. 'Jones belongs at Deepdean.'

'Huh!' said Clementine. 'It's not as though he's one of *us*.' And she walked away.

'Oh, how horrid!' said Beanie. She had gone quite pale. I did not know whether she meant Jones's dismissal, or Clementine's snobbishness. I might have agreed with her about both.

'It isn't just horrid!' said Daisy. 'It's . . . why, it's unbearable.' She looked straight at me, and I have only once before seen her eyes more blue and more desperate: at Fallingford last spring.

I opened my mouth, and then there was a shriek from across the grass. A second former, Daisy's little informant Betsy North, was waving something – a bit of paper – in the air. 'Listen to this!' she cried. 'Oh, just listen to the note I've found!'

Everyone on the lawn turned to her. I looked at Daisy, and saw her shoulders tense.

'*Astrid Frith dyes her hair!*' read out Betsy triumphantly. '*She isn't really blonde.*'

There were gasps. Everyone turned to look at the group of Big Girls, Astrid among them, who were standing watch in the doorway to the Library corridor to stop us going back in before the end of bunbreak. Her hair sang out, bright blonde. Was it true?

But Betsy had not finished. 'And there's another one on the other side of the paper!' she cried. 'It's even better! *Pippa Daventry's parents aren't married. Her father has a first wife in Australia!*' Her friends gasped and squealed, but around them the lawn had gone dangerously quiet.

I could hear a rook high up in the trees call, and rain in the distance. Pippa Daventry, another Big Girl, was shrinking away from her friends, shaking her head. 'It isn't true!' she said. 'Daddy wouldn't!'

'Mine isn't true either!' said Astrid desperately. 'It's natural, it is. I wouldn't ever—'

Daisy sprang into action. She marched across the grass towards the second formers, who stumbled rather as she approached, their faces dropping. Betsy looked rather nervous.

'Give that to me,' Daisy said.

Betsy held it up, but she did not hand it over yet. 'Someone dropped a bit of paper,' she said. 'I found it just by the edge of the grass, there. I'm only reading what it says – it's nothing to do with me!'

'Don't be an idiot,' said Daisy. 'Hand it over now.'

There was a pause, and then Betsy scowled, and put the paper in Daisy's hand.

'Thank you,' Daisy said coldly to Betsy, and stuffed it in her school bag.

'Come on!' said Kitty, motioning to the rest of us, and she went rushing over to Daisy. The other girls were watching, fascinated. Daisy's face as she turned to us was calm, but her fingers were gripping her bag as tight as anything.

'What is it?' asked Kitty.

'I'll tell you later!' said Daisy sharply. That surprised me. Was she stalling? Was it possible that she did not know what she had just been given? Daisy likes to know everything that goes on at Deepdean – she prides herself on it – so for her to have come up against a surprise was truly unusual.

'I say,' said Betsy. 'This isn't fair. I found it. I want it back!'

'No!' said Daisy. The bell rang. 'Go to your lesson! Bunbreak's over.'

'But what does the paper mean?' Beanie asked again. 'I don't understand!'

'Neither does Daisy,' said Lavinia.

The look that Daisy gave her then was furious.

'Oh, Lord!' said Kitty. 'Move it, Pippa's coming over!'

Pippa Daventry was indeed marching towards us, a very cross look on her face, and if the second bell for the beginning of lessons had not gone at that moment, giving us an excuse to rush for Library corridor, away from the worsening rain, I do not know what might have happened.

5

The first lesson after bunbreak was French, and Daisy was mysteriously absent. She stores up excuse letters from mistresses to use in emergencies, and before she slipped away she had pushed one into my hand. I gave it to Mamzelle, who spent the lesson convinced that Daisy was carrying out a most important task for Miss Morris, the Art mistress – although, really, I do not think Daisy needed to bother. Mamzelle was far too distracted by what had happened to Elizabeth.

'Morning, giirrrls,' she said, rolling her Rs in the particularly strong way that I knew meant she was worried. 'Settle down, settle down, *s'il vous plaît*! Silence!'

But we could not be silent after what had happened at bunbreak.

The handy thing about Mamzelle is that she is good at knowing when she is beaten. After ten minutes of trying to discuss the *passé composé* in a room of girls buzzing with horror about Elizabeth Hurst's death and the mysterious notes, she simply shrugged, chalked up *Write an essay about your last weekend* on the board, and sat down at her desk with the latest copy of *Weldon's Ladies' Journal*. I got a creepy feeling – for, of course, this reminded me of last year, when Miss Bell died, and lessons had fallen apart. I knew, from the way Mamzelle was turning over pages, that she was feeling the same.

At last the bell rang, and we all sprang out of our seats. I was desperate to know where Daisy had gone, and what she had discovered.

'Slowly, girls! *Lentement!*' shouted Mamzelle, and was ignored. We poured out into the corridor, and I craned to look for Daisy, but I could not see her. Then, as girls shoved around us, we heard a shriek. There were two Big Girls, one of them weeping.

'That's Heather Montefiore!' hissed Clementine. 'What's happened?'

'There's been another note found!' I heard a third former say next to us. 'There must have been! Ooh!'

'It isn't true!' Heather was saying loudly as we pushed closer. 'It isn't!'

'Then why is it on this paper?' asked her friend. 'You lied to me!'

'It's . . . it was a misunderstanding!' cried Heather.

'That's what Mummy says. Oh, do listen to me!'

'Your uncle is in a loony bin,' said her friend furiously. 'You told me he was a war hero, when really he *deserted*. It's shameful! I shall never listen to anything you say again!'

Now, Heather Montefiore is not particularly nice, especially not this year, but at that moment, as her friend stepped away from her in disgust, I felt dreadfully sorry for her. I still did not understand where these secrets had come from, but I knew that Deepdean was full of awful things; things that no one mentioned, that went bubbling away under the surface of life. What was happening? Why were they all suddenly coming to light?

I turned to see what the others thought of this, and saw Daisy next to me, as though she had never been gone. But she had gone pale, even paler than at bunbreak, with just a burn of colour at the tops of her cheeks. I knew that look – she was quite tearingly angry.

'How dare someone be letting out secrets like this! It's dreadful! Secrets are . . . precious, they mustn't be abused like this! It simply isn't right! It's not!'

I squeezed her hand. I realized that this must be her worst nightmare. She loves to think herself omnipotent, and is terrified that despite all her plotting and information-gathering, she cannot control everything.

'We'll work it out,' I said. 'We always do. And we'll find out who's behind it – who wrote the notes, I mean.'

'Oh!' said Daisy. 'As to that, that's not a mystery. That's where I was, just now. I had a theory, and it paid off.'

'What do you mean?' I asked.

'Exactly what I say,' said Daisy. 'I took that page Betsy found and compared it to a detention list that's pinned up on one of the boards – one that Elizabeth wrote on Monday. The writing matched.'

'You mean the secrets are from Elizabeth?' I gasped.

'Who else? Oh, come now, Hazel, isn't it obvious?'

I did not think so. As we went to Maths, my head was in a whirl. The secrets were Elizabeth's! But if someone had them now, and was releasing them, how had they got them? And – an even worse thought – it was suddenly as though Elizabeth had not died. She could still spread her poison through the school. We were not free of her after all.

6

I could tell that Daisy was now focused on the case like a dog with a bone (she dreamed all the way through Maths, and got all the questions in our test right by mistake), and so was I. I knew we had to break Elizabeth's spell, and save Jones. But certain other members of the Detective Society still needed persuading.

'You still haven't told me why I should bother,' said Lavinia as we walked up to House for lunch. 'What do I care if stupid Elizabeth is dead, and stupid Jones has been blamed for it? What does it matter if Elizabeth wrote down secrets, and some of them have been found?'

Of course, I had made Daisy tell the other three about her handwriting discovery.

'It isn't about whether you care or not,' said Daisy. 'It's about the principle of the thing! And anyway, secrets are private. They oughtn't to be spread. What if one had been about you?'

'But they *weren't* about me,' said Lavinia. 'What do I care about the Big Girls? And anyway, if Elizabeth was writing down those things, why should I care that she's dead?'

'It does make her look even nastier,' agreed Kitty.

'That doesn't matter!' said Daisy. 'It isn't about the victim. It's justice, I said so before.'

'And even if she was horrid, she *died*!' cried Beanie, at the same time as Kitty said, 'Besides, it's the fun of the puzzle, don't you see that?'

I ought to have joined in the argument, but my mind was stuck in the new letter I was composing to Alexander. It was so clear that it almost seemed to float in front of my eyes, instead of the wet grey of the path, and the woolly grey of our uniforms, and the streaked black of the trees. I wanted to tell him everything that had happened, despite Daisy's prohibition – after all, he was Alexander, and he was my friend.

I was so busy thinking about this that I did not expect what happened at lunch. It was minced lamb, with sticky toffee pudding for afters, and we were just clearing away the smeary lamb-plates (I was excited about the pudding) when there was a frantic burst of giggling from the second-form table, which Enid was supervising.

'Quiet!' she said, slapping the table with her open French book – but she was ignored.

The giggling increased, and then Lettice flew up from where she was sitting with the fifth formers and whirled over to the main giggler, Betsy North. 'Stop it!' she shrieked. The second formers all drew in a breath and leaned back slightly. Lettice in a rage is quite chilling. 'Whatever is it? You – North – what's that in your hand? Give it to me!'

'But I found it,' said Betsy, who does not always know what is good for her. 'Again! It's the second time today.' Lettice merely leaned forward and snatched whatever she was holding straight out of her hands. I saw that it was paper – of exactly the same sort as the page from earlier. It was torn too, just like the first piece, and it was not hard to guess that it was from the same place. From Elizabeth.

'Oh!' said Betsy. 'Why does everyone keep taking them away from me? I found both bits, I say!'

'Where did you get this?' Lettice hissed. Her face had drained of colour quite completely. The whole Dining Room had gone still, and everyone was staring at Lettice and Betsy. I looked around at the rest of the Five. Una's pretty blonde face was stark with panic, Florence looked simply ill, Margaret was gulping like a frog and Enid had gone absolutely pinched. I realized something: like Daisy, the Five all knew exactly who the paper had belonged to. And, more than that, what they knew made them afraid. Did this have something to do not just with Elizabeth Hurst, but with the mystery of her death?

'I found this one in a flowerbed,' said Betsy. 'By the entrance to House. Someone must have dropped it just before I came by. Here! Don't!'

She had cried out because Lettice was ripping the paper to shreds. Her long, slim fingers tore it into smaller and smaller slivers until they fell to the floor in a shower of white.

'Clean that up,' she said to Betsy, so quietly that we could barely hear her. 'Clean it up now, you horrid thing. That'll teach you to go about picking up things you oughtn't.'

She had destroyed it, I realized, to stop anyone seeing Elizabeth's handwriting. Our suspicions must be right – this must be a part of the mystery, part of the reason why Elizabeth was dead.

I saw the rest of the Five exchanging looks, and then Florence got to her feet. 'Listen, you lot! If you see any more papers like that, you just leave them be. They're not for you, so you oughtn't to have them. In fact, if we find anyone else with a piece of paper like this, we shall put you in detention all term, and we'll let Miss Barnard know about it!'

It ought to have been an awful threat – it would have been, before Elizabeth died. But now I could feel everyone in the Dining Room not caring. They wanted to know what had been on that bit of paper, and what might be on others that were yet to be discovered. Florence's warning had simply proved that there were more bits of paper and more revelations to come. I knew that after lunch, everyone would be ferociously on the hunt for secrets. It was no good the Five trying to hide them.

'What was on it?' whispered Kitty, craning about. 'What was it this time?'

Lettice shrieked, 'Quiet! No speaking!' but all the same I heard the news pass along the second-form table to the third in a few soft breaths, then along the row and across again, to the person on the end of our table. It happened to be Clementine. She narrowed her eyes in concentration . . . and then she burst out laughing. 'But we know *that*,' she said. 'Everyone knows *that*.'

'What is it?' cried Beanie, bouncing and infected with Kitty's enthusiasm.

'Why,' said Clementine, and she narrowed her eyes like a cat, 'it's perfectly obvious information. It says that Lavinia Temple comes from a broken home.'

Now, Clementine does not like Lavinia (their feud was the cause of last year's Case of Lavinia's Missing Tie), and it is true that Lavinia can sometimes be a beast – but there is such a thing as form solidarity, and this was quite shockingly against it. Clementine ought not to have passed on gossip like that, much less seemed to relish it so much.

We all gaped, and Lavinia gave a cry. She raised a fist, but quick as anything Kitty caught her wrist and stopped her. She rounded on Clementine.

'How dare you!' she cried. 'How dare you say such a thing!'

'You all know that it's true,' said Clementine, rolling her eyes. 'It isn't a secret!'

Lavinia was making a sort of low animal growl.

'Anyway, it doesn't matter if I keep mum about it or not. It was written on that bit of paper, and that means that everyone knows about it now. It'll be all around the school.'

'Oh!' said Beanie, with a sob in her voice. 'How beastly!'

'You think you're so special in your dorm,' Clementine went on fiercely. 'You think you're better than us. When everyone knows that Hazel Wong's father is an opium trader, and Beanie Martineau's never even went to school, and Daisy Wells had a murder happen in her house.'

At that, Daisy simply pushed back her chair, stood up and walked out of the Dining Room. Clementine looked gleeful.

'If you say another word I shall let Lavinia hit you,' snarled Kitty, in a tone of voice that I had never heard before. 'Hazel, let's leave as well.'

And all four of us stood up and followed Daisy. I was so angry that I only thought about the sticky toffee pudding twice on the way out. I was also struggling with Lavinia – I had to help Kitty drag her along, as she had gone stiff with rage.

The whole Dining Room watched us, and I could feel everything that Clementine had said swirling in their minds. I had forgotten how much gossip hurts when it is about you, how it makes your head spin and your eyes smart, and leaves you powerless and in pain. You want to stretch out your hands and snatch it back, but you cannot, and it is even worse when you know the story is untrue. My father, as I have said and said, is a banker, and absolutely honest. He would never touch opium in a thousand years, but it is no good protesting. The story is that he trades opium, and somehow, that is stronger than the truth. I have been followed about by the opium story ever since I arrived at Deepdean two years ago.

I realized something as I walked past the half-open doors of the second-form dorms, the rows of beds inside them neatly made. If Elizabeth really had written down the secrets she knew, she must have written down secrets about the Five as well. And there, perfectly, were the Five's motives for murder. Secrets are the most powerful things in the world – I had felt that in the Dining Room.

I could easily imagine someone killing to keep a secret hidden.

7

'I could punch them,' snarled Lavinia, up in the dorm. 'I could hurt them, I could – I could—'

'Really, don't do that,' said Kitty. 'It's all right, Beanie, we know she won't. Oh, sit down, Lavinia, stop thrashing about, we've all been upset!'

Daisy was perched on the edge of her bed. She was flexing her fingers, and narrowing her eyes, and I could tell that she was focused inwards, on the problem of the secrets.

'I take it back,' said Lavinia. 'What I said earlier. All right, I do care now. I'll do whatever you like.'

What seeing Jones leave Deepdean could not do this morning, the scene at lunch had managed: Lavinia was now desperate to solve the mystery.

'Of course we have to do something,' said Kitty. 'Dorm pride! Those horrid secrets – I admit, I was wrong. It isn't just the puzzle this time. Come on. Detective Society Meeting?'

I got out this casebook, and the rustle of its pages seemed to call Daisy back to herself.

'Yes,' she said. 'Excellent. Watson, assistants, we must detect. We must! It's a matter of honour.'

'It's a matter of lies!' said Lavinia.

'Yours isn't a lie, Lavinia,' said Kitty.

Lavinia scowled at her. 'Yes, all right,' she said. 'Doesn't mean I want it said in public, does it?'

'But where are the secrets coming from?' asked Beanie.

'We know that,' said Daisy. '*Elizabeth*. We always thought that she stored them up in her head, the way I— I mean, the sensible way. But, as I confirmed this morning by matching the sample from Betsy with Elizabeth's detention list, she appears to have written them all down. So, you see, we have a possible motive for our murderer – if Elizabeth knew something secret about one of the Five, and was threatening to reveal it, they might have killed her to stop it getting out.'

Lavinia scowled. 'They can't all have secrets!' she said.

'Why not?' Kitty asked. 'Most of the rest of us do. Isn't that what we've just been finding out?'

'Yes, but even if that's true, how are we supposed to narrow them down?' asked Lavinia. 'Isn't that what detectives do? Rule out suspects?'

'If they *do* all have secrets,' said Daisy, 'which, as Assistant Freebody happens to be correct about, is quite possible, the only way we shall rule them out is by discovering what they are.'

'And how are we supposed to do that?' asked Lavinia, curling her lip. 'They're Big Girls.'

'Easy,' said Daisy. 'We must listen out for gossip. You never know what details they may have let slip.'

'But what about the secrets being spread *now*?' I asked. 'Who's doing that? How does it connect to the Five?' This was a problem I had been stumbling over. If Elizabeth had been writing secrets down somewhere, how were they getting out now? It could not be the murderer, letting them out so freely, could it?

'It can't be the murderer,' said Daisy, as though she had heard my thoughts. 'The grown-ups think Elizabeth's death was an accident and Jones is to blame, so there's no need for the murderer to be dropping secrets to throw investigators off the scent. There won't *be* any official investigators, and no one knows that we've taken on the case.'

'So?' asked Beanie, eyes wide.

'So something else is going on, something we don't understand yet. It seems such an odd thing to do, to let out secrets like this. It doesn't make sense, and that's important. If something's untidy, there's usually a reason for it. That's what Hazel and I have learned in our career to date.'

'So what do we do?' asked Kitty.

'Carry on with our plan of action,' said Daisy smartly. 'But with some additions. We know that Jones was framed, and that we are dealing with a murder. We believe we may know why Elizabeth was murdered – because she had a secret about the murderer, and was holding it over them. So although we must keep on listening for gossip, and collecting alibis, we can begin to be more precise. What do we know about the Five? What might their secrets be? And what more can we find out about Elizabeth and her collection of secrets? Where did these pages come from? How many more are there? And, most importantly, who is releasing them and why?'

'I want to *hurt* whoever it is,' growled Lavinia.

'We can't actually hurt them,' I said. 'But we can find them. That's part of the plan of action.'

'Indeed,' said Daisy, nodding. 'Finally, we need to get back to the crime scene.'

'But how?' asked Beanie. 'They won't let us go up to the sports field! Miss Barnard said so.'

'Of course they will!' snorted Lavinia. 'Miss B just said that for show. I heard her tell the other mistresses that we'll still have Games tomorrow, and that Saturday's match isn't cancelled either. Worse luck.'

'Oh, excellent!' said Kitty. 'You see, we're good at this.'

'Of course we're good at this,' said Daisy. 'We are detectives!'

PLAN OF ACTION

1. ~~Prove that the rake was moved on purpose, and that this really is murder.~~ DONE. We now know that Elizabeth's death was murder.

2. Gather evidence about our five suspects — discover possible motives, and find out whether they had alibis for the ten minutes of the display.

3. Look for clues, especially up at the sports field — do this tomorrow, when we have Games with Miss Talent.

4. Find out the Five's secrets.

5. Discover who is spreading Elizabeth's secrets around the school, and why.

8

I knew what Daisy had said about not mentioning the case, but somehow I could not quite help myself. Alexander already knew there had been a murder, after all, so I owed it to him to keep him up to date with what we had discovered. During English with the new mistress, Miss Dodgson, when we ought to have been writing our compositions, I tucked this casebook on my lap, open on a fresh page. I took out my special pen with its lemon-juice ink, one of two (the other, of course, is in Alexander's school bag), and began to write, the letters fading away almost as soon as I had put them down.

Deepdean School, Wednesday 6th November

Dear Alexander,

The case has moved on since I wrote to you last night.

First, it looks as though our handyman — Jones, do you

remember? — is really being blamed for what happened. He's been made to leave Deepdean. We know he couldn't have done it. He's a very careful sort of person, and he never would have left a rake lying about like that, especially not when he knew we were all going to be running around the field after dark. He can't remember doing it, either, but because Miss Barnard is sure that Elizabeth's death was an accident, she is blaming him. It makes me sure that the person who killed Elizabeth is truly awful. They are framing Jones, making him take the blame for it, and that is terrible. It's quite wrong, and we can't let it stand.

And there is another reason why we must solve the case: people have begun to find secrets all over the school, the sort of secrets people want to keep for good reasons. They're written on bits of paper, and we have discovered that the handwriting on them is Elizabeth's. They must be hers, so they must connect to her death, but how did they get out, and why are they being shared around now? It makes sense to guess that this is the motive for murder — that Elizabeth knew something about one of the Five, and they killed her to keep it quiet — but if so, it can't be the murderer who is behind the other secrets being shared. The Five are terrified, you can tell. They've quite lost control of the younger years, and the mood at school is so strange today.

We're going to try to understand more about the secrets, to find out what the Five could be hiding, and we're also going back to the sports field at the next opportunity, tomorrow, to hunt for clues. Is there anything else you can think of that we ought to be doing?

Hazel

At that point, Miss Dodgson came walking down the rows of desks to see how we were getting on with our work, and I had to shuffle the pages of my letter under an old half-finished composition that I use for camouflage and pretend to be writing that. I looked over at Daisy, and saw with a shock that she was looking back at me, with her eyes very slightly narrowed. It felt like all the fizz in my chest had been sucked away. She must think I was working on this account, surely. But what would she do if she discovered that I was writing to Alexander about the case instead? I looked down as quickly as I could and told myself that I had every right to carry on. He was my friend, after all, and another detective.

I quickly turned back to this casebook, and my usual blue-ink pen, and carried on writing until the bell went. But I was really thinking of something else. Writing the letter had somehow given me a plan, a rather Daisy-ish one, and I wanted to put it into practice.

Now, the first formers happened to have a lesson in the room next door to ours, and so we all came flooding out together at the bell. Just as the crush became truly close, I spilled my books out of my hands, into Lavinia. As I knew she would, she growled, lashed out with her elbow and (I stepped aside as neatly as I could) knocked into one of the first formers, Emily Dow. Emily stumbled, and then Lavinia (being Lavinia) pushed her all the way over. Emily shrieked and fell.

'Lavinia!' Beanie cried, and rushed to help Emily up. 'Don't do that! Poor Emily!' For a moment Beanie looked quite fierce. Emily burst into tears and Beanie put her arms around her protectively. I was glad that Beanie, at least, had not been infected by the nastiness of this year.

'It's Elizabeth,' I said as Beanie and Emily stood up, and Daisy and Kitty pushed over to where we were. 'That's why we're all upset. Lavinia didn't mean it.' (I felt rather guilty as I said that). Everything depended on what Emily said next, and she did not disappoint.

'It's horrid!' said Emily, wiping her face. 'I've been thinking and thinking about it, ever since last night. We were so near, after the end of the fireworks! What if *we* had stepped on that rake?'

'But—' said Beanie, and then she went red. She looked at us helplessly.

'But you didn't,' Daisy said pointedly, and Beanie collected herself.

'It was Charlotte who found her,' said Emily, and I thought of what Daisy says: that if you give people room to talk, they will explain everything without you having to ask. 'She – she *tripped over her*.'

'She was just *lying there*,' said Charlotte Waiting, a little first former with curly blonde hair and eyes even bigger than Beanie's. Daisy made sympathetic noises, and as usual they did the trick.

'It was awful,' Charlotte went on passionately. 'We went over to the bonfire after the display to warm our hands – it was awfully cold – but the prefect beside it—'

'Enid, wasn't it?' asked Daisy casually.

'Oh no, it was Una, she had just put another load of wood on – she told us to move along. She was terribly flustered and cross. So we went back beyond it, towards the pavilion, and that's when we – when I – *trod on Elizabeth*.'

I could have cheered. There we had the beginnings of our first suspect's movements. Una had been at the bonfire just after the end of the fireworks, exactly on the spot to hurt Elizabeth.

A group of third formers shoved past us then, giggling at something.

'Watch it!' shouted Kitty, and one of them (of course, it was Binny) turned and stuck out her tongue. Then all four of them shrieked with laughter and rushed away.

'I don't like the way the younger years are behaving today,' said Kitty crossly. 'Why, if I was in charge, I should—'

'You sound just like one of the Five!' said Beanie rather reproachfully.

Kitty froze. 'I am nothing like the Five!' she gasped.

'Do you think another secret has been found?' asked Emily shyly, looking rather more cheerful. 'I never knew that the older girls had so many. I'm much less afraid of them now.'

Kitty opened her mouth to say something snubbing, caught herself and shut it again. She blinked, as though she had just thought of something. 'It *is* only the older girls' secrets coming out,' she said. 'Goodness. Our form is the youngest that's had anything revealed about them. What if the secret-spreader is one of the younger girls?'

She was quite right. For a moment we all stared at each other in surprise. Had we discovered something else important?

'It might be,' said Daisy thoughtfully. 'But it could also just be a blind. After all, there could be plenty of older girls whose secrets haven't come out yet. I happen to know that Violet—'

Just then, Betsy North came hurrying up to us. 'Psst,' she said. 'Information.'

'What is it, horrid little shrimp?' said Daisy loudly, shooing the first formers away. Then, in a lower voice, 'Go on, tell!'

'Listen to this!' whispered Betsy. 'I heard one of the third formers saying it just now. They were standing near Elizabeth, just before we all formed up in rows for the fireworks, when Lettice came up to her. She was shaking, and she said something about *secrets*. And Elizabeth laughed at her. She told Lettice that *she had better be careful, for the sake of her sanity*. And Lettice looked *terrified*. She went rushing away, and that was when Una came by, to line them all up.'

'Oh, well done!' said Daisy, excited. 'Bunbreak privileges for you tomorrow morning, Betsy, I promise you that! Detectives, we are beginning to gather important information. Now it is your mission to discover what else was overheard on Tuesday.'

That was the beginning of our run of good luck. We spoke to all the younger years – Daisy worked her magic on them, and they melted. There was general agreement that the Five had been behaving even more badly than usual last night. Margaret had shouted at a first-form shrimp, just after we had seen her snap at Astrid. Una had given two third formers detention for pushing out of their line, just as the fireworks were beginning. But we also spoke to plenty of girls who said that the Five were not merely cruel, but upset. Lettice, handing out sparklers, had had tears in her eyes, and before that she had been storming about, full of angry energy and snapping at everyone she passed – we had this from several people. Enid had been distracted, muttering to herself and not even seeing the third formers pretending to fence with their sparklers, although they did it right in front of her.

Each of the Five had been seen speaking to Elizabeth before the fireworks – it seemed as though she had never left her comfortable position near the bonfire. To our sighting of Margaret, and the third formers' of Lettice, were added three more. A second former had seen Enid pausing with a load of wood in her arms to speak with Elizabeth next to the fire, just after everyone had arrived and been greeted. Elizabeth was speaking crossly to her, telling her off, and then Enid walked away again to collect more firewood from the pavilion. The second former thought that this was quite probably what the argument was about: Enid having to collect firewood. 'She's always so busy with her books, she looked as though she hated being away from them!' she said. She was replaced by Florence. Elizabeth had turned and told her (so said the second former, who was feeling very important by now, at having fourth

101

formers listen to her so intently) to be careful collecting firewood, because *it might be too heavy for her*. This did not seem very likely to us. Everyone knows that Florence is strong as an ox and can stride over hurdles in the most terrifying way (women cannot compete at hockey at the Olympics, you see, so she has chosen hurdles as her sport, though during term time she is quite obsessed with hockey). But the second former was very insistent. 'It's what I heard!' she said indignantly. I wrote it all down, frowning rather, but knowing we could not discount information just because it seemed unlikely. We had done that before, to our cost.

Una had spoken to Elizabeth just before Miss Barnard's speech. We'd had to consult one of the fifth formers for this information, no one else had been close enough to the fire at that moment to hear, but apparently Elizabeth had replied crossly to her. It was something about Una's father, the fifth former thought, and Una had been furious – but of course, she'd had to whisper, so as not to disturb Miss Barnard, so the fifth former could not hear properly.

Binny's friend Martha was still spreading her story about seeing a man running away towards the woods, just before the fireworks began. We cornered her on the way up to House after school, and she blushed and said that, no, she had never said she had seen a *man* – only a figure – and it had been very dark, so perhaps . . .

We had plenty of information, but nothing that we could point to and say that it ruled out any of the Five. In fact, everything we had discovered made all our suspects look equally likely. What we did know for certain was that the murder must have happened *after* the fireworks began. Lettice had been talking to Elizabeth just before, so that made her a strong suspect, but the others were all in the right area too, and they had all argued with Elizabeth. Now what we had to do was discover why. There were hints, indications, and now we had to seize on those threads and follow them through to the truth.

PART THREE

THE SCANDAL BOOK

1

Two more secrets came to light at dinner, on two more bits of paper. One was found by a third former, on the walk up to House, and another was found by a first-form shrimp just outside House. One of them we already knew: that Alice Murgatroyd (the fifth former who helped Daisy last year, now a Big Girl) smuggled cigarettes; and one we did not: that Sophie Croke-Finchley had only got a merit in her last piano exam, and her father had paid to have it promoted to a distinction.

Whispers and giggles rushed through the Dining Room. Alice was sitting with her arms crossed, trying to look don't-care, but next to her was a space where Heather Montefiore ought to have sat, and next to *her*, Astrid Frith had her hair hidden under a contraband hat. Nervousness flowed from the Big Girls. They were the subjects of nastiness now, the ones who it was done to.

The other fourth-form dorm surrounded Sophie protectively, daring us with their eyes to even mention what we had heard. Kitty curled her lip at Clementine, and Clementine glowered back. The feud between them was clearly as bad as ever. I ought to have felt worried by it, but somehow I did not. I was thinking about Alexander again, about what he would say about all our new evidence, and somehow that made me feel light, but all the same full up before I even ate a bite. I found I could not manage the last few bits of my rabbit pie, and Lavinia had to eat them off my plate.

'Whatever's wrong?' asked Beanie, concerned. 'Are you ill?'

I shook my head, and avoided Daisy's stare.

'Frith!' said Una. 'Headgear off in the Dining Room! Or do you have something to hide?' Astrid simply stood up with a gulp and ran out of the room. Una caught Florence's eye, and smirked, and I felt indignant. Why, if it was our year in charge, we should never be so dreadful . . . but then I noticed that Kitty was drumming her fingers on the table. No, not drumming, *playing*, as though she was at a piano. Sophie made a gasping sort of sob and covered her face with her hands. Clementine was seething. Beanie looked upset, and I winced. Not even we were above the nastiness.

'Clementine,' said Daisy suddenly. 'How many goals did we lose to Headley House by last weekend?'

For a moment I thought that Daisy was joining in with the cruelty, and reached out to pinch her under the table, to stop her. But then I saw the look in her eyes. Daisy, as usual, did not mean a word she said. She was merely up to something.

'Two,' said Clementine, turning her head. 'Why?'

'And how many goals did you let in?' asked Daisy.

Clementine turned pink. 'You know perfectly well,' she snapped. 'Oh, don't be such a sourpuss, Daisy. It's not my fault the team's losing matches. I heard Florence talking about it with Elizabeth just after we arrived on Tuesday evening, next to the fire. Someone's not properly fit – I didn't catch all of it, but I know that things are about to change.'

'I bet it's you who's not fit,' said Lavinia loudly.

'Rudeness!' said Clementine, blushing brightly with rage. 'You really are a disgusting cad, Lavinia Temple, not a lady at all! No wonder, when you don't even have a father about to teach you manners!'

Lavinia gave a roar, and lunged at her.

Up jumped Lettice at the end of our table (her food was untouched again, I saw) and shrieked, 'Temple! Get up to your dorm at once! Detention!' I saw her hands shaking, the bones of them awfully red and thin, and I wondered about her again.

Lavinia shrugged. 'Don't even care,' she said, then she pushed back her chair and rushed out of the Dining Hall up to the dorm.

Beanie jumped up to race after her, so we all had to follow. The way the Dining Room was that day, no one bothered to stop us.

As we hurried up the stairs, I wondered exactly what Elizabeth and Florence had been talking about on the evening of the fireworks, when Elizabeth had said that the firewood might be *too heavy* for Florence. Clementine must have overheard the same conversation as that second former, but more of it. And what she had heard was odd. Elizabeth had not been particularly sporty, or much interested in that side of Deepdean life. Why would she suddenly bother with the hockey team on the last evening of her life?

2

When we came into the dorm, Lavinia was sitting on her bed. Her eyes were raw at the edges. 'I'm all right,' she said gruffly. 'But when we find who did this, I shall . . . *eat* them.'

'Don't do that!' said Beanie.

'She's speaking metaphorically, Beans!' said Kitty.

'Am I!' said Lavinia.

Daisy sighed. 'Metaphors are not important. What happened at dinner—'

'What happened at dinner?' asked Beanie.

'Florence,' Daisy and I said together. I felt the click between us and I knew, just then, that she was thinking the same thing as me. 'Clementine heard her talking to Elizabeth about the hockey team. What if that's connected to Florence's secret? She might be hiding something to do with the team, or her hurdles training.'

'Yes, but . . . how are we supposed to know for sure?' asked Lavinia. 'We can guess all we like, we still won't rule anyone out.'

'But their secrets must be written down on bits of paper, like the other girls'!' said Beanie suddenly. 'All we need to do is find them.'

Daisy beamed. 'Very true! And I believe I know the perfect place to begin the hunt,' she said. 'The Five's dorm. If they have any secrets in their possession, they are most likely to have hidden them there.'

'But didn't we say the secrets were coming from a younger girl?' asked Kitty. 'This doesn't make sense!'

'Cases never make sense until you have made sense of them,' snapped Daisy. 'We must continue to investigate.'

'Oh, I don't want to go into the Five's dorm,' said Beanie. 'It's terribly dangerous. And against House rules!'

'If you think it's dangerous, then you needn't have anything to do with it,' said Daisy. 'Hazel and I will deal with it together.'

My heart jumped. I had been thinking – well, that Daisy might have been able to tell how distracted I had been at dinner, and why. But now she was smiling at me, and I could feel myself smiling back. We lit up at each other, like an electrical circuit clicked into place.

'You really do commit a lot of crimes, for detectives,' said Lavinia.

'I don't commit crimes,' said Daisy. 'I *catch* the criminals. Don't get confused.'

Lavinia rolled her eyes – but before she could say anything else, the Prep bell went, and we had to rush away without discussing exactly *how* Daisy expected us to get into the Five's dorm.

During Prep, I wrote to Alexander again. *Dear Alexander, I think we are making headway with the case* . . . I wrote and wrote, my arm curled to hide the fact that what I was doing was not a History essay or a Maths problem at all.

I looked up once, and saw Daisy looking at me. Her lips were pursed, and she flicked her eyes from my face to the casebook, and then up again. I froze, and I felt my face giving me away. Did Daisy . . . know?

As always, one of the Five was taking our Prep, but luckily for me, it was Enid. As I have said before, Enid is our best hope for a university place this year (you see, not all of our Big Girls go to university. Most are only presented at Court and go on to marry Lords with no chins). She works without stopping, always head down in a book, and that means that you can get away with almost anything when Enid is on Prep. It did make my heart race, though, to be so close to one of our suspects. What if Enid was the murderer? What if she decided to hurt us too? I got shivers all over my body, thinking about it.

But then I looked at Enid with my eyes, instead of with my imagination, and saw how small she was, and how pale, and how her brow wrinkled as she read. Could Enid really lift that heavy rake, and bring it down on the back of Elizabeth's head hard enough to kill her?

There was a History book in front of her this evening. I had heard her mentioning an important test earlier, and from her look she was concentrating hard on it. I frowned at her, and she blinked up at me with unfocused eyes and then looked back down at her page. *Distracted*, I thought, and then, *by her work*. And I felt a connection between us, for although I have learned to hide it at school, I do love to learn as well.

Then I felt a nudge in the small of my back. I put my hand out automatically and felt the bit of paper passed into it by Kitty's hand.

Midnight feast, it said, in Daisy's writing. *Top Secret. You know what to do.*

This was a cover, I understood at once. Daisy would not simply suggest a midnight feast at a time like this without good reason. But why had she not told me beforehand? What did it mean? I felt confused.

3

I went back to the dorm, and changed, and went to toothbrushes, but I could not think of anything but Daisy. I was still trying to understand why she had planned a midnight feast without telling me. Why would she do such a thing? It could not have anything to do with Alexander's letter, could it?

At toothbrushes, Lettice and Florence were supervising, and I could feel the distrust in the air. There was so much that was not being said, and I understood as never before that every moment of unity between the Five was only a front. Behind that, they were divided.

'Hurry up, you horrors, or you'll send Lettice quite potty!' said Florence, and Lettice flinched, then took a step backwards.

'Don't shout, Florence!' she said in a furious, scratchy little voice. 'You've got to be careful of yourself, you know.' Florence cast an absolutely hateful look at her, and I felt thankful that we could escape to our dorm. But all the same, I wanted quite desperately to know what Lettice and Florence would say to each other when they were alone. And at that moment, as though the thought had jumped straight from Daisy's head to mine, I knew what she was planning to do.

We crept back to our dorm almost unnoticed (the other fourth-form dorm were having a row about Sophie's exam results), and turned off our light.

'What do we do now?' whispered Beanie.

'Wait!' hissed Daisy. 'Wait until things go quiet!'

So we waited. I heard the House hum around me, pipes and shouts and thumps as doors slammed and windows were hauled open (as I have said before, Matron is very fond of fresh air, even in winter). It made a living rhythm, and I was soothed by it.

The House sighed, one more door hushed shut, and there was quiet. 'All right!' hissed Daisy, and she sat straight up in her bed like a rocket. Kitty sat up too.

'Ooh, is it time for the feast?' whispered Beanie, bouncing into a sitting position and clicking on her torch enthusiastically.

'It is indeed,' said Daisy. 'Or at least, it is time for you to provide cover for *me*. You shall be holding the mid-night feast while *I* am detecting. I am about to put myself in terrible danger for the good of this investigation.'

'Ooh!' said Beanie, digging through her tuck box and unearthing an enormous box of Sharp's creamy toffees and another of Turkish Delight. 'On your own?'

'Oh, I don't want to put any of you in danger,' said Daisy, and there was a funny flicker in her voice.

My heart stuttered. What was Daisy doing? First she had not told me about her plan, and now she seemed to be deliberately leaving us – me – out of it. Earlier today, Daisy herself had said that we would handle this bit of the investigation together. What had changed?

'But what if *I* want to put myself in danger?' I asked. 'I've been in at least as much danger as you have. Let me come with you.'

There was that funny flicker again. And then . . . 'Oh, if you must,' said Daisy quickly. 'You can stand at the window and watch for me.'

'No!' I said. 'I want to come with you, all the way up to the Five's dorm. That's where you're going, isn't it?'

Daisy scowled. 'Yes, you're quite right,' she admitted grudgingly. 'I'm going to climb up to the Five's dorm. I'm going to spy on them. I'll bet anything they've been waiting all day to talk to each other safely. Now is the perfect time, and I mean to be there to hear it.'

Beanie gasped, and even Kitty's mouth fell open a little way.

'You know I ought to be there,' I said. 'I know shorthand, after all, and you don't. I can take notes.'

I am proud of the fact that I have become quite good at shorthand over the last few months.

'True,' said Daisy. 'But . . . I'm not sure the drainpipe will take two.'

I felt that jibe. I know I enjoy bunbreaks, but so does Daisy, only she shows it less.

'Well, I shan't fall,' I said.

'I shan't either,' said Daisy, rather stiffly. It was very odd – it almost felt as though we were arguing. Where had that come from? 'Now, are you ready? You three, get out your midnight feast things at once. We are relying on you to provide cover. If any of the other girls come in, tell them that we're off creating a prank, and if it's Matron, she'll be too busy confiscating things to notice that we're gone. We'll be back as soon as we can.'

4

We eased up the window. The night was very dark and rustling. Behind us, Beanie was arranging the midnight feast things on the rug, dropping them nervously and saying, 'Oh! Sorry. It'll go back together again . . . look—'

'Beans, that fruit cake's Fortnum's!' said Kitty reproachfully. 'It's from Granny, you can't just *drop* it.'

I stuck my face outside, into the cold breeze, and wished very much that I could go and sit down next to Beanie and eat that cake. I would not even mind the little bits of floor dust on it. But Daisy, hair done up in fresh plaits and socks rolled down, was putting her hand on my shoulder and hoisting herself up onto the sill. She crouched there for a moment, legs bent and fingers still gripping the cloth of my pyjamas, and wobbled, so I gasped and put out my hand to steady her.

'Do let go, Watson,' said Daisy sharply. 'I'm quite safe. I've done far worse than this before. Why, last year

I climbed to the very top of the Secret Tree. Not even Bertie's ever done that and he's supposed to be good at climbing. You know he's joined some sort of midnight climbing society at Cambridge? Why, he's not half as good as I am. Just because he's a boy!'

'Daisy!' I said, letting go of her.

'Do stop fussing!' said Daisy. She turned her head to look at me, and I saw her face blazing with excitement. She seemed to have forgotten to be annoyed at me for a moment, but I had not lost the upset in my stomach. There was something wrong between us, I knew it. 'Now, are you ready? We are about to embark on a most exciting and important mission.'

I swallowed, and nodded.

'Hazel,' said Daisy, and she leaned forward until her nose was almost level with mine, staring into my eyes intently. 'Watson – Detective Society for ever, yes?'

'Detective Society for ever,' I said, and my heart jumped with guilt. It felt like a test, but I did not know if I had passed.

'Good,' said Daisy, pulling away. 'I'll go first. Wait five minutes, and then follow. All right, wish me luck.'

And in one swift movement she stood up on the windowsill, spun, bent forward and launched herself out onto the drainpipe. I had one sheer dreadful moment when I thought she had not done it, but then there was a small ladylike clank and I saw that she was gripping onto it, arms and knees wrapped around it like a monkey. Then she began to climb.

Up and up she went, the white from her socks flashing like semaphore. I had a heart-in-my-throat second as she reached the place where the roof turns out, but she was up and over like a cat. Then I could not see her any more. The prefects' dorm is at the very top of the House, and its window is hidden from us down below by the lip of the roof. So there was nothing for me to do but wait. I couldn't concentrate on anything but what was ahead of me. For once I could not even draft a letter in my head.

I waited for what felt like five years, which were only five minutes by my wristwatch, and then it was time for me to follow. I tucked this casebook into my pyjamas, took a deep breath, and leaned out of the window.

5

I craned upwards. Daisy had made it look easy and not perilous at all, as though it was quite ordinary to be clambering up the side of a building in the middle of an English winter night, on the way to spy on five murder suspects. It was not. When I launched myself at the drainpipe, I nearly missed it, and had to scramble and clank, shaking, for what seemed an endless minute. I began climbing, and my legs ached and my arms twisted and my fingers scratched against the peeling paint of the pipe. I felt my whole body tremble, but I could not stop or let go, so I hauled myself upwards, inch by grim inch, trying not to make too much noise, or slip, or cry. At last, and I thought the moment would never come, my hands found the lip of the roof and I dragged myself over it to safety, washed through with nerves.

I had only ever seen the roof of our House from the road before, and I had only the vaguest impression of it as being rather normally roof-shaped. Now that I was up on it, though, it seemed as though there was not a flat place on the whole roof space. It was all peaks and dips and turrets, and I was tremblingly certain that if I let go my hold for even a second, I would simply roll off again. I also knew that Daisy would have had no difficulty with it at all. She does have quite marvellous balance. That is why she is so good at Deportment.

Once I straightened up (shaking) I looked for her, but found myself quite alone. Daisy had not waited. The prefects' dorm was on the other side of House, and so I had to creep my way across the roof on my own; it seemed suddenly as large as the world and twice as confusing. I was trying desperately not to breathe too loudly as I inched round a particularly pointy outcrop – and there in front of me was the peak of the window of the Five's dorm. Crouched over it, like a gravestone angel, was Daisy. She was bent away from me, her head inclined downwards, so I could see the edge of her hair, paler in the darkness, and the outline of her fingers gripping the tiles. I crept over to her and nudged her shoulder, and she nudged back automatically, without looking at me. She was already listening, and so I pulled this casebook out and began to listen too.

We were helped, once again, by Matron's obsession with fresh air. Like every window in House, the Five's dorm window was open, and the blowing wind that raised the hairs on my arms and made me shiver (Daisy held still as a statue) also whipped their conversation straight past our waiting ears.

And it was a conversation worth hearing. It must have begun before I arrived, before even Daisy had, but now it was in full swing.

'They hate us!' That was Lettice, her voice high and worried. 'Since Elizabeth . . . something's changed, haven't you noticed? They won't take orders.'

'Oh, let them,' said Florence's voice, snorting. 'They can't hurt us.'

'Yes they can,' Una said. 'If they knew—'

'I don't want to talk about this,' snapped Enid. 'Can't we go to bed?'

'Not until we've discussed Elizabeth's Scandal Book,' said Florence.

Daisy and I both heard those words hit home. There was a hiss from Enid, and a whimper from Lettice. Daisy sat up, and I leaned further forward. What did she mean? What was the Scandal Book?

'What about it?' asked Una coldly, and I heard the way that she and Florence were taking over leadership of the Five, now that Elizabeth had gone, trying to fill the space that she had left and not quite managing it. I made a note, next to my shorthand dictation.

'*What* about it?' echoed Enid sharply, when Florence did not answer. 'Don't you know that pages from it are

124

being spread all over school? Who's doing it? Who's got it? Is it one of you?'

There was a silence.

'None of us has it?' asked Lettice. 'Really?'

'Would those secrets be getting out if it was one of us?' snapped Florence. 'Someone else has found it, somehow. It must have fallen out of Elizabeth's pocket on Tuesday evening. She was taunting us with it earlier that day, after all. Or—'

'Or it was stolen,' said Una.

'We have to get it back!' said Lettice. 'We must!' She sounded quite panicked.

'And how do you propose we do that, *Lettice*?' asked Enid. 'Do we go up to the thief and ask nicely? *Excuse me, may I have our secrets back?* You're mad if you think—'

'Stop it,' said Una. 'We shall all suffer if that book isn't brought back safely. It must be one of the younger years. You've seen how unruly they've been. And none of *their* secrets have been revealed.'

'I'd watch the second formers,' said Enid. 'Betsy North, especially.'

'Oh yes,' said Margaret. 'She found those first two pages. And if not her, one of those first formers. They're terribly forward.'

'Good,' said Florence. 'Watch them all. Punish them if necessary. One of them must have it, and we'll get it back. We must stick together until this is cleared up.

Oh, Elizabeth! Even the accident hasn't stopped her secrets getting out.'

'An accident!' said Una. 'You really think it was an accident?'

'What do you mean?' asked Lettice in a strangled voice.

'Of course it wasn't an accident,' said Margaret scathingly. 'We wanted to step down as prefects, stop helping her. We didn't want to do what she said any more, we made that quite clear. And she was going to punish us for it. She would have, if she hadn't died. Quite lucky for us, wasn't it, that she never got the chance?'

There was a cold, cold silence as Margaret's words sank in. I was writing so quickly the symbols blurred.

'I didn't kill her!' said Lettice shrilly. 'I would never!'

'It goes without saying that none of us are going to admit to it, anyway,' Enid said, after a pause.

Lettice made a strange noise, as though she was about to cry. I flinched, and under my feet a tile suddenly slipped. I gasped, and Margaret said, 'What's that? Outside the window?'

'There's someone there!' cried Florence. I heard a noise, and then a rattle. Florence must be sticking her head out into the night. Then – 'It isn't anything,' she said. 'Must have been leaves off a tree. It's quite all right.'

Then she slammed the window shut, and our way into the Five's conversation was quite cut off.

6

'Hazel,' breathed Daisy. '*The Scandal Book!* Oh, but – how, Hazel, how could this happen? How could there be a book, an actual *book* of secrets, at Deepdean? How could I not have known about it?'

She was gripping my arm really quite tightly.

'Daisy!' I said. 'Daisy! Ow!'

'Do be quiet, Hazel, this is important. Hazel, a *book*!' She was reeling, as though she had suffered a blow, and I suppose she had. The world of Deepdean had burst open. There was a whole side of the school that was a surprise to her. 'We have to find it!' Daisy was rattling on, and I was glad that the window was closed. 'We have to get it back from whoever has it. Before the Five do, we *must*!'

'Of course we must,' I said, trying to be comforting.

'But Hazel, you don't understand, we *must*!'

'I know we must! Daisy, I have been listening.'

'We must actually get into the Five's dorm too, tomorrow, while they're out. We must make sure that the book isn't there, that they aren't lying. One of them must have been lying about the murder, after all.'

'But I don't think they *were* lying about the book,' I said thoughtfully. 'If one of the Five killed Elizabeth to stop her spreading their secret – and I'm sure one of them *did* – then why would she start letting out *other* girls' secrets? The killer doesn't need to throw suspicion onto any other girl at Deepdean, after all. Miss Barnard believes Elizabeth's death was an accident, so no one apart from us is looking for a killer. It's what we thought, that it doesn't make sense for them to begin spreading other people's secrets.'

'Yes, Watson,' said Daisy. 'They all seemed genuinely afraid, didn't they? They all have secrets, and they all know each other's, you could tell. If one girl's secret gets out, then she can drag the others down. So someone *else* has the book. It really does seem as though we are dealing with two quite separate crimes, which is terribly interesting. Goodness, what a complex case! We are dealing with a murderer *and* a thief.'

'Let's go back down,' I said. I really was beginning to shiver in the night. 'Tell the others.'

'Yes,' said Daisy vaguely. I could tell that her brain was clicking away like a calculating machine – in the excitement of the case, she had forgotten to be short with me. 'All right. I'll go first.'

Without waiting for my reply she rushed away across the roof, moving fast and gracefully. I heard a clank and a rattle as Daisy clambered down the drainpipe, and then a light click as she stepped over onto our dorm's windowsill. I waited again, and then crawled over to the pipe myself, struggling down it clumsily. I was so distracted that I almost missed my footing twice, and almost did not care. I had not forgotten how Daisy had been behaving, even if she had, and I also had the Five's conversation to worry about.

I stepped onto the sill, and there was the open window, the curtain waving in the breeze. I climbed back into the warm, breathing dorm with a gasp of relief. Hands reached out to catch me – Beanie and Kitty – and I was safe again.

7

'I can't believe you were nearly caught!' gasped Beanie.

'We were not!' said Daisy, taking a large bite of cake. We were both wrapped in blankets, plates of cake on our laps. My fingers were sticky with Turkish Delight, and I was leaning against Beanie's bed. 'We were quite safe, really. Spies never get caught, not if they're really good. And I am an excellent spy. And anyway, look at what we've uncovered! *The Scandal Book.*'

Daisy and I had explained what we had discovered: that something called the Scandal Book existed, and that it was missing; and that we were looking not only for a murderer, but a thief.

Beanie shuddered. 'What if the Five find the person who stole the book? What will they do?'

There was a very loud pause. I took a large bite of cake, and choked a little. What if the Five *did* discover who had been releasing the secrets before we did? If it was a shrimp, as they guessed it was, how could she hope to stand up to the Five, and how could she stay safe from the murderer? I shivered. For once, it was not us who were in the most danger. It was the unknown thief.

'We shall just have to find them first,' said Daisy briskly.

'Oh, of course,' muttered Lavinia.

'We shall!' said Daisy. 'We are very good at finding things, aren't we, Hazel? Really excellent. We must look for the book as hard as we can. And we must also do something else we planned: now that we have confirmed that the Five all have secrets, we *have* to discover exactly what they are.'

I could see Kitty perking up at that.

'And the easiest way to do that is to keep watch on them. Tomorrow, between lessons, we must tail them. It's quite neat, really: five of us and five of them. I'll take Enid, Beanie takes Florence, Kitty can stay on Una, and Lavinia can have Lettice. And Hazel, you take Margaret.'

I thought about this. As always, Daisy is clever with people. Florence would not notice Beanie, Lavinia is too slow to get on Lettice's nerves, and Kitty and Una have the same sort of sniffishness about younger girls. Was giving me Margaret a jibe – saying that I was slow and dull? I swallowed unhappily and pushed my mind back to the case. Daisy had given herself Enid, which was interesting. She always liked to follow the person she considered the most likely suspect. Could she be right? I was not sure. As I had thought before, Enid seemed far too small and mousy to hit anyone over the head.

'Ooh!' said Beanie, wriggling. 'Exciting!'

'It's crucially important that we watch them!' said Daisy. 'We must convene at bunbreak to discuss what we have discovered. Once we know their secrets . . . why, we'll have practically found the murderer!'

Daisy always does make things seem so easy.

8

In Prayers the next day the rumours about Elizabeth's death – her murder, it was still being whispered – were unabated, and I saw more clearly than ever why the Five were so sure that a younger girl had the Scandal Book. The littler girls were giddy, nudging each other and gazing at the Big Girls far more boldly than they would have dared to on Tuesday. The older girls, though, were silent, withdrawn, nervous. Those of them who were already the subject of gossip – Astrid, who kept on touching her blonde head nervously; Heather Montefiore, pale and tragic – hunched into themselves in shame, and all the others were almost as bad. I knew why. It was that they were all afraid that they would be next.

Suddenly the younger years held the power, and they knew they did. It was as though the whole Deepdean system had been put on its head, the shrimps sure of themselves and the older years wavering. The gold had

133

cracked off the older girls, and what was revealed was that beneath it they were only skin after all, like the rest of us. It was a shock, and that, I understood that morning like never before, was the power of secrets. They could change a person, change the very shape they made in your head. Until yesterday we had all known that Sophie Croke-Finchley was a musical prodigy, but now we looked at her and saw a new girl, one who did not think in waltzes. Whether the secrets were true or not had almost nothing to do with it. The rumour about me was a lie, and I was almost sure that Astrid's hair really was naturally golden, but that did not matter. Once it had been said, there was no taking it back.

I suppose this is something that Daisy has understood for a long time, and why she was so upset after what happened at Fallingford last spring. She trades on her reputation, and you cannot trade on a reputation that is broken. I imagined the secrets of the Scandal Book dripping out one by one and rising to fill the school with rumour.

Miss Barnard was reading the announcements. 'Girls,' she said. 'It has been decided that the memorial service for Elizabeth will take place on Saturday morning, here in the Hall. In the meantime, there will be a condolence book open in my office, for any girl to sign if she would like. I will also be on hand to speak to any one of you who wants to talk about Elizabeth.

I do appreciate that this is a difficult time for many of you, and though I know that the school will carry on, you must all feel this loss greatly.'

Once again, I did not recognize the Elizabeth in Miss Barnard's speech at all, the Elizabeth who was missed, and who ought to be celebrated. That was the Elizabeth she had known, but the Elizabeth whose death we were investigating had schemed and hurt until she had been killed for it.

Then the organ blared and we began to file away to lessons. As we left the Hall, I slid from our line into the line of third formers next to us, who were being led out by Margaret. Her face was flushed red. I wondered whether Miss Barnard's words were what had upset her. Binny and her friends were whispering about something as usual, causing a stir, and Margaret, hearing it, swung about in annoyance. 'You!' she growled. 'Stop it at once!'

The third formers hushed for a moment, and then the whispering carried on. As Binny snickered and whispered something, I saw Margaret's fists clench and her jaw set – and her eyes shine. She was near tears. Did this mean she was upset about Elizabeth's death after all, or that she was guilty, and regretting what she had done?

I made sure to keep following Margaret as she left the third formers at the door of their form and started back down Library corridor, towards Big Girls' Wing.

She wiped her eyes on her jumper and squeezed her fingers together tightly, so busy with her own thoughts that she did not notice me.

Then, just ahead of us, I caught sight of Astrid Frith. I saw Margaret give a start – at last, she came out of whatever funk she had been in. She sped up to reach Astrid, and as she did so Astrid jumped and stopped in her tracks. I pulled back, hovering next to one of the windows and pretending to be hunting through my school bag for something.

'What do you want?' Astrid asked.

'Why should I want anything?' said Margaret, her voice so loud that I could hear it quite easily, although I stayed a careful ten paces behind her. 'I only— See here, are you all right?'

'I'm perfectly all right,' said Astrid sourly. 'Why do you care?'

'See here,' said Margaret again. 'I – I wanted to say that on Tuesday night—'

At that moment, up came Lettice. Lavinia was lurking behind her. She was making a botch of it. She was much too far away to hear anything, halfway down the corridor, picking at her nails and yawning.

Margaret caught sight of Lettice and froze. 'I meant what I told you then,' she said loudly. Her mood had changed as abruptly as if she had flicked a switch. 'Your hair *does* look utterly fake.'

Astrid gasped, her face crumpling. 'Oh!' she choked out, and then she turned and hurried away, almost at a run. Lettice nodded at Margaret, but although Margaret nodded back, her face was stiff.

'It's the only way,' said Lettice.

'Don't!' said Margaret miserably, and I was more sure than ever that she would have said something quite different if Lettice had not arrived. I thought of what we had seen on the night of the murder. Margaret had seemed to be going out of her way to be nasty to Astrid then, and she was doing it again now, but at the same time I felt that she did not really dislike her at all.

The bell for lessons rang, and I had to hurry not to be late to Latin.

9

That morning, lessons happened like pauses in a sentence when it is spoken aloud. Most of what I remember of it I spent lurking about at the bottom of the stairs to Big Girls' Wing, pretending not to see Lavinia and Kitty and Beanie as I was doing so, and trying not to catch Beanie's eye as she grinned and wriggled at me. I barely saw Daisy – she is annoyingly good at this part of detection, while I really do dislike tailing people. It is such a bother. This mission was even more frustrating than usual. The Five are Big Girls, and that meant, under Deepdean rules, that they could go places that a fourth former simply cannot. There was so much that I knew I was missing that it made my teeth clench.

But despite the fact that I struggled to overhear anything really useful, what I saw was almost more important. The Five were skirting around each other, tense and mistrustful, but all the same they kept on coming back to each other. The loss of Elizabeth had stuck their group together with the most awful glue. They were all suspecting one another, and unable to say it. That made them hate each other, but need each other more than ever.

I saw Enid hiss something in Lettice's ear that made her blanch and rush away. I saw Una mutter something to Florence that made Margaret, overhearing, blush bright red with rage. They could not seem to leave each other alone.

And although I was looking at the Five, I was also seeing *us* – Kitty and Beanie and Lavinia and Daisy and me. I saw the way Kitty and Beanie have their own slightly private language and the way Lavinia is jealous of it, although she hides it beneath her general crossness. I saw that Kitty and Lavinia both want Daisy to notice them, and fight for it (while Beanie simply assumes that Daisy will not notice her, and has taught herself not to mind). And once again I saw the odd new way in which Daisy was looking at me, as though she had something on her mind that she could not say out loud. This case, it seemed to me, was becoming as much about us as about the Five.

At bunbreak we convened on the North Lawn, munching our Chelsea buns. 'All right, Detectives,' said

Daisy. 'What have you discovered? And if you didn't see anything, you weren't looking properly.'

'I did,' said Kitty. 'Or, well, I think I may have done. Una's in a terrible pet. She hates that the younger girls aren't being respectful. She tried to give some third formers detention, but they *ignored* her. Then, after Latin, there was something else. Miss Lappet came to talk to Una. She had today's *Times* under her arm, she must have just read it. "These new laws of Herr Hitler's," she said. "Very tidy – no room for doubt now, is there? Your father must be pleased, Miss Dichmann."'

'What laws?' whispered Beanie.

'About Jewish people,' I whispered back. Since this summer, I have become rather interested in Europe, and what is going on in Germany in particular, although not because I like it. Hearing about it gives me a sick feeling, but all the same I cannot look away. 'In Germany, there are lots of things you can't do any more if you're Jewish, and Hitler and the Nazis are making a special list of all the Jewish people, so there won't be any mistake about who can do things and who can't.'

'That isn't very nice,' said Beanie, frowning. 'Are you sure? Why would anyone do that?'

I did not know how to answer that, so I only shrugged.

'So? Why does any of this matter?' asked Lavinia.

'Because Una looked ill to death,' said Kitty. 'And I thought . . . well, that might be important. You know her father's something high up in Hitler's government? She usually boasts about him, but she didn't today. And I thought that might be important.'

'Oh! Remember what that fifth former said, that Elizabeth was speaking to Una about her father on Tuesday night?' I said. 'What if Una's secret is about her father and the Nazis? What if he's not as close to them as he pretends to be?'

Kitty looked pleased. 'That's what I think,' she said. 'It fits – and, oh, if you'd seen Una's face! She was terrified.'

Daisy clapped her on the back. 'Assistant Freebody, this is excellent work!' she said. 'Well done. Now, who else?'

We all hesitated. It was difficult to follow that.

'Lettice isn't eating,' said Lavinia. 'I stole her bun just now, and she didn't even notice.' She held it up to show us.

'Yes, well, she never eats, does she?' said Kitty. 'But that's not a secret.'

'Why doesn't she get hungry?' asked Beanie. 'I've always wondered. She's so thin . . .'

Kitty put her arm around her. 'Oh, Beanie,' she said.

'She's looking for paper too,' Lavinia went on. 'She's pouncing on any bits of paper she finds, and then, when none of them are secrets, she looks as though she doesn't know whether to be pleased or even more afraid. The only time she stopped hunting was to have a boring conversation about some dress she's having made.'

'Some dress!' said Kitty. 'That isn't *some dress*. You mean her coming-out gown, for her presentation at Court in January. I've heard about that. She's having it made specially in London, by the same dressmaker who dresses the Queen. It'll be peach satin, with a bow, and—'

'*Yawn*,' said Lavinia rudely.

'It's what I heard!' said Kitty defiantly. 'I'm only reporting it. She even went to finishing school in Switzerland this summer, Lausanne, I think, to prepare for the ball properly.'

'If I have to hear any more about that dress I shall be sick,' said Lavinia, stuffing bits of her stolen bun into her mouth. 'She talked about it with three different people. The same conversation! And nothing about her secret at all.'

'Beanie?' asked Daisy, raising her eyebrow. I could tell that she was not impressed with Lavinia's detective skills.

'Florence is very quick,' said Beanie, flushing. 'I didn't quite— Sometimes I couldn't—'

'Admit it, you couldn't keep up with her,' said Lavinia.

'No!' said Beanie. 'I mean . . . I did *sometimes*. I know she rushes about all over the school like a mad thing when there are other people about, but when she's alone, she *breathes*.'

'*She breathes?*' said Daisy and Kitty together.

'She *breathes*,' repeated Beanie. 'Stops and breathes. Like *this*.' She put her hand on her chest and blew out her cheeks, leaning sideways against Kitty.

'Whatever are you doing?' asked Kitty sceptically. Daisy was watching her with narrowed eyes. I could almost see her thinking.

'I don't know!' said Beanie. 'That's what she did. It was as though she wasn't feeling well. But the rest of the time she was striding about like anything and shouting at people about top buttons and detentions and things, so perhaps I misunderstood.'

'Humph!' said Daisy. 'That *is* interesting. What if Florence really isn't well? This – it may be important. Now, Hazel, you've been quiet. What did you discover?'

'Er,' I said. 'Margaret . . . I think there's something going on between her and Astrid. They met in the corridor, and they were speaking about Tuesday evening, but as soon as Lettice arrived, they stopped.'

'What's this?' asked Daisy, ears pricked. 'Lavinia, why didn't you mention it?'

'I didn't see it,' said Lavinia, sighing. 'Anyway, Hazel's told you now.'

'It was strange,' I said. 'Margaret was being quite nice to Astrid, but then, as soon as she saw Lettice, she said something horrid to her, and Astrid ran away. It was rather like what happened on Tuesday, actually.'

'Interesting!' said Daisy. 'Very interesting. Now, shall I tell you what I saw Enid do?'

'Work?' asked Lavinia sarcastically. 'Like she always does?'

'She was *trying* to work,' said Daisy. 'But she was terribly distracted. She kept darting in and out of rooms, and while Miss Lappet was busy talking to Una she went into the History room for almost five minutes. When she came out she looked dreadfully guilty.'

'So?' asked Lavinia again.

'So,' said Daisy, 'it's interesting, that's all. Perhaps she's looking for the Scandal Book as well – but if she is, she's being very careful not to show the others.'

'Oh!' I said, remembering something. 'The Big Girls have an important History test next week. I heard Enid mention it before Prep yesterday.'

'Watson!' gasped Daisy. 'You genius! Why – this could be the link. What if Enid wasn't looking for the Scandal Book? What if she was hunting for Miss Lappet's test paper?'

'You mean, you think she might be cheating?' whispered Beanie.

Daisy nodded, cheeks flushed. 'It does fit!' she said. 'Imagine! A cheat, at Deepdean. A cheat, cheating her way to university! Why, it's dreadful.'

There is a funny thing I have noticed, about the English and cheating. When you cheat in England, it becomes more than just the fact of cheating, it becomes part of who you are.

'But you can't know it's true, not unless you catch her at it!' said Kitty. 'We're only guessing, really.'

'Kitty's right,' said Lavinia. 'You're just making things up. Is detecting always like this?'

'We aren't *guessing*,' said Daisy crossly. 'We're theorizing. And we have four theories: that Enid is a cheat; that Una's father is not as close to the Nazis as she has been saying; that Margaret and Astrid have some sort of secret together; and that there is something wrong with Florence's health. Now all we have to do is prove our theories *right*, and to do that we need to search the Five's dorm, like I said. We must do it as soon as possible. The only suspect we haven't made headway on is Lettice, and so it's especially important that we search her dorm area. You never know what clues we may find.'

The bell for the end of bunbreak rang then. We were further along with the case, closer and closer to the Five's secrets. As we pushed through the throng into Library corridor, I was already composing another letter in my head. I turned and looked at Daisy, expecting to see her smiling at me – but instead I caught her giving me a very sharp stare. My stomach sank. I had thought that Daisy and I were all right again after this morning, but it did not seem to be true. And if we were not, I could guess why.

10

All the rest of that morning, I kept on getting the most unpleasant creeping feeling, as though all the air was being let out of me, as though I had made a horrid mistake that I could not put right. Could Daisy really know about Alexander's letters? And if so, could she really hate me for it? Surely not. But then, I had the evidence of my own eyes. Something was wrong with her.

It did not help that another secret had come out. This had been found lying on the path to House, by the third former Alma Collingwood, and it was the most scandalous one yet.

'Emmeline Moss killed her twin!' gasped Kitty. 'Apparently it was when they were very young. They were both standing next to a pond, and Emmeline pushed her in, and she drowned.'

'Oh!' cried Beanie, eyes welling up. 'Oh, how awful! It can't be true! It must be a mistake.'

'That's what the secret said!' said Kitty.

'It doesn't have to be a fact!' I said. 'Some of the secrets in the book are lies. You know there's that one about my father!'

Kitty looked rather guilty. 'Oh,' she said. 'I forgot – well, I suppose they're not *all* true. But most of them are.'

We stepped through the front door of House. The smell of steak and kidney pudding gusted about us, but for once it made me feel ill, rather than hungry.

At that moment Emmeline Moss herself, a fifth former with dark hair and a thin face, came pushing past us out of the door. She had tears in her eyes. Someone in the hallway laughed, a nasty sound, and everyone else turned to look at the door, and us. I felt again how horrid gossip could be, whether or not there was truth to it. It would be impossible to see Emmeline from now on, and not think of her twin, and wonder whether it had been an accident.

'Ooh, the post's been!' said Beanie. I turned to look at our pigeonholes, and I saw Daisy's head snap round as well. There was a letter for Kitty, and one for Clementine, and . . . one for me, in the handwriting I knew very well.

'What's that?' asked Daisy coolly, from behind me.

'Nothing,' I said, feeling myself flush scarlet. 'Let's go to lunch.'

'But you've got a letter,' said Beanie. 'Look!'

I froze. 'It's from my cousin,' I said. I was suddenly tingling all over.

'Hazel Wong, you haven't got a cousin,' said Daisy. And she reached forward and picked up Alexander's letter by its edge, dangling it between her fingers. 'So who could this be from?'

I felt my face going red. 'I do!' I said, following her as she walked through the doorway into the Dining Room and fighting not to snatch the letter away from her. 'You just don't know about her.'

'That isn't true,' said Daisy, and little pink spots appeared at the tops of her cheeks. 'You know it isn't. And I can tell when you lie.'

'I am not lying!' I said, and my own cheeks were burning again.

'Yes you are,' hissed Daisy, sitting down in her seat at the table, just too far away for me to be able to reach for her. 'I know you, Hazel Wong, I know you inside out, and I know what you've been doing.'

'No you don't,' I said, my stomach churning.

The whole table was watching us now. I hated the eager look on Clementine's face. I could feel a new story starting, more gossip about me, and it would all be Daisy's fault.

'Of course I do! You've been writing to *a boy*, Hazel Wong! You've been doing it all term, and you thought

149

I wouldn't notice!' She lowered her voice. 'Just tell me you haven't told him about the case,' she hissed. 'You haven't, have you?'

I felt dizzy and thin, as though I was hovering somewhere above all our heads like one of the ghosts we used to try to summon with our Ouija-board rituals. This could not be happening. 'I—' I said. 'But . . . he's a detective too, you know that, I was just—'

Daisy went white. 'You broke the Detective Society pledge!' she hissed. 'How could you? You . . . *enemy*!'

'No,' I said, the words stumbling out of my mouth. 'Daisy—'

'And the worst part is,' said Daisy at last, very quietly, although I could see every movement her mouth made, 'that he doesn't even *like* you like that, Hazel.'

I slapped her. My hand moved on its own, as though we were two parts of a magnet. I heard the crack of it, then Beanie's wail. Daisy did not make a noise.

The whole Dining Room gaped, and then Florence stood up from the end of our table. She shouted, 'Stop that at ONCE! Wells! Wong!' Then she put her hand on her chest, and I saw what Beanie had meant about her *breathing*. Her face looked pale, and I could believe at that moment that she really was ill.

But I could hardly think about that. The dizzy feeling was worse than ever, and I got up, snatched the letter from where Daisy had dropped it on the table, and rushed out of lunch into the corridor. I raced up the stairs – someone shouted after me, but I ignored them – and before I knew it I was in the airing cupboard where once Daisy and I had held our first ever Detective Society meeting. I crawled into the very lowest space, among the crackling fresh sheets that smelled of starch and coolness. We keep a spare torch there, and I dug it out and clutched it, and my letter, and this casebook. How could I have done that to Daisy? How could she have done that to me?

I tore open Alexander's letter, heated it against the torch, my fingers shaking, and read.

11

Dear Hazel,

Really? A murder at Deepdean? Murder does follow both
of you around. Of course, if you think it was murder, then
I believe you. George and I agree that it could not have
been Jones, and so he must have been framed by one of the
prefects. No one else could have done it, it's so neat, really,
perfect, except that it's going to be terribly hard to narrow
them down any further. Do any of them have alibis? Do you
know their motives? I suppose clues will be particularly
important in this case. Have you been able to go back to the
scene of the crime yet? I wish we were on the spot with
you. Listen to gossip as well. You never know who may
have seen something important. What does Daisy always

say? *Constant vigilance.* Good luck, and keep us up to date. I wrote this as quick as I could and sent it by return of post.

Alexander

I crumpled the page against my knee. It was exactly what I had wanted to read – Alexander must have read my first letter yesterday afternoon, and replied immediately by the second post – but all the same, it had been the cause of the most terrible rift between me and Daisy. Her words floated back through my head: *he doesn't even* like *you like that, Hazel.* It made me furious. Alexander and I were friends, that was all. Why did Daisy have to be so cruel and twist it into something awful?

The airing-cupboard door creaked open and I froze. But then . . . 'Hazel?' whispered Beanie.

'Here,' I whispered back in relief, and Beanie came burrowing into the sheets like a little animal. She huddled up close to me, and after a moment she patted my arm. 'Hello,' she said. 'Are you all right?'

'Yes,' I said miserably. 'No.'

'I don't think Daisy meant it,' said Beanie. 'I don't think either of you meant it. Kitty's terribly cross with her for teasing you. Were you really writing to a boy?'

'Daisy always has to be right,' I said. 'And yes, to

153

Alexander. Remember I told you about him? We met him on the train this summer.'

'Oh, I remember,' said Beanie. 'He sounded nice. It'll be all right. I know it will. You and Daisy are friends, always.'

I was not sure about that, but I did not want to hurt Beanie by saying so.

We sat leaning our heads together and not speaking for a while. I felt my breathing steady and my heart calm in my chest. Beanie was enormously comforting.

And then the airing-cupboard door opened again.

I nearly opened my mouth to say, *Who is it?* but something made me pause, just in case it was Daisy. And a moment later, I was gladder than anything that I had stayed quiet – for the person who came through the door was not Daisy, but Florence.

I saw her worn-in brown shoes and her legs, very long and rather trunk-like (from all the sport she does, of course), with fine reddish hairs on them, and I could smell her, like grass and exercise. Then someone else came through the door behind her. These legs were blonde and shapely, and the shoes at the bottom of them were glossy and quite new. They belonged to Una.

Beanie had her fingers around my arm, quite painfully, and I said, '*Shh!*' in her ear. I felt her give a jerky little nod, and knew that she would be quiet. I was amazed. Beanie and I, quite by accident, had managed to be on the spot for the sort of meeting that we had wanted to overhear, and assumed that we never could.

'I don't see why we have to meet in the airing cupboard,' said Una, sounding rather snobbish about it.

'Oh, do be quiet, it's the only secret place in this wretched House,' said Florence. Her voice was rough, and she moved restlessly.

'So, what do you want to say to me?' asked Una, her slight German accent coming out more than usual in her words. I wondered if she was nervous. 'And why can't you say it in front of the others?'

'You know perfectly well,' said Florence. 'Elizabeth. If she had told those secrets, she would have ruined us all. It was enough for any one of us to—'

'To kill her?' asked Una. 'Ah, you've thought of that too. It's certainly true. You think one of us *did* do it. But which? Or is this your confession?'

She said it coolly, as though it hardly mattered, but I could feel shivers of tension run through the space between them.

'Of course not! I'm innocent. But one of us isn't.'

'So why ask me here? It could be me. I might be the murderer. And then what would you do?'

'Nothing,' said Florence. 'Because I won't tell. And I know you won't either. Because your secret isn't just about you. It's about your father – your whole family.'

Una tensed. 'Is this because of the Games?' she asked. 'Are you afraid that if my father is removed from the Party you'll have no one to stay with in Berlin next summer?'

'Don't be slow,' said Florence. 'You know what I'm trying to say, more than any of the others would. No matter who is guilty, we can't let on what we know, because if one of us falls, we all do. If it's discovered that Elizabeth's death wasn't an accident, all our secrets come out. Whoever did it would have no reason to keep them hidden any longer. You lose your family. I lose the Games.' There was almost a sob in her voice as she said that. Florence, who had seemed so hard and strong! 'You know, I don't think Elizabeth ever really understood what our secrets meant. To her, they were just . . . ways in. It was the only way Elizabeth knew to be close to someone: by keeping their secrets. She didn't see why we should be hurt by them. But you do, and that's why I asked you here. You understand that more than anyone. We have to stick together and make sure what happened to Elizabeth officially stays an accident. Jones has been blamed for being careless about the rake, but that may not be enough.'

'I know,' said Una. 'We must get hold of that book. Then we'll be safe. And Elizabeth won't matter.'

'Whatever it takes,' said Florence, fierce again.

'Indeed,' said Una. 'I may have an idea about that. We shall see. And in the meantime, we don't say anything about Elizabeth, or who might have done it. We keep the secret. We're good at that, by now.'

They shook hands. Then the airing-cupboard door opened once, twice, and we were alone again. I could feel Beanie shaking next to me, like a little dog, and I put my hand on her shoulder. Daisy and I might be arguing, but in the face of the astonishing things we had just heard, that hardly mattered. When you are a detective, some things are more important than yourself.

PART FOUR

THE DETECTIVE SOCIETY IN DANGER

1

Beanie and I raced back to the dorm, but when we arrived, only Kitty and Lavinia were there. 'Daisy's gone,' said Kitty. 'She said she had to do something.'

That ached, but I was not surprised. Of course Daisy would not be here. She was in another part of House, following her own leads. It was my punishment for what I had done. I thought about what Florence had said, that knowing secrets was the only way Elizabeth knew to be close to someone. And I thought I knew who else that sounded like.

'But just listen to what we heard!' said Beanie. In a flood of words, she poured out what we had seen.

'But do you really think they were telling the truth?' asked Kitty.

I nodded. I did not want to detect, not at all, but I had to hold myself together. 'I don't see why they wouldn't,' I said. 'What Florence said about the Games next summer – that's the Olympics, of course. And when we put that together with what Beanie saw, I think she really is ill, and hiding it because she wants to go to Berlin.'

'Oh!' said Kitty. 'Why, of course! You know, my cousin knew someone who had something wrong with her heart, and she'd pant after she went up the stairs.'

'Ooh!' said Beanie. 'Yes! That's just like what I saw. Oh, poor Florence! Imagine!'

Despite myself, I began to feel excited. 'And Una—' I said.

'Una's *is* about her father and the Nazis!' said Beanie.

I thought about some of the things I had learned this summer on the Orient Express, and what Miss Lappet had said to Una.

'What if Una's father is secretly Jewish?' I asked. 'Or someone in her family is? If the Nazis found out, he'd have to leave the Party. Her family might even have to leave Germany. That would fit, wouldn't it?'

'Yes!' said Beanie. 'Oh, poor Una!'

'Beanie, stop feeling sorry for everyone!' said Lavinia. 'One of them's a murderer, remember?'

'Even murderers are people,' said Beanie. 'And they both said they didn't do it.'

'You can't just believe them, Beans!' said Kitty. 'But we *can* write both motives down on our suspect list now, can't we?'

'We do still have to make sure we're right,' I said. 'We need to get proper evidence. A conversation, even that one, isn't enough.'

'Do you think Daisy will still let you—' Kitty began. There was a very still, uncomfortable silence.

'We'll see,' I said. 'I'll write them down anyway. The suspect list needs to be updated.'

I hoped they could not see my hands shaking.

SUSPECT LIST

1. *Una Dichmann.* Was near the bonfire when Elizabeth was killed. She was seen by a fifth former having cross words with Elizabeth as the sparklers were being handed out, and was then seen beside the bonfire again by two first formers just after the end of the fireworks. NOTES: We believe we have uncovered her motive. She had an uncomfortable reaction to Miss Lappet's mention of the Nazis (witnessed by Kitty Freebody), and from this and her conversation with Florence we suspect that her father or someone in her family may be secretly Jewish. This would be an excellent motive for murder. Now we must confirm it is true.

2. *Florence Hamersley.* Was near the bonfire when Elizabeth was killed. Seen arguing with Elizabeth just after the younger girls arrived at the sports field by second formers and Clementine. NOTES: Beanie Martineau and Hazel Wong overheard her speaking about her secret to Una. She seems to be hiding an illness in order to go to next summer's Olympics. If true, this would be an excellent motive for murder. Now we must confirm it.

3. *Lettice Prestwich.* Was near the bonfire when Elizabeth was killed. Seen crying while handing out sparklers, clearly very distressed. Also heard arguing with Elizabeth just before the fireworks began. NOTES: She has been very nervous, and has not been eating. She is also clearly hunting hard for the Scandal Book. Is this her guilty conscience, or is it merely because she is afraid of her secret getting out? We must investigate further.

4. *Enid Gaines.* Was near the bonfire when Elizabeth was killed. Was seen standing with Elizabeth next to the fire just after everyone arrived, Elizabeth speaking crossly to her. NOTES: She

has been very preoccupied, although Elizabeth's death has not stopped her working entirely. Daisy Wells saw her going into the History room while Miss Lappet was out. Hazel Wong overheard her mentioning that the Big Girls have a History test coming up. Could the two things be connected? Is Enid trying to cheat? We must investigate further.

5. *Margaret Dolliswood*. Was near the bonfire when Elizabeth was killed. Argued with Astrid Frith, and was also seen arguing with Elizabeth before the fireworks display. NOTES: She has since been seen with Astrid Frith by Hazel Wong. What is going on between them? We must investigate further.

The bell for the end of lunch rang. 'Ugh!' groaned Lavinia. 'Games!'

Kitty looked at me. '*Games*,' she said, raising her eyebrows. 'Didn't you say we needed to look for clues?'

I could feel my heart speeding up. Although Games meant facing Daisy for the first time after our argument, it also provided the perfect opportunity to hunt for clues at the scene of the crime. I realized that I was actually looking forward to getting onto a sports field.

2

It was a cold, wet English day outside. The trees on the sports field stood up ghostily out of the mist at the edges of the pitch, moisture shivering off them onto the grass in heavy patters.

It was strange to step through the gates and see the field again, the grass hardly even showing a mark of all the feet that had crossed it on Tuesday evening. Except there, between the lines of the hockey pitch and the pavilion, and showing up horridly darkly against the silver-green ground, were the remains of the bonfire, and close to that was the spot we all knew to avoid, the place where Elizabeth Hurst had fallen on Tuesday night. The rain had made all the blood wash away. There would be no clues there.

The changing room in the pavilion was subdued. Even Clementine was dampened, and Beanie whimpered as she pulled on her games knickers. I felt like whimpering too, from the cold and the upset in my chest. Daisy kept glaring at me, but not speaking to me. I knew that I had been the one to slap her – but she had been so awful to me. How were we to make it up this time, and if we could not, what would it do to the case? I had not yet told Daisy about what Beanie and I had overheard, and I did not know where she had gone at lunch. Neither of us had ever solved a case without each other before. How were we to deduce the answer to this one without sharing all the information that we needed?

'Buck up, Beans,' said Daisy, with one more flick of her eyes at me, and she put her chin up and marched out onto the pitch. Beanie, Kitty and Lavinia all looked from me to Daisy, unsure what to do. Then, of course, they followed her. 'Sorry, Hazel,' Beanie whispered to me as she went.

'It's all right,' I said stupidly, stumbling after them. But I did not mean it.

Third and fourth formers take Games together on Thursday afternoons, and when we arrived outside again, most of the third form was already waiting, Binny Freebody in the lead. She smirked at Kitty, and Kitty glared at her and muttered about impertinent little sisters.

'I heard that,' said Binny, scowling. 'And see here, Kitty Freebody, you may think you're so grown up, and you and your friends know everything. But you don't. You're just as in the dark as anyone, all you bigger girls. You'll see. There are things about this school that only we younger years know, isn't that right?'

All her friends shifted about and nodded, although I saw little Martha Grey blush. Once again, I had the feeling of power shifting. The third formers ought to be afraid of us fourth formers, but now it was us who stepped back from them. Sophie Croke-Finchley clutched her hockey stick protectively, and Rose Pritchett looked pale.

Kitty, though, snorted. 'You are quite the worst little sister imaginable,' she said. 'If only someone would bump *you* off next!'

'Ooh!' said Binny with relish. 'That's a horrid thing to say. Don't let a mistress hear you talking like that!'

Just then Miss Talent, the games mistress, strode up, glaring and tugging at the whistle on a string around her neck. 'Form up into teams, girls!' she barked. 'You! You! You! And you! You're one team, and the rest of you are the other. Stop groaning! You! Fetch the hockey sticks. You'll have to get out one of the spares – there's been one missing since yesterday. Hurry up, we don't have all day! Now come back here and jog. Go! Down to the end of the field and back. And don't look so lumpish! At the double, girls, quick!'

I never thought I would miss Miss Hopkins, our old games mistress, but, well, life is surprising. Miss Talent's Scottish barks followed us down the field as we ran on our warm-up lap, cross about that missing hockey stick. She seemed half convinced that the third formers had hidden it – which, I thought, they probably had. My neck was warm and the chilly air clung to my arms and legs, making me feel uncomfortably hot and uncomfortably damp and short of breath, even in the cold. I watched Daisy lope away at the front of the pack, Kitty just behind her, and was resentful.

By the time we began the hockey game proper, I was already wheezing. Lavinia and I hovered back in our usual spot in defence (the little third former Alma was in goal, looking very nervous behind her padding). Binny and her friends had all managed to get themselves on our team, with Clementine, while Kitty, Daisy and Beanie were on the other. I could see from Kitty's face that she was still cross with Binny, and even before they clashed sticks and began, I knew it would not be a friendly match at all. Kitty had her teeth set, and she began to make great lunges forward, passing back and forth with Daisy, leaping high over attacking sticks and almost bowling Clementine over as she went.

Daisy came down the field towards me, and dread pooled in the pit of my stomach. She looked so determined. How could I stop her? I readied myself, stick out – and she whisked round me as though I was not even there, putting the ball neatly in the back of the goal. She had not even met my eye.

But then Kitty began to exhibit some very odd behaviour indeed. She pelted down the field towards Lavinia and me again, and I readied myself for another awful steamrolling. But then, instead of passing sideways to Daisy, she seemed to stumble, and the ball went flying to the left to land in the long grass under the trees.

Lavinia grumbled, and went lumping off to fetch it, coming back a few minutes later with her legs and games socks covered with leaves. It made me think of something . . . I almost remembered it . . . but then it was gone as Miss Talent shouted at us.

'Hit it, Temple! Good grief, girl, hit the ball! Have you learned nothing in four years?'

Lavinia managed a weak, resentful hit, glaring hotly at Miss Talent as she did so, and the ball was back in play. But only a few minutes later, Kitty came pelting at us once again, and the same thing happened. Off the ball flew, thunking against a tree trunk this time and dropping out of sight.

'FREEBODY MAJOR, BADLY PLAYED!' roared Miss Talent. 'Wong, fetch it now!'

I sighed. I did not at all want to go digging about in the mould at the bottom of the trees, but the key to surviving Games is to seem vaguely willing, and anyway, it was better than facing Daisy again. So off I went at a stumbling jog (I have perfected this – you appear to be making an effort, when really you are moving no quicker than walking) after the ball.

3

Kitty really had hit the ball hard. At first I could not find it. I stared about, disgusted at the thought of digging my fingers into the black bits of leaf and the wet leaning grasses.

'HURRY UP, WONG!' roared Miss Talent behind me. 'Ach, Wells, fetch a new ball! We can't wait!'

Then I saw the ball, tucked under a bramble just where its thorns would bite my fingers trying to pull it out. I stepped forward to get it, but at that moment, most luckily, I realized what was really going on. I was not *supposed* to find this ball straight away. Kitty is an excellent shot, and so she must have sent it deep under this bush on purpose. And I saw her reasoning. There might be a clue here. We had heard that rumour from Martha about someone rushing towards the trees at the edge of the field, just before the fireworks went off. Kitty was giving me an opportunity to see if it was true, and if it was connected in any way with Elizabeth's death. It was an excellent piece of detective work on her part.

So I crouched down, as though I was still hunting for the ball, and began to work my way across the ground. I still did not want to touch the wet leaves, so I took up a twig and poked my way into hollows and lumps of grass. Raindrops fell on the back of my neck, making me shiver, and I kept glancing across at the game. I could tell that Kitty was doing her best to distract Miss Talent while I worked, and that Beanie and Lavinia were helping her. Then Daisy suddenly made a most impressive play, and scored a goal. She went into an enthusiastic victory dance with Kitty, and Miss Talent grumbled and tried to break them apart. My heart did its own strange dance in my chest. Had Daisy noticed what I was doing? Was she trying to help as well?

But then she did glance my way with a most bitter glare, and I realized I must have been mistaken. I looked down quickly, my heart thumping, and kept on searching.

I found a pair of games knickers, and a sock, waterlogged and fading. A Fry's chocolate wrapper (no chocolate inside). And then I saw something else that made my heart race. It was a hairclip, a pretty silver one with a delicate filigree flower. It looked clean, only a very few leaves covering it. It could not have been here long. This was contraband, not regulation at all. Very few girls could get away with it without a mistress ordering them to remove it.

But a prefect could.

4

'HURRY UP IN THERE, WONG!' bellowed Miss Talent, and of course I had to jerk upright, clutching the ball in one hand and tucking the clip into my games knickers with the other. I came galloping back onto the field rather awkwardly, as the clip burrowed down and dug determinedly into the top of my leg, and nodded at Kitty. I wanted to tell her that I had at last found a clue.

She must have understood my meaning, for she waved her stick at me, and so the message passed between the members of the Detective Society. I saw Daisy raise her hand – it might have been to me, or it might have been to tuck a flyaway piece of hair behind her ear – and then the game continued. I felt broken by what had happened between us. It was truly dreadful, to be fighting with someone who ought to be your friend and to be hiding things from them. In a way,

I was almost glad that she knew about Alexander . . . at least I was no longer lying.

I wondered if this was how the murderer felt, how all the Five were feeling. And I had a rush of pity. It hurts to do bad things, even the small sort of bad things that I have done. I have been part of investigating four murders now, and I am just as sure as I ever was that murder is never worth it. It does not make you happier, or better. It only tears you apart.

Kitty did not fling the ball away again. She did not have the chance. The third formers on our team got the bit between their teeth and began to score goal after goal. It was nearly a rout. Daisy and Kitty's team lost by four goals to fifteen.

Binny and her friends all jumped about cheering, and I clutched my stick tight in my hands. They were still chilled and damp from the leaves, and quite uncomfortable. I felt just as uncomfortable inside. Daisy would not even look at me.

Then Lavinia came up to me and gave me a bump, shoulder to shoulder. 'Chin up,' she said, peering at me with her face frowning as it always does. I think that was Lavinia's way of saying that it would be all right, though how she knew the sad things I had been thinking, I do not know. Perhaps Lavinia is more noticing than I have always thought.

5

To Kitty's great annoyance, Binny and her friends went off on a jubilant lap of the pitch, while Miss Talent shouted at them. The rest of us congregated by the pavilion.

The remains of the bonfire were piled up, just where they had been, the charred sticks all horribly damp and black, quite soggy in the rain. I looked between them and the heap of fresh firewood that hadn't been used up on Tuesday, still stacked in the dry next to the pavilion. It was twenty paces between the two, and the dry wood was so close to the pavilion that it would have been the easiest thing in the world for the murderer to scoop up the rake from where it was leaning, under cover of going back for more wood, and take it to where Elizabeth was standing.

Lavinia went up to the bonfire and began to kick through it with the toe of her shoe.

'Ugh!' said Clementine. 'Leave it!'

'It's only fun,' said Lavinia, kicking away, but I saw her flash a glance at me, eyebrows frowning, and knew that she had only said it for the benefit of the other dorm. Lavinia was hunting for clues in her own way. 'Don't be such a bore, Clementine.'

'You are disgusting!' said Kitty, understanding. 'Really, Lavinia!'

I wriggled as the clip dug into my thigh again. I still had not had a chance to take it out and hide it somewhere safer, or to tell the others about it.

Daisy finally gave me a look, up and down, and I quailed a little. Then she stepped forward and began to toe through the rubble herself. She made it look as though she was doing it idly, but I knew that was all show. Daisy can never be still, but she never makes a motion that does not have a reason behind it. Then I saw her stiffen, a movement that I knew like looking at myself in the mirror.

'Golly,' she said. 'How odd! That bit of wood there, it's not a piece of wood at all. It's a hockey stick.'

'Oh!' said Beanie. 'It must be the missing one, the one Miss Talent was cross about! But how did it get *here*? And why is it . . . *oh*.'

I froze. I could feel my heart pounding. We all stared at one another, and I could tell we had all had the same thought. Here was the missing stick, found mysteriously half burned on the bonfire. The rake had been found next to Elizabeth's body, so we had assumed that it must be the murder weapon – but a hockey stick was really a much better weapon. It was exactly the right shape for hitting someone, after all. I had often thought how dangerous those sticks were when Daisy and Kitty were waving them about during matches. What if the rake had not been responsible at all? What if *this* was the murder weapon, and the rake just a blind? But how were we to examine it without the other dorm noticing?

Then Kitty stepped up in the most marvellous way.

'Do you know what I think?' she said to Clementine. 'I think that your team cheated just now. Why, I saw you – that flick's outlawed!'

Clementine, predictably, swelled with outrage. 'How dare you!' she cried. 'You're a rotten loser, it's bad form!'

'I say you cheated too,' said Lavinia, moving to stand next to Kitty.

'Lavinia Temple, we were on the same team!' hissed Clementine. 'You other dorm, you're all awful!'

Lavinia curled her lip, and Kitty squared her shoulders. Clementine had been rude about our dorm, and that was not acceptable. Then Lavinia put out her hands and shoved, and that was that, it was all-out war. Clementine shouted and Lavinia pinched her.

It was the perfect cover. I crouched down – and so did Daisy. It felt like the most dangerous thing I had ever done. I looked at her, waiting for her to tell me to go away, but she was staring straight at the stick, running her eyes across it greedily.

'Oh!' she breathed, pulling an absolutely minuscule magnifying glass out of the pocket of her games skirt and squinting through it. 'It *is*! Look, look at these stains, they're blood, I'm sure of it! Oh, Watson—'

She looked up, and for a moment we were eye to eye. She had said it without thinking, I knew, for she flushed, and looked away again.

'How do you know it's blood?' I asked gruffly.

'Oh, just look!' said Daisy, holding out the magnifying glass to me, and I saw.

The stick looked as though someone had stuffed it into the bonfire by the handle, but it must have rolled off again, for it was only charred, not burned. The face of it was blackened, but I could still see that there was something on it, a dark, dirty stain with something clumped on it.

'Blood!' whispered Daisy. 'And hair! See? Hazel, what if the murder weapon wasn't the rake at all? What if it was *this*?'

Once again, we looked at each other, and this time we did not look away. Detective excitement crackled between us, and for a quick singing moment everything was right.

'We need to hide it!' I said. 'In the pavilion?'

'No!' hissed Daisy. 'We have to take it back to House, we can't leave it!'

'We'd be seen!' I said. 'It has to be the pavilion.'

'Hazel,' Daisy said. 'Don't be an idiot. You—'

Miss Talent was approaching. 'Girls!' she said. 'What are you doing? Really! Put that bit of wood down at once! You'll get your games kit dirty!'

Daisy dropped the stick and hid the magnifying glass in her hand. 'Sorry, Miss Talent,' she said. 'We'll go tidy up now, Miss Talent,' and back into the pavilion we had to go, leaving the stick behind. Our argument had cost us a most important clue.

As soon as we were back in the pavilion's changing room, Daisy turned on me.

'You're a prize idiot!' she hissed. 'Why didn't you go along with what I said?'

'Because it was silly!' I said. 'We'd have got caught!'

'We were caught anyway! And now we don't have any evidence. Just after we discovered the real murder weapon, too! Ugh, I could scream!'

Beanie, Kitty and Lavinia came rushing in then. Daisy turned to them, ignoring me, and I sat down heavily on a bench.

My heart ached. I had been thinking about the hairclip. Which of the Five's was it? I thought again about the person running into the woods. What if it was not a man at all, but one of our suspects? If so, we would be able to rule one of them out at last. After all, they had been seen fleeing before the fireworks began, when Elizabeth was still alive. If they were in the woods while the fireworks were going off, they could not have been killing Elizabeth. But which one of the Five did it belong to?

These were important questions, I knew it, but I did not want to show the clip now, when Daisy was behaving this way. So I put it in the pocket of my skirt and did not say a word.

6

Dear Alexander,

We have had some important developments in the case. We have discovered that the murder weapon was not the rake at all. It was a hockey stick! The murderer tried to burn it, but it was no good, we found it in the ashes of the bonfire this afternoon. There was still blood on it, and Elizabeth's hair (which is quite gruesome, I know), but before we could hide it, we were moved away. It is most annoying. We will have to have the stick in our possession if we are to prove the murderer guilty, and Jones innocent, but we are not sure when we can get to it again. I do feel dreadful about Jones. I wish we could simply go to Miss Barnard and ask her to bring him back, but I know that will do no good. She will not believe us unless we present her with a truly perfect case.

Our suspects are the problem. They all have secrets, but we have not yet found them out. We think we are close to most of them: we believe that Florence may have an illness that she has not told anyone about, that Una's father may be Jewish, and hiding it, that Enid may have been cheating in tests, and that Margaret may have a secret with another of the Big Girls, Astrid, but it is hard to know for certain. We are going to try to break into the Five's dorm tomorrow, to confirm our suspicions, but of course, that's terribly difficult, and I don't know if we will be successful.

But at Games this afternoon, when we found the stick, I discovered one more important clue: a hairclip, under the trees at the edge of the pitch. It must be one of the Five's, and it will rule whoever it is out, for someone was seen running away to the woods just before the time when the murder must have taken place.

We will keep on following the Five, and their secrets must come out eventually! I only worry about the person letting out the secrets. It can't be one of the Five, for they have no reason to, and every reason to keep the secrets hidden. Our friend Beanie and I overheard Florence and Una talking about it, and it sounds as though the Five really are not the ones responsible. They are trying to find out who it is as much as we are, and I am worried about what will happen to that person once they are found. I think they must be in one of the younger years. What if the Five – or the murderer – gets to them before we do?

Write back,
Hazel

'What are you writing?' asked Beanie, leaning over to peer into my lap. It was after tea, and we were all up in the dorm. I shut this casebook quickly.

'Only case notes,' I said.

Daisy made a small snorting noise. 'She's writing to Alexander again,' she said. 'She can't stop letting out facts about the case.'

I withered. 'Why shouldn't I?' I asked. I was trying to sound bold, but it only came out harsh and weak. 'He might be able to help.'

'Boys are distractions,' snapped Daisy. 'And Alexander especially so. Hazel, he is in a rival detective society – that is most dangerous!'

'It is not dangerous!' I cried. 'Alexander is our friend, yours as well as mine. You know he'd never tell anyone else!'

'I know you're being a fool,' said Daisy.

My eyes smarted, and I gulped.

Then Kitty came rushing into the dorm. 'Oh, do come quickly!' she cried, without noticing how Daisy was flushed, and I had turned away. 'Another secret's come out. It was in the front hall, lying in the very middle of the carpet. It must just have been put there, it wasn't there when we came in from Games, remember?'

'Who's it about?' Daisy asked quickly.

'Another Big Girl,' said Kitty. 'Of course.'

'Oh dear,' said Beanie sadly. 'This is all so dreadful.'

'Matron's terribly angry,' said Kitty as we rushed downstairs. I was glad to be thinking of something else, although this new secret did not sound nice at all. 'She's shouting at everyone.'

And indeed, I could hear her voice, bellowing out questions.

'Stop it! What is this?'

I realized that this was the first time a grown-up had really seen the effects of a Scandal Book secret. Was this a good thing? Might this finally stop them coming out? Or would it make things even more terrible?

7

There below us in the very middle of the House hallway, under the big clock that measures out our lives, stood Matron, shoulders back, legs apart and hands outstretched. On her left was Elsie Drew-Peters, and on her right was Jennifer Stone, and they were both leaning towards each other, teeth gritted.

'GIRLS!' bellowed Matron. 'Stop at once! This is not ladylike!'

'It's her!' screamed Jennifer. 'She did it!'

'I never!' cried Elsie. 'I never, it wasn't me—'

'You liar! Why, the note says what you did!'

'It isn't like he was *yours*! Why, he wouldn't even have looked at you if his mother hadn't made him! He likes *me*, not *you*, you fool!'

'*You?* Why, your nose is crooked.'

'You've red hair! It's a wonder you don't dye it like Astrid.'

'You're horrid! I can't imagine how he could stand to look at you.'

'Well, he did more than that this summer, I can tell you.'

Jennifer gave a shriek and lunged out at Elsie.

'They've been carrying on with the same boy,' whispered Kitty gleefully. 'Lord Edgemire's son, Charles. They only discovered it just now – that's what the secret said. Isn't it *funny*?'

I did not think it was funny at all. My stomach crunched up sickeningly, and I heard again Daisy's voice in my head saying, *He doesn't even* like *you like that, Hazel. You're being a fool.*

I looked down at my feet and clenched my fists.

'Not all of us are mad about boys, Kitty Freebody,' said Daisy. 'Not all of us are like you and Hazel.'

'You say that now,' said Kitty in a superior way. 'You'll see. Why, as soon as you're presented at Court you'll be married. It won't even take a month!'

'Really, I don't see why I should bother,' said Daisy. 'A husband would only get in the way.'

'Not all girls want to be married, you know,' said a voice behind us. I turned. Clementine was standing there, watching the row. She had a rather nasty spiteful expression on her face. 'Sometimes things go wrong in their brains. Don't you remember Miss Bell and Miss Parker?'

Daisy turned on her. 'Be quiet, Clementine!' she hissed.

'And it's not just the mistresses who're like that,' said Clementine, curling her lip. 'Some girls are too. It's terribly shocking, but it's true. That's what everyone says.'

I bit my tongue. Clementine was being horrid, but something had just slotted into place in my head. Everything around me had gone very bright and clear. Some girls are not interested in boys. I know that, although it is an odd thought. At Deepdean, a girl who likes another girl – I mean, more than just a pash – is laughed at for it, and looked at oddly, or worse, sneered at. So a girl who liked another girl would try to hide it, especially if she was something important at Deepdean like a prefect. What if that was the answer to the mystery of Margaret and Astrid? What if Margaret *liked* Astrid?

I wanted to blurt out my thoughts, but knew how dangerous that would be.

'I wouldn't listen to gossip, Clementine,' said Daisy, without missing a beat. 'You might hear something about yourself.'

Clementine gasped. 'I have nothing to hide!' she said.

Daisy caught hold of her arm. Clementine stumbled, and I saw Daisy put her lips against Clementine's ear, and whisper something into it. Clementine's foot buckled and her wrist went limp in Daisy's grasp. 'Should you like me to spread that more widely?' asked Daisy, louder this time, just as the dinner gong went.

'Take your hands off me!' whispered Clementine. 'No!' And she went hurrying down the stairs, stumbling in her haste.

'What did you say?' asked Kitty.

'Nothing much,' said Daisy, but spots of colour had appeared at the tops of her cheeks. 'It's not just Elizabeth who knew things in this school, that's all.'

'Oh,' said Beanie sadly as we began to move down the stairs in the general dinner rush, everyone around us exclaiming about Jennifer and Elsie, who had been dragged off to Matron's office to face punishment for fighting. 'I don't like any of this. I don't think we'll be the same again, will we? Everything's changed.'

'Huh!' said Lavinia. 'Nothing really changes in this dire place. If only it would!'

But I thought to myself that of the two of them, Beanie had it right. We all knew things now that could not be un-known, and that is the problem with knowledge. It stays in your mind, even when you wish it would not.

During Prep, I looked over at Daisy, and got a nasty shock. Now, as I have said before, Daisy is always very careful to look industrious, and to take twice the amount of time she needs to do every bit of Prep, to hide the fact that she is cleverer than most of the rest of the form put together. But I know her and her work very well, and I saw at once what she was doing. The heading at the top was THE FACTS IN THE CASE, and below it ought to have been a list. It began well, in neat columns, but then Daisy's enthusiasm had taken over and her pen had gone rushing too fast for the lines. Her thoughts exploded in scribbles and scrawls and circular maps with question marks all around them.

I felt sick. In the Detective Society, I have always been the Secretary and the Vice-President, and Daisy is the President. That Daisy was trying to be the Secretary alone now only meant one thing – she was trying to do without me for good.

I wished I could talk to Daisy. I wanted us to detect together, but our friendship had been upset. It had changed, like Deepdean, and I did not know how to put it back together again.

8

I stayed up late on Thursday, writing all that up, and so I was bleary when I was woken early the next morning, Friday.

I remember feeling someone shaking my foot, and thinking confusedly that something was tied to it, something unpleasant. I groaned and flinched away from it, and then I heard Kitty's voice saying, 'Hazel. Hazel!'

I opened my eyes, and said, as civilly as I could, 'What is it?'

'Rose Pritchett has run away,' said Kitty. 'Her bed's empty, and the other dorm's going quite mad. Jose is crying. Clementine loves it, of course.'

'But why?' I asked.

'New secret,' said Daisy. She was standing by the doorway, I saw, fully dressed, hair brushed and cheeks clear of pillow creases. 'It came out last night, after you were asleep. Rose is a thief.'

The twins Rose and Jose Pritchett are in the other dorm with Clementine and Sophie Croke-Finchley. They are blonde, with round ordinary faces and a slow way of speaking in rhythm with each other. Daisy would say they were *not interesting*, although now that I write this, I see that my opinion of them was one of Daisy's that I had taken on without considering it. What I ought to have learned from this term is that Daisy should not always be believed. I ought to have been watching the twins as much as anyone else.

'She's been pinching things from the shrimps,' Kitty went on as Daisy stood back, arms folded, and watched me clamber out of bed and shove my feet into my slippers, her lip very slightly curled. 'At least, that's what the secret said. Jose covered it up for her. But last week Rose went into Matron's office and stole her brooch. You know, that annoyingly pretty one.'

I remembered Matron crashing all over House the week before, hunting fruitlessly for the brooch. The world seemed to spin again, and set itself down in yet another new place. Was nothing I had thought really true? I remembered how pale Rose had looked, and knew I ought to have seen what that might mean.

'But then a secret was left in Matron's office late last night, saying that Rose was to blame. So Matron went straight into the other dorm, and found the brooch.

She was going to call Rose's father this morning, only when we woke up, Rose was already gone!'

'She won't get far,' said Daisy dismissively. 'She'll have gone on foot through Oakeshott Woods, so she'll be fearfully tired and dirty by now. No motorcars will pick her up, and the first grown-up who sees her will report her to the police station. She'll be back here in disgrace by lunch time.'

'But she's missing!' I said. 'Anything might have happened to her!'

'Don't be dramatic,' said Daisy. 'Nothing has. You'll see.'

'That's an idiotic thing to say,' I snapped, before I could stop myself. Daisy and I glared at each other. Once again, it was war between us.

'Oh, do come on and let's go see what's going on!' said Kitty hurriedly.

We all rushed out of the dorm. It was mad in the corridors. All the shrimps were running about almost at will, forming into little groups, whispering and then moving on. Binny and her group of friends came striding past, Binny looking almost insufferably smug.

'I knew it was her,' said Binny. 'I knew Rose was the thief. I said so last week, when my pen went missing. Didn't I?'

Martha Grey nodded encouragingly.

'Oh, you did not,' said Kitty. 'Stop making things up, you insufferable liar.'

'I did!' cried Binny. 'See here, I know plenty of things. More than *you* do. You think you're so grown up, but you're only a year older than I am.'

'Which means you ought to listen to me, and be polite!' said Kitty. 'If you had known anything, you would have said. You're rotten at keeping secrets.'

'Hah!' said Binny. 'That's what you think. You'll see. Come on, everyone. Let's leave these idiots to their own devices.'

And she swanned away. Kitty had gone red.

'Little sisters are dreadful,' said Daisy, as though she was not one herself.

It is funny how public the English are about disliking their families, even when it is not really true. Love is a secret to them, hate, far less so.

9

When we peered through the door of the other dorm, we saw Jose Pritchett sobbing, and Sophie Croke-Finchley comforting her. There was Rose's bed, neat and un-slept-in, her chest of drawers half open and her school bag missing. So she really was gone. Then Clementine caught sight of us and simply slammed the door in our faces. It made me feel briefly more kindly towards Clementine. At least she had some sense of dorm pride.

The breakfast bell rang, and we all streamed down-stairs. The front door of House slammed shut as we clattered down, and I saw a brief flash of hats and three prefect scarves through the front windows. As we went into breakfast, only Florence and Enid were in the Dining Room, and once we had all taken our places, Florence stood up, motioning for quiet. She looked tired and cross.

'You lot,' she said as Enid hovered behind her, her ever-present History revision books clutched in her hand. 'Listen up. An idiotic fourth former has gone missing. Rose Pritchett. You all know her, don't you? Just nod, don't speak! Stop snickering, Freebody Minor. All right, she's gone, and she left some time in the night. The police have been called, and the other prefects are out looking for her until they get here, but you lucky things still have Enid and me to watch over you. Now, if any of you know anything about Rose, where she might have gone, and why, you need to speak up now. If you don't, and we find out you knew anything once she's back, you'll be in really horrible trouble. Isn't that right, Enid?'

Enid nodded and glared about the room.

'So speak up now! No, no crying. Stop that!'

'But what if she's dead as well?' wailed the little first-form shrimp Charlotte.

'She isn't, and if you keep saying she is, I shall strike you,' snapped Florence. 'Now, we'll give you two minutes to come up here and confess. All right?'

Of course, no one did. We all sat quite still, and I saw that we were not frightened any more, or at least not simply afraid. It was a sort of silent rebellion. We would not listen to the Five any more.

But I was thinking. The police were on their way, and that meant Inspector Priestley. He had helped us before with two of our cases, and I knew that if anyone would believe us about Elizabeth, it was him. This was an excellent chance. And it was a chance to do something else as well. If the Five were distracted looking for Rose, we would never have a better opportunity to search their dorm.

We all joined up in groups as we walked down to school, older girls talking to younger in the most mixed-up way. Everyone was properly mutinous about the Five at last. There was a camaraderie between the younger years that I had never seen before.

'If they were proper prefects, Rose would never have run away!'

'If they'd been proper prefects, Elizabeth wouldn't have died!'

There was a pause as everyone thought about this, and an unspoken moment when everyone agreed that perhaps it was not *altogether* a bad thing. I felt rather a pang. After I had heard what Florence had said, I felt I understood Elizabeth rather better. She had been cruel because she had not known how to be kind, because all she knew how to do was manipulate and push. Perhaps she had thought that the Five *were* her friends. Perhaps that was why she had threatened to expose them when they told her they would not work for her any longer. Had she had time to be shocked when one of them crept up behind her and brought the hockey stick down on her head?

I shook my head, and brought myself back to the conversation.

'I heard they had something to do with Elizabeth's death!'

'They helped Jones do it!'

'No, *they* did it! All of them!'

'That isn't true!' Kitty said to the third former who had spoken. We were all of us rather nervous, I could tell, about the fact that the Five were at last being mentioned as suspects. If the murderer realized that she was suspected, might she not also discover that we were looking into the case? Then it would not just be the mysterious secret-spreader who was in danger.

'It is!' said the third former – she was one of the Marys, Marion. 'The Five, they're all liars. Lettice didn't even go to finishing school this summer!'

'Of course Lettice went to finishing school,' said Kitty, who could still not get used to all this impudence from the younger years. 'We all know it.'

'That's what everyone *says*, but she can't have done,' said Marion. 'Not really. You see, my cousin's friend Margery, whose father is the Austrian ambassador, went to the same school, the one in Lausanne, and they both came with Mummy to take me to tea last Exeat. Margery was being an absolute bore about her time there, so I asked her about Lettice and she didn't know who I meant!'

Daisy kept on walking quite calmly, but I could see the set of her shoulders change. I could feel the breath become short in my chest. Was this a clue to our last secret?

'I expect she just forgot,' said Daisy.

'Or didn't notice her,' said Lavinia. 'What? It's possible, isn't it?'

Marion shook her head. 'No. I asked twice; she certainly wasn't there. Margery remembers everyone's name, and she didn't know Lettice. *She wasn't there.*'

'But where was she?' gasped Beanie.

'Shh, Beanie,' said Daisy smoothly. 'D'you know, Marion, I wonder whether Lettice has been lying to us about *which* school it was she went to. I heard that her father might be having money trouble. Perhaps he scrimped, and she was too embarrassed to say anything about it?'

'Ooh!' gasped Marion. 'Do you really think so?' And she went rushing away to where the other two Marys were walking.

We turned to Daisy. She rolled her eyes. 'I had to say something to make her go away,' she said. But I knew why she had said it – to put Marion off the scent. What Marion had said was important. If Lettice had not been at finishing school this summer, where had she been, and why?

10

School that morning felt strange. We ought to have had double Science with Miss Runcible, but she had been called into the search for Rose, so we were put into Art with the fifth form instead. The new Art mistress, Miss Morris, put an arrangement of fading autumn branches in front of us, their gold leaves drooping off onto the wooden desk and a soft, ageing smell coming from them, and we all drew in silence.

I sketched away rather discontentedly, going round and round the outlines of my leaves until they were fat and black and out of proportion, and then I was cross at myself for ruining my drawing. I am not an artist, but all the same I do not like to destroy things. My stomach hurt. What if that was what I had done to Daisy? What if I had destroyed our friendship for ever?

At bunbreak (gingernuts), rumours were everywhere. The Five really were being blamed for Elizabeth's death now. The five of us huddled together, Daisy and I carefully keeping Beanie between us, for the day was cold and our pinafores and jumpers thin, and breathed on our hands while we ate and talked about the case. But we seemed to be going round in circles, and everything felt miserable. I wondered if the police had arrived yet, and whether Rose had been found.

When we arrived back at House for lunch, I saw a new letter poking out of my pigeonhole in the hallway.

I snatched it up, cheeks heating, and turned to see Kitty, Beanie and Lavinia all watching me. Daisy had turned away, and was whispering with a fifth former.

'It's nothing,' I said, louder than I needed to.

'It's lunch time,' said Lavinia as the lunch gong went. 'Honestly, sometimes you all wear me out. Can't anything be simple?'

I had a sudden longing ache. Why *couldn't* anything be simple any more? Why did everything have to be difficult, now we were older?

We were walking through the doorway into the Dining Room when the little third former Martha Grey half blocked our way. She was nibbling on her hair nervously and blinking, and I could see that something was upsetting her. As Kitty stepped forward she shrank back. 'I—' she said. 'I . . . er . . . Binny—'

'Oh, spit it out!' said Kitty. 'What has that little toad done now?'

'Oh!' said Martha with a gasp. 'It – it's nothing. I think the new bracelet she's wearing isn't hers. She says it is, but—'

'New bracelet!' raged Kitty. 'Why, that's mine! How dare she!' And she rushed into the Dining Room, on the hunt for her sister.

'Was that really what you wanted to say?' I asked Martha.

'Yes,' she said hurriedly. 'I have to go sit down.'

I almost went after her, but I was thinking about my letter. I wanted to know what Alexander thought of the case. So I did not press her.

11

As we were eating (Kitty clipping her bracelet back on under her jumper sleeve in triumph), Beanie nudged me.

'Have you heard?' she whispered. 'Kitty and Daisy are going to search the Five's dorm! Betsy North's providing the distraction.'

'They are?' I asked, putting down my fork. I had been thinking of exactly that, but to hear that Daisy was going to do it without me—!

'Oh,' said Beanie. 'They – we – I mean, we all are. Lavinia and I are coming too. And you, of course.' Then she blushed.

I could tell that Beanie was lying, or at least, that she was trying to cover up the truth. Daisy had wanted to leave me out. That was why I was only hearing of it now.

'I'm coming too,' I said, and I looked up to where Daisy was sitting. Her nose was wrinkled, and she gave me a very cool stare. I stared back. The Hazel of a year ago might have begged for forgiveness, but I would not.

The prefects on duty had changed. Florence and Enid had gone out to join the hunt for Rose, and Lettice and Margaret were in their place. Lettice trembled with nerves, and looked quite exhausted, and Margaret was scowling and distracted. I had heard that the police were here now, and searching, but that they still wanted everyone they could helping them. I wondered if Inspector Priestley would come to House, if he was wondering about where we were. But perhaps he would not think of us, if he believed he was simply investigating a runaway child? He had no reason to know that there was a body behind it all.

Pudding plates were cleared away (apple crumble and custard), and Betsy's distraction began. I saw Daisy nod at her, and Betsy nod at her year – and then they all went quite wild. They began shrieking at each other like monkeys, chasing about the Dining Room in breach of the rules, and Margaret and Lettice could not cope.

'Stop that!' Lettice screamed, and Margaret put her hands up to her face in distress. They did not even notice the five of us slipping out of the room.

As we crept up the stairs (avoiding the creaks), Daisy turned to us. 'There are rather a lot of us,' she hissed, 'so we must be extra careful.'

'Isn't it a good thing, though?' I whispered back, as shouts echoed below us. 'We can each take a sleeping area. There are five of us, and five of them. The search will be over quicker.'

'Yes, thank you, Hazel,' said Daisy, and we glared at each other. I hated it. We were so far apart, and it hurt so much.

We climbed another flight of stairs, and another one (as I have said, the Five's dorm is right at the top of House). It felt quite wrong to be so high. It is drummed into us all that you cannot go up to the top of House unless you are a Big Girl.

But finally, there at the end of the dim corridor was the door to the Five's dorm.

'Golly!' whispered Beanie. 'Are we really going to do it?'

'Of course!' snapped Daisy. 'And quickly. We've got to be in and out by the end of lunch break!'

And she pushed open the door with all her usual confidence.

12

It felt very odd, being in the Five's dorm – not only because it was *theirs*, but because it was so similar to *ours*. Their five beds were laid out just as ours were, and they each had their little chest of drawers and tuck boxes under their beds, just as we did. The only difference was that their furniture was all rather newer (the Big Girls get things first, and then, as they become older and more worn-down, they are brought down to the younger girls' dorms), and there were more personal touches allowed in their areas: a patterned throw on Una's bed, a little glass ornament on Lettice's chest.

'Split up,' hissed Daisy. 'One bed each. Lavinia, you take Margaret. Kitty, take Una. Beanie, Lettice. I'll take Florence. Oh, and Hazel, I suppose you can have Enid. Remember, you are looking for evidence of their secrets, and also for any indication that one of them is the murderer. A bloody glove, or a burned scarf, any small thing may give us the crucial clue.'

I felt the sting of being the afterthought. I did not look at Daisy. I only made myself think how interesting it was that she was giving herself Florence now. Did that mean her suspicions had moved on?

'I don't like this!' whispered Beanie. 'What if they come in and find us?'

'Enid, Una and Florence are out searching, and Margaret and Lettice are distracted. And if you're still worried, you must just hurry and not get caught,' said Daisy. 'Come on, then!'

I moved over to Enid's bed. I was looking for stolen test papers, I reminded myself. For proof that Enid was a cheat.

Enid's chest of drawers was tidy, the clothes neatly folded. I lifted them all up carefully, but there was nothing hidden beneath them.

'Got something,' said Lavinia gruffly from beside me. 'Under Margaret's mattress. It's all ripped, but I think it used to be a letter. It's signed *A*. That must be *Astrid*. Ugh, it's all goopy and romantic. They really *do* like each other.'

'Ooh, I've got something as well!' cried Beanie. 'Here – it's a diary! Oh no, it isn't. How funny, it's a sort of log book. She's recording . . . oh dear, she's recording her weight, and what she eats every day. It starts in July this year, and at the beginning it says "At the request of Doctor Forel of Prangins Psychiatric Hospital, I am writing this record . . ." Oh, this isn't very nice. I don't want to read it any more.'

So it really was true! Lettice had spent her summer in a hospital, not a finishing school. If it was discovered that her head was not well, she would never find a husband at all – and I knew that was all she hoped for.

I moved on to Enid's tuck box. I had a wormish feeling in my stomach. Going through suspects' things is never very nice, but this felt particularly awful. These were secrets that the Five were desperate to hide, that one of them had killed someone for. And we were pawing at them, pulling them out into the open. It felt wrong.

'Hah!' said Daisy suddenly. 'Here, look at this. A bottle of pills in Florence's tuck box. *Digoxin.*'

'What's that?' asked Lavinia. It sounded as though she had stood up and stopped her search.

'I'm not entirely sure,' said Daisy. 'But I know how I can find out. I'll telephone Doctor Cooper back at Fallingford and pretend to be Mummy so he'll tell me what they're for. Matron isn't in her office because she's chasing shrimps, so I can creep in quite easily. This is all excellent. Kitty, anything from you?'

There was a shuffling noise. 'Perhaps,' said Kitty. 'She's got some pictures hidden under her blouses of some old people. On the back it says, er, "Oma und

Opa, Juni 1934". That's German, isn't it? They must be her grandparents, but I can't see why . . . they don't look Jewish, do they?'

'Let me see,' said Daisy. I stuck my head inside Enid's tuck box and dug. There were piles of paper, all revision notes. I began to look through them.

'*Kitty!* What do you mean, *not Jewish*? D'you see that candelabra thing behind them? That's a menorah. It's part of what Jewish people have instead of Christmas.'

'Why don't they have Christmas?' cried Beanie, horrified. 'Poor things!'

'Beanie, they don't— Oh, never mind. The point is, Una's got Jewish grandparents. Excellent work! Now Hazel. What have *you* found?'

She sounded accusing, and I was cross, because I had not found anything.

'Here,' I said, snatching up the first document that came into my hands and thrusting it at her. 'Here you are!'

Daisy and I locked eyes, and she glared. I could feel that I was glaring too. 'This, Hazel,' she began, 'is quite—' Then she stopped. 'This appears to be a letter from Enid's father,' she said.

'Ooh, is it important?' asked Beanie.

There was a pause. 'Yes,' said Daisy at last, quietly. 'I think it is. It's from a few weeks ago. Mr Gaines is talking about universities. He says, "I was sorry to hear of your latest History mark. Remember, Enid, that your mother and I expect to hear that you have been accepted by Oxford at the end of this school year. You are clever enough, if only you apply yourself. We have put so much into your education, and expect to get proper returns. Your sister sends her regards. As always, she wishes she could be with you, but of course finances will not allow it. I hope you are putting in the study that we discussed." Goodness, it goes on like that for simply ages.'

She looked up from the page, and I caught her eye. I knew what she was thinking. I could suddenly see from that letter how exam marks *might* seem like life or death to Enid. If she failed to get into Oxford, after her parents had spent so much money on sending her to Deepdean – why, they would not forgive her. Cheating would seem like a sensible answer.

My parents have never had to worry about money, but all the same I know what it is like to be expected to do well. I have to prove to my father that I deserve Deepdean, now that he has given it to me – that I ought to be here, and that it is worth sending my first little half-sister, who is eight, here when she is old enough. I am the first, and that is sometimes a difficult thing to be.

I opened my mouth, but Daisy turned away.

'Well,' she said to Kitty and Beanie. 'There we have it. Now, shall we go, before we're caught? I have a doctor to telephone.'

13

Down we went to the main hallway. The shrimps and Betsy were still doing a marvellous job of running riot, and the door to Matron's office hung open, with no one inside. We had heard her shouting at them somewhere on the first floor, so we knew we were safe. But the clock on the wall gave us only ten minutes until we had to walk down for afternoon school. We had to work fast.

'All right,' said Daisy. 'I'm going in to use the telephone. You four, stay out here. If you see Matron, or one of the Five, do your best to distract them, as loudly as you can. I only need a few minutes – *if* Doctor Cooper is in his office. We must bank on that.'

'Good luck!' whispered Beanie nervously. I did not say anything at all.

'Thank you, *Beanie*,' said Daisy, and then she whisked away into Matron's office with one glance back at me that, if it had been from anyone else, I would have thought was full of hurt.

A moment later, we heard her voice, sounding very crisp and grown up. 'Hello? Operator? Fallingford 214, please. Yes, Doctor Cooper's practice. Yes, I can hold.'

There was a pause. Then Daisy's voice again: 'Oh, good afternoon, Doctor Cooper! No, no, you must have been given the wrong number. This is Lady Hastings, and I just have a *little* query for you—'

'Fourth formers!' said a voice. 'What are you doing here?'

We all whirled round. We had been paying attention to Daisy, and had forgotten to watch out, as she had told us to. But the front door of House had opened, and now Enid was standing before us.

Kitty coughed, I cleared my throat, and Lavinia stuck out her chin and said, 'What are *you* doing here?'

'I was looking for the missing girl,' said Enid coldly. 'I was sent back. There are branches covering the path and I'm not strong enough to lift them. Why are you all standing about? Are you waiting for someone?' Her head turned towards Matron's office.

'Yes!' said Beanie suddenly, so loudly it was almost a shout. Enid started, and we all stared at her. 'We . . . we were waiting for Matron! Because . . . because' – we all heard Daisy's voice again – 'BECAUSE I'm so terribly

213

UPSET! POOR ELIZABETH, and all the HORRID things that have happened since then. It's AWFUL!'

'Oh, it IS!' cried Kitty, sniffing and wiping crocodile tears off her face. 'DREADFUL!'

They were making such a lot of noise now that Daisy was quite drowned out. Enid looked nervous, and when Beanie stepped forward, holding out her arms to be comforted, she backed away in horror. She was too preoccupied to notice the moment that Daisy slipped out of Matron's office, looking very cheerful. She was beside Lavinia before Enid noticed her, and then she nodded her head in greeting and said easily, 'Leaving a note for Matron. After all, it's time to go down to school now, and she isn't back yet.'

Enid looked uncertain for a moment, but then the bell did ring, and she had to let us go. She was still standing in the hallway when we rushed out of the door, feeling as though we had had quite a few lucky escapes for one lunch time.

'What did you discover?' whispered Kitty to Daisy as we walked down to school in a fine drizzle. 'Did you find out what Dig— whatever is?'

'Yes!' said Daisy. She was glowing with excitement. 'I pretended to be Mummy, and told Doctor Cooper I'd found it in my cabinet and wondered whether I could take it for my headaches. He got most dreadfully upset and told me absolutely not, that it was heart medication, for people with *very serious heart diseases*.'

'No!' cried Kitty.

'Yes!' said Daisy. 'Oh, it was the easiest thing in the world. And there you have it. Our last motive, confirmed! Florence really is ill, and hiding it. If this got out, she'd never be allowed to go to the Olympics. Isn't this marvellous?'

'But we still haven't ruled anyone out!' I said. I suppose I was trying to needle Daisy – but all the same, it was true. All our hunting for motives did not really seem to have got us anywhere.

'That,' said Daisy airily, 'will come. *If* you have faith in the Detective Society. Do you, Hazel?'

There was nothing I could say to that.

14

In History I scribbled down our escapades at lunch time, and then I settled down to read my letter at last.

Weston School, Thursday 7th November, morning

Dear Hazel,

I'd only just sent that last when I got your second letter. Things are moving so quickly. I wish George and I were there. Has the handyman been arrested? Or do all the grown-ups still think it was an accident? And have you found out any more about who is spreading those secrets, and why? Have the Five's secrets been shared yet? Who was the person running away into the woods?

I'm sorry for all these questions, but this is the most exciting thing that has happened to us all term. Nothing has happened here, you really do have all the luck. We ought to come to Deepdean, then we'd have some fun. Although they'd never let boys in, which is a real pity.

George and I have been putting our heads together to think about how we can help from where we are. We've not been much use. All I can say is, don't worry too much about the motives. You know all your suspects had them, and that's enough. The important thing isn't why, it's *how*, isn't it? They all could have done it, but only one of them did. It's a simple logic problem – who was in the right place at the right time. Maybe a re-creation would help you work it out. Have you done one yet?

Don't give up, Hazel. Of course I know you never would, not like most of the people I know. Perhaps that's not very British of me to say, but sometimes I think that's what makes us good detectives – that we're not quite British. Funny that, of the four of us, only Daisy really is English. Perhaps that's why you work so well together, and why you're such good friends.

Alexander

I had gone shivery all over, with something that felt halfway between excitement and illness. I was glad to read the letter, of course, but it was not just that. There was something very important in what Alexander had said, something that exactly answered the question I had asked on the way down to school. He was not on the spot, so there was plenty about the case that he could not see (and he was working from my second letter on Wednesday, he was hopelessly out of date).

All the same, he had seen something that we had overlooked. We had become so obsessed with secrets, and gossip, and motives, that we had forgotten to look at this case *as* a case, as a logic puzzle. The more we investigated, the more Elizabeth's death seemed inevitable, a fact. Elizabeth had been a person who had made so many people hate her that her murderer could have been anyone. But it was not. The Five had all had motives, but only one of them had done it. As Alexander had said, it was a simple question of who had been in the right place at the right time. That was what we had to discover. Why had we not done a re-creation of the crime yet?

It was a crucial thought, I knew, and I had to tell the others. But I did not want to speak to Daisy. I was afraid that she might not listen to my idea at all if I admitted it was from Alexander.

I was still struggling to think of how to tell her at dinner. I was very carefully looking down and taking great forkfuls of food without really tasting it. I became aware of a buzz all around me, people speaking louder than usual, far louder than they are usually allowed at dinner. I bit down on gluey stew, and then someone tugged at my elbow. I looked round, and there was the little third former Martha Grey.

'Excuse me,' she said, 'but have you seen Binny?'

PART FIVE

KIDNAPPED

1

'Binny's hiding,' said Kitty, twenty minutes later. 'She must be. Ugh, that little beast, I shall kill her when she's found. Oh, don't squeak, Beanie, of course I don't mean it. But I know what she's done. She was jealous that Rose was getting all the attention, so she's pulling some silly stunt. She'll be in the airing cupboard, you'll see, or under a table somewhere. She'll have asked Martha to bring her food.'

But Martha, when questioned further, denied it. 'It's been hours,' she said, pink-eyed and trembling. 'I haven't seen her since the end of school. She said she had to meet someone, and that she'd come up later with Alma. Only Alma says she came up with the Marys, and Binny wasn't in the common room, and she wasn't at dinner either. Do you think she's all right?'

'Of course she is!' cried Kitty. 'I told you, she's hiding.'

Matron seemed to agree with her. She was in an absolute rage. To find that another girl was gone was more than she could bear. She went storming all about House, shouting about ridiculous third formers.

Only Binny did not appear. We all went looking for her, but she was not in the airing cupboard, nor under the beds, nor even lurking in the washrooms or the cabinets. She was nowhere. And although I began the search feeling rather distracted, I soon started to worry. I could feel Kitty wobbling, something inside her buckling a little more with every new room that was empty. I thought of what the Five had said, that they would find the person responsible for spreading the secrets of the Scandal Book and deal with them, and I began to feel really concerned.

I was searching in a small alcove on the second floor when a little voice behind me said, 'Hazel?'

It was Martha. Her eyes had gone from pink to red, and she looked terribly distressed. 'Are you all right?' I asked.

'No,' said Martha, lip wobbling. 'I couldn't say earlier, but I really think something terrible's happened to Binny!'

'What do you mean?' I asked.

'She didn't run away because of Rose!' cried Martha. 'That's what Kitty said, and what Matron thinks, but it isn't true. Binny's been acting strangely all week. She kept on telling me that she knew something, that she had a secret, and of course I thought it was just talk, but then – well, I began to think that *she* was the one spreading the secrets. I tried to tell you at lunch, but you were busy. And now she's gone! Oh!'

There was another 'Oh!' from behind me. I froze.

'Hello, Daisy,' I said.

'Watson,' said Daisy. I spun about, furious, because it was not fair of her to use that name, and I saw her standing there, nose crinkled and eyes very blue. She gave one small shake of her head, and in a moment, like letting go of a ledge, I understood. It was not the time to argue any more.

'You really think Binny has gone?' asked Daisy. 'You aren't just making things up?'

'No!' said Martha, hurt. 'Never!'

'Run away?'

'I don't know! What if . . . someone took her?'

'The most likely explanation is still that she is hiding somewhere,' said Daisy. 'But – you think she was behind the spread of the secrets?'

'Yes,' said Martha, tears standing in her eyes. 'I'm almost sure. She was being so odd about them. Binny does make things up sometimes, but this wasn't like that. When you're friends with someone, you *know*.'

'I know,' said Daisy. 'Friends can always tell.'

Martha ducked her head to swipe her hands across her eyes, and I caught Daisy's eye. My throat felt full.

'Come with us,' said Daisy. 'Come to our dorm. We'll get to the bottom of what's been going on, won't we, Hazel?'

I nodded.

2

'Tell us everything,' said Daisy, sitting down on her bed. 'When did you last see Binny?'

Kitty, Lavinia and Beanie were clustered around her, and Martha was standing at the head of the bed. I was at its foot, taking notes.

'Last lesson this afternoon was French,' said Martha. 'When we got out, Binny told me that she had to stay down at school.'

'Be more specific,' said Daisy. 'Every detail, no matter how small, could be important.'

Martha took a deep breath and squinted. 'She said she was meeting someone, and she'd come up later with Alma. But Alma says she never did.'

I had a sudden horrid memory of our case last year, and of Miss Bell, off to her meeting in the Gym – the meeting that ended in her murder. I shuddered, and Beanie made a little noise. I could tell the others were having the same thought, though none of us wanted to say it.

'All right, so she was meeting someone,' said Daisy, pulling us back. 'Who?'

'I don't know,' said Martha. 'She didn't say!'

'Someone from school, or the town?'

'If it was out of school, she'd have had to leave the grounds with me, or Alma, or *someone*,' said Martha, showing impressive logic. 'You know we can't go out on our own. She didn't leave with me, or any of us in the year, and so she must have stayed down at school.'

She was certain, and I knew she was most likely right. But I could not help imagining Binny being bundled away into the night, long after everyone else had gone. If that had happened, then by now she could be anywhere.

I thought back, and saw the pattern: the way Binny had been boastful and smug and full of her own secret. She had discovered a crucial piece of the puzzle, and once again we had all been looking in the wrong direction, and missed it. I felt shame flowing through me. I had listened to Kitty, and seen Binny as a little sister, not a person.

I realized then that I was imagining the worst. Binny had known something important, and now she was missing. It was not much of a leap to assume that the person who had killed Elizabeth really had taken her.

But what would happen to her now? Surely the murderer could not do anything, not to a little half-shrimp like Binny. She was foolish, and loud-mouthed, but she was not bad. But . . . the Five were serious about keeping their secrets, I knew. We had heard Florence and Una promising to hunt for the thief. And the murderer had already killed Elizabeth . . .

'Binny's going to be all right,' said Kitty, after Martha had left, still sniffling. 'She bounces. She's like an ant, terribly difficult to kill.' But her voice sounded wan and wobbly. 'Mummy will never forgive me if something happens to her,' she said, and Beanie squeezed her hand.

'We'll find her,' said Beanie.

'Yes,' I said. 'We will.'

'We all will,' said Daisy.

I turned to look at her.

'Watson,' said Daisy. 'I think we need to talk.'

3

Daisy led me through the shouting, running, exclaiming House, everything upside down and inside out (Matron had decided to call the police again, and so Binny was now officially missing), to the long wide window on the second floor that sits just above a little ledge. The older girls sometimes go and sit on it to smoke without Matron catching them, but now it was empty. Daisy pushed open the sash and slipped out onto it, and I followed her.

'What do you want?' I asked, once we were sat, being stung by the wind and by little speckles of rain. It was a hard night to be outside. I thought of Rose, hiding somewhere in Oakeshott Woods, and then I thought of Binny. Where was she? Was she safe?

'I needed to speak to you, Hazel,' said Daisy. 'Alone.'

'Now?' I said. I was cross. 'Not before? It's your fault – it's *our* fault that Binny's gone. If we hadn't been so busy arguing, this would never have happened. What if something's happened to her?'

'If something's happened to her, it's too late,' said Daisy. 'But if it hasn't yet, then it's up to us to find her before it does. I know you'd rather detect with someone else, but can't you pretend, Watson? Just for a while?' Her voice had gone very fierce, and even in the dark I could make out the wrinkle at the top of her nose.

'What do you mean?' I asked.

'You'd rather detect with Alexander than me!' said Daisy. 'You're writing to *him*, and asking *him* for help and . . . not me!'

I opened my mouth and then closed it again. 'He's my friend,' I said.

'*You're* my friend!' said Daisy furiously. 'My *best* friend – or at least, you were! You've been *betraying* me with a *boy*, and it isn't fair!'

'Why do you have to say things like that?' I asked. 'That's horrid. I can be friends with you as well as him. One doesn't have anything to do with the other.'

'Really?' asked Daisy. She sounded puzzled. 'I don't— Are you *sure*? You've changed.'

I looked at her, and suddenly I saw the last few months from her point of view. Daisy was Daisy still, with her peculiar Daisy-ishness the same as ever, and she had not known what to do while I had been writing letters and thinking about someone other than her. To her, I had gone away and left her lost.

'Of course!' I said, and my eyes stung. 'You're *Daisy*, you're my best friend in the world. Or you *were*, until you said those horrid things about me and Alexander.'

There was a pause. The wind licked around us and ruffled my hair, and a spatter of rain cooled my face.

'Hazel,' said Daisy, after a while. 'Have you not been explaining things properly to me? Is Alexander *not* your best friend now?'

It was such an absolutely Daisy-ish thing to say that I had to stifle a gulp. 'Of course not!' I said. 'You idiot. Alexander is a boy, and my friend. But he isn't you. Neither are Kitty or Beanie or Lavinia. And you ought to know that. You shouldn't be angry with me for writing to him.'

'Oh, of course I am,' said Daisy matter-of-factly. 'But I see now that you were only hiding the letters because you thought I would disapprove. And I – I overreacted, I suppose. I ought never have said what I did. It wasn't good form. Can't you forget it? What matters now is Binny. She is missing, and I am sure that her disappearance has everything to do with Elizabeth's murder. It is reasonable to assume that the person who killed Elizabeth has taken her, to stop her revealing their secret. So to find her, we must solve the case. And I can't do it without you, Watson.'

I blinked, hard. 'Oh,' I said. 'All right, then. I'm sorry, Daisy. I shouldn't have gone behind your back.'

'Detective Society for ever?' asked Daisy.

'For ever,' I said, and almost before I knew what I was doing, I put out my hand, and we shook. We leaned together, with the rain on our cheeks and the cold dark of the evening all around us, and I was happier than I had been all term.

4

'Now,' said Daisy, leaning back against the bricks of House. 'How are we going to go about solving the case?'

I knew she was smiling. So was I.

'I've realized something,' I said. 'We've been going on and on about motives and secrets. But they don't matter, not really. We know all the Five *have* motives, and that's enough. The important thing is *who had the opportunity*. That's how we'll solve the case, and how we'll get to Binny. We need to do a re-creation of the crime.'

'Lord!' said Daisy. 'You're right! We've been so focused on the secrets, when— Why, Watson, we've been chumps! Why didn't we think of it before now?'

'It wasn't me who thought of it at all.' I stared her straight in the eye. 'It was Alexander. He can be useful, don't you see? He isn't here, so he can see things differently. I think he can help us, just like he did before.'

Daisy flinched. There was a silence. 'All right,' she said, at last. 'I see what you mean. We must do a re-creation of the crime. Oh, if only we hadn't had to leave that hockey stick!'

'We know it exists, though, and anyway, we don't have a fingerprint kit!' I said. 'What could we tell from it, even if we had it?'

Daisy sighed. 'It *is* a problem that we don't have a proper kit,' she said. 'I mean to ask for one for Christmas.'

I grinned. 'Oh!' I said. 'I found something during Games yesterday. Remember when Kitty sent the ball flying into the woods? I think it might be a clue. I put it in my games knickers for safekeeping, and then my pocket.'

I took out the clip, and showed it to her. The little silver flower glinted dully, although there was not much to make it shine – no moon, and only the dimmest light filtering through the heavy House curtains behind us.

Daisy, though, gasped. 'Hazel!' she said. 'You had this all the time? Don't you know whose this is? Oh, why don't people ever *see*?'

I thought that was rather rich, for we had come upon just such a clue during the case of Miss Bell, and Daisy had not known who it belonged to then, until it was almost too late.

'All right, whose is it?' I asked.

'Lettice's,' Daisy breathed. 'I know it, she wears it all the time. And let me see . . .' She closed her eyes and frowned, as if thinking hard. 'Yes, I'm almost certain I remember her wearing it when she was handing out sparklers, just before the fireworks. But I can't recall seeing it since then. And if it was in the woods, why, that means that Lettice was there on Tuesday.'

'She must have been the person running away just before the fireworks began!' I said. 'Her Deepdean coat does make her look bulkier. I suppose that's why Martha didn't recognize her. Oh, and – I remember now! When Lettice came into House after Elizabeth had died, she had a leaf on her sock, exactly like Lavinia did when she came out of the woods during Games. It all fits!'

'Yes! What if she got so upset after her argument with Elizabeth that she ran away? If so, she couldn't have done the murder!' cried Daisy. We beamed. We were catching each other's thoughts again, and it felt wonderfully right.

'We've ruled someone out!' I said.

'At last!' Daisy agreed. 'My goodness, that was unexpectedly easy, after all this time. There, that's the lovely thing about having clues! So – pax? For good?'

'Pax,' I said, still smiling.

'Excellent,' said Daisy. 'Now, let's go down to the dorm and inform them of our fantastic deduction and of the reconstruction we are planning. I think I know the perfect time. On Saturday, when we go to the sports field for the match against Fareham Ladies' School, everyone will be distracted. No one will be looking at us. Goodness, in a way it's just like it was on the night of the murder.'

'That's awful,' I said, suppressing a shudder.

'I know,' said Daisy gleefully. 'But it is most important. If we want to find Binny, we must solve Elizabeth's murder. And that means discovering the alibis of our remaining suspects. Actually, Hazel, I have had an excellent idea about that.'

5

Daisy and I came back into the dorm, and Beanie took one look at us and squealed with happiness. 'Oh!' she said. 'You're friends again! Oh, goody!'

Kitty burst out laughing, and even Lavinia made a snort that sounded almost friendly.

'I suppose we are,' said Daisy, and she grinned at me. I grinned back. 'Now, assistants, shall we all find Binny together?'

'Yes,' Kitty said. 'Please. I know she's a toad, but she is my sister. *You* know.'

We all nodded. I thought of my little half-sisters, back in Hong Kong. They had really been very small when I came to Deepdean the year before last, and I had not seen them much since then, but all the same, I understood. They were part of the very centre of me, just like my mother and my father, and hurting them meant hurting me. And, I realized with a little jolt, it was the same with Daisy. *She* was my family too, my family in England. I realized that the sickness in my stomach I had been feeling had come from that. I had only been pretending not to care.

I felt terribly ashamed, but also better, just like the time I had woken up after a fever and felt cool again for the first time in weeks.

'Excellent,' said Daisy. 'Now, Hazel and I have been doing some detecting together, which we are allowed to do, because we founded the Detective Society. It is ours. We have realized some very important things. First, that Binny has most likely not run away. She has been taken, and we believe that she was taken by the person who killed Elizabeth, because they realized that she was the one spreading the Scandal Book's secrets and they feared that she was about to reveal theirs.'

'Oh!' said Kitty. 'That fool Binny! Why, if I'd known . . .' She lapsed into miserable silence.

'Therefore it is crucial that we work on solving Elizabeth's murder, and the next step in that is reconstructing the crime. Tomorrow's match against Fareham Ladies will be the perfect opportunity. But there is one of the Five that we will not need to consider. Hazel's excellent detective work has ruled out the first of our suspects!'

'I found something in the woods,' I said. 'A hairclip. And Daisy recognized it: it's Lettice's. She was wearing it on Tuesday, so she must have dropped it then – and I remember seeing her with a leaf on her sock when she came back to House that evening. She must have been in the woods, and since we all saw her beside the bonfire before the fireworks—'

'*She* must have been the person Martha saw running away into the woods just before the display!' Daisy butted in. 'And that means she can't have killed Elizabeth during the display. She wasn't in the right place to do it!'

'Oh!' said Beanie. 'Oh, I'm glad!'

'You're soft-hearted, Beans,' said Kitty. 'We know *one* of the Five did it, even if it wasn't Lettice.'

'I know,' said Beanie with a frown. 'I wish it wasn't true, though.'

'So now we have to narrow down our four suspects to one,' said Daisy. 'And to make sure that tomorrow's reconstruction is as good as it can be, and we stand the best chance of discovering the murderer and finding Binny, we must look again at the facts we have about the movements of Una, Florence, Enid and Margaret on Tuesday night. It's crucial that we understand as much as we can!'

We looked again at my notes from Wednesday, and a pattern emerged. As we knew, the Five had spent the evening bringing fuel to the bonfire, and they had done it in shifts, with a strict order and in five-minute intervals. Enid, of course, had taken several loads at the beginning of the evening, between 7.05 and 7.10, during which time she had paused to speak to Elizabeth. She had been replaced by Florence at about 7.10, then Lettice at 7.15. Margaret had stoked the fire at 7.20, and then Una had taken over at 7.25, while Lettice and Enid handed out sparklers – which, of course, was when *Una* had spoken to Elizabeth.

During Miss Barnard's speech at 7.30, the Five had all paused to listen, and the fire had dipped slightly. Then the round had begun again. Enid had taken the next shift at 7.35, as we were all being lined up by Una, Florence and Margaret. That, of course, was when Elizabeth and Lettice had had their argument, and Martha had seen the figure running into the woods, the figure we now knew was Lettice. Enid had been taking a last load of wood to the fire when the display began at 7.40; Florence should have then taken over (of course, we could not confirm this). Lettice was due to take over at 7.45 – but, of course, she could not have been there. Then it was Margaret's turn at 7.50, and Una's at 7.55.

'Well,' said Daisy as we all stared at the list of timings we had made, 'we know exactly when the murder took place, at last.'

We all realized what she meant. Although both Florence and Enid had the opportunity to kill Elizabeth during their shifts, Lettice's absence meant that there was a much more promising gap of five minutes in the rota. No one else was supposed to be near the fire, which meant any of our four suspects could have used that window at 7.45 to creep over to where Elizabeth was standing and hit her with the hockey stick.

'Wait,' I said. 'There's something else too. Look at what Charlotte says, here. When the display was over, she went over to the bonfire and *Una* was there. Not Margaret. Then Charlotte tripped over Elizabeth's body . . .'

'Una might have just taken over from Margaret,' said Kitty. 'It was nearly her time, after all.'

'She might,' said Daisy. 'She might, but none of the others took over early. If anything, the schedule was running slightly behind. That's why Enid was still working when the display began. And see what Charlotte said, that Una was *flustered*. She would be, if she noticed that the fire was burning down, and had to step in unexpectedly. Put that together with the murder weapon – remember how it wasn't burned properly? What if Lettice and Margaret *both* missed their places in the rota, and that's why the fire died down?'

'That's all guesswork!' said Lavinia.

'So it is,' said Daisy. 'But there's someone else we can ask to confirm what I'm suggesting, someone we know must have been near the bonfire, and Elizabeth's body, after the display. Martha.'

'Martha?' said Kitty. 'But—'

'Be logical,' said Daisy. 'Elizabeth kept the Scandal Book on her person all the time. We heard the Five say that. Let us assume that the murderer stole it from her as they killed her, and then dropped it somewhere in the dark between Elizabeth's body and the fire. Binny must have found it wherever it fell, so she must have been near the fire, and Martha is most likely to have been with her at the time. Therefore we need to speak to Martha again. Do you see?'

Lavinia nodded grudgingly. Beanie beamed. 'You are clever, Daisy!' she said.

'I know,' said Daisy. 'Bring in Martha Grey!'

6

Martha was called in again, and she backed up everything Daisy had assumed. Daisy really does have all the luck, sometimes.

'We went to the bonfire just after the display was over,' Martha said. 'It had died down a bit, and Binny wanted to get close to it to make it flare up again. She was being awful, kicking it with her foot and making sparks fly up. The prefect stoking the fire, Una, shouted at us. She looked awfully hot and bothered, and I turned to her to say sorry. When I looked back, Binny was bent over something on the ground, near the fire. She stood up when she saw me looking. I asked her what she'd found, and she said it wasn't anything. Oh, I wish I had made her tell me! If she had—'

'It's a very good thing you didn't ask,' said Daisy. 'Otherwise you might be missing now as well. Was that when Binny began to behave strangely?'

'Yes!' said Martha. 'Although I didn't really begin to notice until the next day, when the first secrets were found.'

'Thank you,' said Daisy to Martha, very queenly. 'You have been terribly helpful, you know.'

'But will you find Binny?' asked Martha. 'She's still missing!'

'Of course we will! But now you must go away so we can do it. All right?'

'All right,' said Martha obediently, and left us.

'Well!' said Lavinia. 'What do we do with that?'

'It ought to be perfectly obvious,' said Daisy, 'We have another witness saying that the fire was low, and Una was flustered after the end of the display. We know that Lettice missed her turn, so it would have burned down, but why didn't Margaret come after her, and build it up again? It's a crucial question, and one that we must discover the answer to. And to do that, we must go straight to the source.'

'Margaret?' asked Kitty, shocked.

'Why not?' asked Daisy. 'She wasn't where she ought to have been.'

'But she could be a murderer!' said Lavinia. 'This is a stupid plan.'

'It is not!' said Daisy. 'Don't disrespect your president, Assistant Temple. I say it's a good idea, and it is. Anyway, you don't have to do it. Hazel and I will speak to her.'

'We will?' I said. 'I mean – of course we will.'

'But what if she kills you?' asked Kitty nervously.

'She won't,' said Daisy. 'Because we know her secret.'

That made me uncomfortable. It seemed to me that if Margaret was the murderer, and we came to her with the secret that she was so desperate to protect, she might do something awful. As far as Daisy's ideas went, this was one of my least favourites.

So as Daisy and I set off together to find Margaret, I was feeling distinctly unhappy. Were we about to make a terrible mistake?

7

We found Margaret trying to tell off one of the younger girls – who, of course, was ignoring her. Daisy cleared her throat, and Margaret swung round to face us. The bottom dropped out of my stomach.

'What do you want?' Margaret asked.

Now, Daisy is very good at confrontations. She always seems to know the right thing to say, and the right wedge to drive straight into the heart of the person (not a real wedge, that would be too much, even for Daisy). This time, she merely stared at Margaret, sharp and blue, and it was Margaret who blinked first.

'What do you *want*?' she repeated, flushing angrily. 'Stop that.'

'I'm not doing anything,' said Daisy silkily as the shrimp Margaret had been shouting at scuttled away nervously, leaving us alone with our suspect. 'Wong and I – we've only come to ask you something.'

'What's that?' asked Margaret.

'Did you kill Elizabeth Hurst?' asked Daisy.

'What?' cried Margaret, and she went redder than ever, red with panic and horror. Her mouth was open, gaping, and her hands were clenched. 'Don't be an idiot! Elizabeth's death was an accident—'

'It was not,' said Daisy. 'You know that perfectly well. The whole *school* knows that by now. She was murdered, and it was one of you prefects who did it. That's what everyone's saying, do you know that?'

'No!' said Margaret. 'That's—'

'*True*,' said Daisy. 'You know it is. There, you're flinching. And you're going to be blamed for it.'

'I am not!' said Margaret.

'You are,' said Daisy steadily. 'Elizabeth was killed during the fireworks display. You were supposed to be stoking the fire at 7.50, just as it ended, but you didn't do it, did you? Because you'd just *murdered Elizabeth*.'

She sounded so terribly certain. I knew that in her head, she had leaped to the conclusion. She was seeing Inspector Priestley drag Margaret away in handcuffs. But—

'I didn't!' cried Margaret. 'It isn't true.'

'Then prove it,' said Daisy. 'If you don't, the others are going to pin it on you. We heard them talking about it. Una and Florence, they're plotting against you. They don't really like you.'

In my ears was that echo – *He doesn't even like you like that, Hazel* – but I shut it off. This was different. Daisy was just trying to get a confession, as fierce as the Spanish Inquisition. She must be hoping that Margaret had seen Florence and Una slipping away together on Thursday.

'They wouldn't do that!' said Margaret, and I knew that Daisy's shot had hit home. 'And none of us would have killed Elizabeth, anyway – we were friends.'

'That's a lie,' said Daisy. 'You wanted to kill her. Do you want me to tell you why?'

'I – I don't . . .' blustered Margaret.

'Very well,' said Daisy. 'Hazel, why are people so slow? You wanted to kill Elizabeth because she was threatening to let out your secret – that you and Astrid Frith are in love.'

All of the colour dropped out of Margaret's face. 'We are not!' she whispered. 'I hate her!'

'No you don't,' said Daisy.

'It's – it's just a pash.'

'It isn't that either. Don't bother trying to lie to me. You're in love with her, and Elizabeth knew. She put the secret in her book, and she did the same with the secrets about the other four. You've all got entries that could ruin you.'

Margaret was gulping like a frog. 'Please,' she said weakly. 'Please don't tell anyone. My parents . . .'

'So I'm right?' asked Daisy.

Without warning, Margaret lunged at her. But Daisy is surprisingly strong. She caught her about the wrists and held her. 'Hazel!' she said. 'Help!'

I did not need telling. I jumped forward and seized Margaret about the waist, trying to pull her off Daisy. She did not let go, and I gave her a swift kick to the shins (I ought not to admit it, but I rather enjoyed that. It was fitting punishment for all the kicks Margaret has given to us this year).

'Ow!' howled Margaret. 'How dare you – little beasts!'

'If you keep making a noise, Matron will come, and I'll tell her what I've just told you!' panted Daisy. 'Confess! You killed Elizabeth, didn't you?'

'No!' said Margaret. 'I didn't! You're right about the fire, but I didn't kill her! I promise. And I can prove it.'

'What?' said Daisy. 'Of course you did! Confess!'

'Daisy,' I said. 'Let her explain.'

'I've got an alibi!' panted Margaret. 'There's a reason I wasn't by the fire when I should have been! Give me a moment. Let go of me!'

'Do you promise not to kill us?' asked Daisy.

'Yes!' said Margaret. 'Get off me! I won't hurt you.'

Daisy did not move, so I knew I had to. I let go of Margaret's waist and stepped backwards. Margaret was panting, and so was I, but when I looked at Daisy, only one golden strand of hair was out of place, and only two pretty spots of colour were visible high up on her cheeks.

'Come into the airing cupboard,' I said, 'and you can explain.'

'All right,' said Margaret. 'But if it gets out . . .'

'*Some* of us don't tell secrets,' said Daisy. '*Some* of us have honour. And anyway – see here, I don't care about Astrid. I don't care what you do. It's no one's business but yours and hers.' I looked at Daisy, but for once she was not looking at me. She had got the pink in her cheeks again, and her nose was wrinkled. 'Anyway,' she said, 'I think I can guess. You were with *her* during the fireworks, weren't you?'

'Yes,' said Margaret. 'I was with Astrid. I wanted to apologize. Elizabeth had seen us together earlier. She wanted me to be cruel to Astrid, and I had to, don't you see? But then, after she had gone . . . I couldn't stand leaving Astrid like that. So while we were lining up the forms I pulled her out to pretend to tell her off for having a non-regulation scarf. I told her to come with me, but instead of taking her to Elizabeth for punishment, I led her away from the fire, and we stood together, away from the others, for the whole display. I missed stoking the fire for the second time, I know, but that was because I was with Astrid.'

'Were you next to the pavilion?' asked Daisy sharply.

Margaret shook her head. 'We were on the other side,' she said. 'Closer to the woods. We'd just got there when the fireworks began to go off, and we didn't go back towards the bonfire until the shout went up about the body.'

'And Astrid will agree with you?' asked Daisy.

'She must!' said Margaret. 'She was there!'

Daisy made a lunge towards the door then, and stuck her head out into the corridor. 'Hey!' she shouted. 'You – Betsy! Go get Astrid, all right? Bring her to the airing cupboard, now!'

8

'Now,' said Daisy, 'while we are waiting, you can explain what happened on the evening of the murder. Why was it that night, rather than any of the others? What did Elizabeth do, exactly?'

She knew, of course – we had heard it already – but Daisy does like to dig.

'That afternoon we'd told Elizabeth that we didn't want to help her any more,' said Margaret. 'That we wouldn't work for her, and we didn't think that she deserved to be Head Girl. We'd been talking about it for weeks, but that day was when we decided to do it. And she went mad. Funny, she seemed more *hurt* than anything else. As though she had thought we were her friends! But, you see, it went wrong. We'd thought that if we all stood up to her, she couldn't do anything. But she was stronger than us. She said that she could get new prefects – better ones – and that she was going to expose us to Miss Barnard the next day. She took out her book and waved it at us, and then she tucked it back into her pocket, where we couldn't get it. We all panicked. We begged her not to, but that only made Elizabeth more determined.

'At the bonfire everyone went up to try to talk her out of it, but she ignored us, or said something spiteful. That's when she was horrible to me, about Astrid. But I realized – well, if she was going to tell everyone anyway, I might as well have one more evening with her. So I took Astrid away before the fireworks, and that's where I was when Elizabeth was being murdered.'

'So you didn't see anything?' asked Daisy.

Margaret shook her head. 'Nothing. I was . . . with Astrid, like I told you. The funny thing about the murder is, I didn't do it, but I was thinking of it. I really was. So when the shout went up, and the body was found, a bit of me thought that perhaps I *had* had something to do with it. I'd wanted it so much, and then it really happened. And all my problems were solved.' She had gone very red, and I could see the tears at the corners of her eyes.

'It's all right,' I said, and Daisy shot me a look that I knew meant I ought not to be so soft with suspects. But I really did feel sorry for Margaret now, and for all the Five.

'I'm glad she's dead,' Margaret went on. 'Once she latched on to something, she never let go. She's – she was – like a terrier, or a leech, something horrid. And she got to me. All last year, and this term, she wouldn't let go of what was between me and Astrid! I kept on telling her that it wasn't anything, and she'd just laugh and say, *Of course it isn't. But it is in the book, Margaret. I've got you in the book, and once you're in the book, there's no coming out of it.* But now she can't say that any more. And as soon as we find that book again, all our problems will be solved.'

I shot Daisy a look. Margaret had just all but said she did not know who was responsible for the Scandal Book's secrets getting out. Her alibi *sounded* plausible, but the fact that she had not connected Binny's disappearance with the book was almost more of a confirmation. Were we really about to rule out a second suspect?

9

At that moment there was a knock on the airing-cupboard door.

I stuck my head outside cautiously, heart pounding. I was suddenly afraid it might be Matron – or worse, one of the Five – but standing outside the door was Astrid Frith, and with her was Lavinia.

'What are *you* doing here?' I asked Lavinia. 'Where's Betsy?'

'Betsy told me I ought to get Astrid,' said Lavinia, sticking out her chin defiantly, 'so I got her. You'd better want her now.'

I almost laughed. Lavinia, shaking the hair out of her face and scowling, looked most fierce, while poor Astrid looked absolutely bewildered.

'We want her,' I said. 'Bring her in. She's Margaret's alibi.'

'Come on!' hissed Daisy behind me, and Lavinia practically dragged Astrid past me into the dim airing cupboard. I saw Astrid twitch as she caught sight of Margaret, and Margaret clench her fists. She did not seem able to look Astrid in the eye.

'Look here!' said Astrid nervously. 'Do let go of me!' This to Lavinia, who was grasping her quite punishingly by the wrists.

'Not until you confess!' said Lavinia.

'Lavinia, she's not confessing,' I said. 'She's an *alibi*.'

'Oh, let me talk,' said Daisy. 'Astrid, who were you with on Tuesday night when the fireworks went off? Tell us all about it.'

'Margaret,' said Astrid, sounding rather afraid. 'She came to get me when we were lining up. She – er – I was wearing a non-regulation scarf—'

My heart jumped. Astrid was corroborating the lie that Margaret said she had told. So far, their accounts matched.

'We know,' said Daisy scornfully. 'We know that she pretended to be punishing you, but that was a lie. The two of you went off to stand beside the bonfire, didn't you?'

'No! The other prefects were there. We went further away, towards the trees – wait, how do you know we were lying? Margaret! What have you told them?'

'I had to,' said Margaret, looking miserable. 'They know everything. They think . . . somebody killed Elizabeth.'

'No!' said Astrid. 'It was an accident . . .' Her voice trailed off, and her face went pale. Then she blurted out, 'But even if it *was* murder, you didn't do it, Margaret!' She sounded quite panicked.

'It's all right,' I said. 'We know she didn't. You've proved it.'

'Yes,' said Daisy. 'My Vice-President is correct. Margaret, you have been ruled out. You are free to go.'

Astrid still looked rather frightened. 'Margaret!' she said.

'It's all right,' said Margaret. 'Don't worry, Aster.'

She put out her hand, as though she was about to take Astrid's, but then pulled away at the last moment. They both blushed. Lavinia made a face.

'Excellent,' said Daisy. 'Thank you. Now go away. We have things to discuss.'

So Margaret had not done it! I thought. We had narrowed down our suspects again.

'Suspect list!' said Daisy quickly, as though she had read my mind. 'Watson, what's the latest?'

Lavinia, Daisy and I peered at the updated list.

SUSPECT LIST

1. *Una Dichmann.* Was near the bonfire when Elizabeth was killed. She was seen by a fifth former having cross words with Elizabeth as the sparklers were being handed out, and was then seen beside the bonfire again by two first formers, as well as Binny and Martha, just after the end of the fireworks. NOTES: ~~We believe we have uncovered her motive.~~ ~~She had an uncomfortable reaction to Miss Lappet's~~ ~~mention of the Nazis (witnessed by Kitty~~ ~~Freebody), and from this and her conversation with~~ ~~Florence we suspect that her father or someone in her~~ ~~family may be secretly Jewish. This would be an~~ ~~excellent motive for murder. Now we must confirm it~~ ~~is true.~~ Her motive has been confirmed by Kitty Freebody, who found a photograph in the Five's dorm that shows her grandparents are Jewish. If this were to be discovered, her father would lose his place in the Nazi Party, and her family would have to leave Germany. She was seen stoking the fire straight after the display, at approximately 7.52, by both Charlotte and Emily. This is earlier than was scheduled, and she seemed flustered. Was she just

annoyed because Margaret had not appeared, or did she have a guilty conscience?

2. *Florence Hamersley.* Was near the bonfire when Elizabeth was killed. Seen arguing with Elizabeth just after the younger girls arrived at the sports field by second formers and Clementine. NOTES: ~~Beanie Martineau and Hazel Wong overheard her speaking about her secret to Una. She seems to be hiding an illness in order to go to next summer's Olympics. If true, this would be an excellent motive for murder. Now we must confirm it.~~ Her motive has been confirmed by Daisy Wells and Doctor Cooper: she is taking Digoxin for heart disease. If this were to be discovered, she would not be allowed to compete at the Olympic Games. She was stoking the fire between 7.40 and 7.45, during the fireworks. Did she use this opportunity to kill Elizabeth?

3. *Lettice Prestwich.* ~~Was near the bonfire when Elizabeth was killed. Seen crying while handing out sparklers, clearly very distressed. Also heard arguing with Elizabeth just before the fireworks began. NOTES: she has been very nervous, and has not been~~

eating. She is also clearly hunting hard for the Scandal Book. Is this her guilty conscience, or is it merely because she is afraid of her secret getting out? We must investigate further. ~~RULED OUT: Although her motive for murder is clear (she was in a psychiatric hospital this summer, instead of a finishing school, as she claims) Hazel Wong discovered her hairclip in the woods. This, as well as a sighting by the third former Martha, proves that she could not have been beside the bonfire at the time the murder took place. She did not kill Elizabeth. But her absence (she should have been stoking the bonfire between 7.45 and 7.50) gave the murderer the perfect opportunity to carry out the crime.~~

4. *Enid Gaines.* Was near the bonfire when Elizabeth was killed. Was seen standing with Elizabeth next to the fire just after everyone arrived, Elizabeth speaking crossly to her. NOTES: ~~She has been very preoccupied, although Elizabeth's death has not stopped her working entirely. Daisy Wells saw her going into the History room while Miss Lappet was out. Hazel Wong overheard her mentioning that the Big Girls have a History test coming up — could the two things be connected? Is Enid trying to cheat?~~

We must investigate further. Her motive has been confirmed by Hazel Wong: a letter from her father proves that she is under pressure to get a place at Oxford. She must be cheating to ensure she is accepted. She was stoking the fire between 7.35 and 7.40. Could she have killed Elizabeth after that?

5. *Margaret Dolliswood.* ~~Was near the bonfire when Elizabeth was killed. Argued with Astrid Frith, and was also seen arguing with Elizabeth before the fireworks display. NOTES: She has since been seen with Astrid Frith by Hazel Wong. What is going on between them? We must investigate further. RULED OUT: she was standing with Astrid Frith during the fireworks. They are in love, Margaret's secret, but Margaret did not kill Elizabeth. She did not go near the bonfire during the display, and this means that she did not stoke the fire when she was supposed to, at 7.50.~~

We really had ruled out two suspects, but we had also proved that there was a window of five minutes when any of our remaining three could have very easily killed Elizabeth. We were closer, but we were not there yet.

10

Then someone ran past in the corridor outside. 'She's back!' they shouted. 'She's back!'

The three of us stared at each other, and then Daisy turned and dashed out of the airing cupboard, Lavinia and me just behind. My heart was beating madly. Had Binny really been found?

We reached the top of the stairs and looked down into the hallway. There was a girl in Deepdean uniform, hair tangled and shoes muddy. Matron had her by the shoulders and was shouting at her, face close up to hers with rage, while behind her Una shrugged off her coat and brushed down her skirt.

It was Rose. She was wet through, and muddy, and there were tear tracks on her cheeks.

Behind me there was a groan. I turned to see Kitty, her hands clapped over her mouth and her eyes wide. She saw me looking, and took a step backwards. 'Of course it isn't her,' she choked out. 'That little idiot! I should have known she wouldn't be found so easily.'

Worry settled in my stomach.

'Go upstairs!' Matron bellowed at Rose. 'Get out of my sight! Prefects, look after the girls. I must telephone the police.'

Rose made a sobbing noise and fled up the stairs towards us. Jose was there to meet her, and Kitty turned away from them as they met.

Daisy took my hand then, and I started. Her eyes were glittering and her colour high. For a moment I thought she was *glad* that Binny was still missing, and Kitty was aching about it, but then I understood that she was only determined.

'Watson,' said Daisy in a quick whisper meant only for me. 'We're close. But if we don't solve the mystery . . . *you* know.'

I nodded, very slightly. We had to solve the case. Binny's life now depended on it.

PART SIX

HOLMES & WATSON

1

After toothbrushes we all climbed into bed, and I huddled under the blankets to write all of that last up in the glow of my torch. I could hear Kitty and Beanie whispering, or rather Beanie whispering soothingly, and Kitty giving short, jerky responses. I knew that she was still most terribly worried about Binny, and I was as well. We were doing all we could, but would our help still come too late?

At least Daisy and I were friends again. That thought gave me a warm glowing feeling in the pit of my stomach, exactly where the ill sensation had been before. It really was odd how much better I felt after our conversation. It was as though the world was back in place.

I wrote and wrote, balancing my torch on my shoulder (it wobbled about, but I was used to that by now). Then there was a soft noise, just outside the blankets. I paused, and heard myself breathing, and other breaths too – dainty, measured ones.

'Daisy?' I whispered, although of course I knew.

'Coming in, Watson,' said Daisy, not asking for permission, of course, because that is not ever her way, and then the bed bounced and the covers dipped back and she was squeezing herself in next to me, her elbow digging into my side.

'Ow!' I said quietly.

'Shush, Hazel,' said Daisy. 'The others are only just asleep.'

'Kitty's not,' I said.

'How do you know that?' asked Daisy. 'Although as it happens, it's true. She's not breathing right. I think she's pretending.'

I did not bother to explain how I knew about Kitty. There are some things that I feel, that Daisy never will. It is what makes her Daisy, and me myself.

'How far are you?' whispered Daisy, craning over my shoulder. She saw this casebook, and then she saw Alexander's latest letter, unfolded next to it. I had wondered, when she appeared, whether to hide it, but I did not want to any more. If we were to be friends again, for good, then I did not want to hide anything from her.

'Alexander?' asked Daisy, though of course she knew. I nodded against the side of her head.

'I suppose he's all right,' said Daisy, after a pause. 'If you do *have* to be telling someone about the case, it might as well be him. And – well, good work, using lemon juice, so as not to be detected. Very resourceful.'

'Thanks,' I said. 'And . . . Alexander and I really are only friends, Daisy. You said so yourself.'

'Oh, very well. We're Detective Society again, aren't we?'

'We are,' I said, and I bumped her shoulder. 'And I've nearly caught up with the case. What's wrong?'

'Binny,' said Daisy. 'I couldn't say it earlier, but I think it might be too late.'

'Daisy!'

'I'm only being realistic. Someone has to be! I'm not cruel, Hazel, I'm just truthful. She hasn't come back on her own, and no one heard her being taken. She's so loud – if she's trapped somewhere, why hasn't she been screaming? I couldn't say any of that to Kitty, of course, but I've been thinking it.'

This, for Daisy, was quite restrained. I was rather impressed by her.

'Of course, we keep on trying to find her tomorrow,' said Daisy. 'If anyone can find her, we will. *Before* the police.'

'The Detective Society will,' I agreed.

I think both of us thought we were lying.

2

There was a part of me that had been hoping, despite our conversation, that Daisy and I would wake up to find Binny back and annoying people, but the wake-up bell went on Saturday morning to find House still in chaos, Binny still missing and a peaky look on Kitty's face that deepened as we dressed and went down to school.

'They must have called Mummy by now,' she said. 'I wonder what she'll think? Daddy's away on business – I'll bet you anything Mummy will think Binny'll be back in the end, when she's bored. Binny's run away from home before, you see, for the attention, but she never stays away long. Mummy won't even come down until—'

Until they find her, I thought. We had to hurry.

'D'you know,' said Lavinia as we walked through Old Wing Entrance, 'there's something that *hasn't* happened.'

We all looked at her.

'There haven't been any more secrets released, not since yesterday. So Binny really *must* have been behind them.'

'Assistant Temple,' said Daisy, surprised, 'you are quite right!'

'Gosh!' said Beanie, rather sadly. 'So it really was her!'

'We already knew that!' said Daisy. 'After all, why else would someone take her? We must work on the assumption that the person who killed Elizabeth has Binny, and keep watch on our remaining three even more closely this morning. It's Elizabeth's memorial service, after all, the perfect opportunity to observe them. Are you agreed?'

We all nodded.

'What I want to know, though,' said Lavinia suddenly, 'is why no one heard Binny yelling when she was taken. She's terribly loud, isn't she? Why didn't she scream?'

It was exactly what Daisy and I had been wondering last night. I felt ill, and Kitty turned positively green.

'I expect they muffled her when they took her,' I said quickly. But in my head, I was coming to think something different. What if Binny really *was* the second victim?

The memorial service was horrid. It took place in the Hall – we all filed in for Prayers, and then stayed, in awkward, shuffling rows. Elizabeth's parents were there, her mother very small and mousy and her father very large and unnervingly like Elizabeth, with a square face and clenched jaw. Neither of them cried, although her mother looked as though she might break at any moment. No one else from outside the school came.

'*No one*,' whispered Kitty wonderingly. 'Imagine!'

I imagined. No one else caring whether you were dead or not. No uncles and aunts, or nursery friends, or servants. Suddenly I remembered what Florence had said, that gathering secrets was *the only way Elizabeth knew to be close to someone*, and I felt desperately sad. Poor Elizabeth.

I also watched our three remaining suspects. Enid looked pale, and cross, and harassed. She had her hands folded to her chest as though she still thought there was a school book there, and she did not look at Mr and Mrs Hurst once. Una, though, seemed not to be able to look away from them. She stood tall, her knuckles clenched around the chair in front of her, and stared and stared at the Hursts. Florence, three seats away, leaned against a pillar and looked ashen. She really did look ill, and I felt concerned. She had to read a poem, and I thought she would not be able to bear it.

'*They shall not grow old, as we that are left grow old . . .*' Florence read, with shaking hands and short breath, and for a moment it looked as though she would crumple.

'Touching,' muttered Miss Lappet behind us, and I caught Daisy rolling her eyes. I knew what she was thinking: that grown-ups can be so trusting sometimes.

Then I craned round a little more, and felt a little jump, like a shock from a woollen jumper. There was a man standing at the back of the Hall, hands folded respectfully over his hat and his head bent. I knew that coat, and that crumpled forehead. I knew the man very well indeed. It was Inspector Priestley. He was here! Even though I had guessed he would be one of the policemen here to help with the search for Binny and Rose, it was still a shock to see him. The last time I had encountered him was at Fallingford, after what happened to Mr Curtis. I wondered if he knew about Elizabeth's death, and whether he also suspected there might be more to it than just an accident – and if not, would Daisy and I get the opportunity to explain things to him?

The organ blared for one more hymn, and then we were filing out of the Hall at last. 'Daisy!' I hissed, nudging her and nodding my head – but the Inspector was already gone.

3

The rest of that morning was terribly tense. We followed our three suspects as best we could. At bunbreak (squashed fly biscuits) Una went to the Hall to tidy the hymn books, and Florence disappeared to talk tactics with the hockey team, but otherwise we didn't let them out of our sights.

In Prep I could not work. I composed a letter to Alexander that simply said, *A girl has been kidnapped. We are on the trail of the murderer, her kidnapper, but I am not sure that we will be in time.* It felt soothing to admit this to someone who was not Daisy, and at that moment I really saw how I could be both Daisy's friend and Alexander's. I could be honest with both, but I did not have to give them the same part of myself. There were some things that Daisy did not need to know, and plenty that Alexander could never understand.

Lunch was a rarebit, with spotted dick for afters. I thought I could not eat, but then Beanie and Kitty could not either, and I ended up eating both of theirs. I felt rather ill after that, and could not decide if it was nerves or stodge. Every ring of every bell was bringing us closer to the hockey match and our re-enactment of the crime. The hockey team were all gathered on one table, talking. There was Clementine among them, looking rather smug to be with so many Big Girls and with Florence. I thought Florence was looking pale against her red hair, but I could not be sure.

They all trooped off down to the sports field, and we followed, wrapped up in our House scarves. Daisy held hers up to her face and whispered orders through it. 'Now, Beanie, Kitty and Lavinia, once the match begins, you must be our three suspects. Beanie, you'll be Una, while you, Kitty, can be Florence, and Lavinia can be Enid. I want you to follow what we know of their movements on the night. Of course, the bonfire is where it was, and we know that Elizabeth fell between it and the pavilion, just far enough away from the fire to be out of the light.'

'What about you and Hazel?' asked Lavinia, scowling.

'We shall observe you,' said Daisy smoothly. 'Hazel will be Lettice until the moment when she ran away, and then Margaret, and I shall be Elizabeth. But we will both also chart your movements. We must do this scientifically.'

'Last time we used dolls!' said Beanie.

'I said *scientifically*,' hissed Daisy. 'We are far older now, and dolls were inappropriate last time, anyway. Are we all understood? You will begin as soon as I give the nod, and I want you all to time yourselves carefully. Remember, we think Elizabeth was killed at 7.45, as the fireworks display was in full swing. Do you all know where you are supposed to be at each time?'

Lavinia, Kitty and Beanie nodded.

'Good,' said Daisy. 'You're quite ready, then. And there's a crowd around you, watching – it's as close as we'll be able to get to Tuesday night. I want all three of you to try to see if you can go to the pavilion, collect the stick and the rake and then get to Elizabeth – me – without coming too close to the bonfire. Hit me, steal the book from my pocket and then go back to the fire to drop the stick. Is that clear?'

I was nervous. It did feel so dreadfully unsafe. What if the murderer should see us and realize what we were doing? But there was nothing else for it. There was no other way we could do this without attracting real notice. We would just have to accept the danger, and hope that everything would be all right.

We went through the gates together, just as we had on Tuesday night, and I felt, as I always do when we begin a re-creation, that we were stepping back in time, back to the night of the murder. I think I have a little too much imagination for re-creations. I feel it, I don't just see it. Daisy, though, only sees, and sees everything. The emotion behind it all does not affect her. She is merely watching a play in her head, whereas I feel the horror of what happened, and what the murderer felt – and can almost begin to imagine why they did what they did.

4

Though it was early afternoon, not evening (the day was bare and pale, a white sky above us so blank it made me shiver even in my heavy woollen coat and hat), the crowds all around us, chattering so excitedly, really did drag my mind backwards to the Tuesday of Bonfire Night. I could still see the burned-out pile of blackened sticks beside the pavilion, and I knew without looking the spot where Elizabeth had fallen.

There were crowds of Deepdean girls, in their grey coats and striped House scarves, and smaller clumps of Fareham girls in the purple and yellow of their school. Out of the pavilion jogged the teams, and a cheer went up.

'Go it!' shouted Kitty, getting into the spirit at once. 'Play up!'

Our team looked cheerful as they waved their sticks – they had been training hard, I knew, and great things were expected from them this year. Only Florence was serious. She looked as impressive in her sports kit as ever, but under her blaze of red hair her face was now undoubtedly pale and drawn. She turned to her team, though, and spoke to them just as a captain ought, and I could see that they were all ready to do their best. The captains' sticks cracked against each other (I flinched a little at that) and then the team took up their positions on the field. Daisy nodded at the four of us, and we knew, as much as Florence turning to *her* team, that that was our cue. We clasped our hands together – Lavinia's rough and rather pinching, Kitty's firm and slender, Beanie's small and fluttering and Daisy's easy and familiar as my own – and then slipped away to our positions. We had agreed to begin our re-creation with the moment Miss Barnard began to speak, at 7.30.

We threaded our way through the crowd and all stood together between the bonfire and the pavilion, where Elizabeth and the Five had been on Tuesday; Beanie as Una, Kitty as Florence, Lavinia as Enid, myself as both Lettice and Margaret, and Daisy as Elizabeth. On the field, the sticks cracked again, and the game had begun.

I stared at my wristwatch. I knew that Daisy would be timing us all. Miss Barnard's speech had gone on for five minutes, and in that time no one had moved, not even to stoke the fire. I stood still as the noises of play washed over me. The hands of the watch moved. It was 7.35. Miss Barnard stopped speaking. Lavinia as Enid began to walk between the pavilion and the blackened pile of sticks as though she was carrying wood to the fire. Una and Florence (Beanie and Kitty) walked away from Daisy and me towards the pitch and the place where the younger girls had been lined up to watch the fireworks. Of course, Margaret had gone with them on Tuesday, but now I had to be Lettice, and re-enact her final argument with Elizabeth.

I turned to Daisy, and she winked at me. She positioned herself in the very spot where Elizabeth had fallen, near the pavilion, just outside the circle of the bonfire light. I looked at my wristwatch again – 7.39, and the moment that Lettice ran away into the woods. Enid was still stoking the fire. As Margaret, I moved towards where the Big Girls had been standing, paused for a moment and then walked back towards the woods, exactly what Margaret had done with Astrid. Margaret and Lettice were now both out of the action, and it was 7.40, time for the fireworks to begin.

As Florence, Kitty moved forward to stoke the fire, taking over from Lavinia. Enid drew back from the fire, towards the pavilion – which of course was what must have happened. If Enid had gone towards the trees, she would have stumbled across Margaret and Astrid. But she was now blocking Florence's path. Florence had to walk round her to reach the wood pile. Kitty, as Florence, walked back to the bonfire, dropped her invisible wood and turned back to the pavilion. I saw something, then. Although Enid and Una were in darkness, outside the light from the bonfire, Florence would be constantly watching. If someone else had tried to get to the bonfire during the time she was stoking it, she would see them at once. On her second trip to the pavilion, though, Kitty paused for a moment longer, scooping up not just the wood from the pile, but pretending also to pick up the rake and the hockey stick. She began to walk back towards the fire, and then paused behind Elizabeth. In one smooth movement she raised her right hand, the one which must be holding the stick. Balancing the wood and the rake under her left arm, she brought her right down over Elizabeth's head. Then she bent, put down the rake and went rifling through Elizabeth's clothes. It was all over very quickly, and she resumed her walk back to the fire, throwing the wood and the hockey stick in quite casually, before turning to go back for more fuel. Florence could have committed the murder.

After the next trip, Kitty stopped. It was 7.45, and the moment when Lettice should have taken over stoking duty. But, of course, she had not – now was the most likely time for the murder. But who would move first, Una or Enid? Then Lavinia sighed and shrugged.

As Enid, she had been standing quite close to Elizabeth, but now she turned and walked the four paces to the side of the pavilion. I counted the seconds in my head as she bent down, picked up an armful of wood, and then picked two objects up from the side of the pavilion. The rake and the hockey stick, of course. Unlike Kitty, she made her arms look rather full, and she moved quite slowly back towards Daisy the way Enid would have, as though she did not want to drop anything. I realized how heavy the armful must have been for Enid, and how difficult to balance. It would certainly have taken a great deal of strength and skill to hit Elizabeth with the hockey stick without dropping the wood and the rake. Tall, well-built Una might have done it, and muscular Florence, as we had seen, but Enid, who had been too weak to lift branches in Oakeshott Woods? It did not seem likely.

Lavinia went walking up to Daisy, moving slowly and carefully (she had been thirty seconds now), then raised her right arm and made a hitting motion towards Daisy's head. Daisy turned and raised an eyebrow at her, and Lavinia grinned. Then she mimed bending down over the place where Daisy ought to have fallen and putting something next to the body – the rake. She went rifling through Elizabeth's pockets (she had been seventy seconds now), then straightened up again, as though she had just noticed the time. Indeed, it was

280

7.49 now, and the final fireworks were going off. Lavinia had to rush towards the fire, but as she arrived, Beanie came over to stand beside her.

'What are you doing?' I heard Lavinia say crossly.

'I'm being Una!' said Beanie. 'It's 7.51 – I have to be here now, don't I, otherwise Charlotte couldn't see me stoking the fire a minute later.'

'But—' said Lavinia. 'Oh. You're right!'

She was, I realized, and that meant something else. Charlotte had *not* mentioned seeing Enid next to the bonfire after the fireworks, so she could not have been there. Therefore there was no time for her to have done the murder, and no way for her to get back to the bonfire and leave the stick without it seeming suspicious. We could rule her out!

'Then the shout went up,' I said, my words masked by another cheer. 'And . . . there, she's been found.'

I turned, and went back to Daisy. There she was, quite unharmed still, standing above the spot on the grass where Elizabeth had been discovered.

'Perfectly on time,' she whispered. 'Deductions, please.'

5

'Enid couldn't have done it!' said Kitty and I at the same time.

'Florence stopped stoking the fire at 7.45,' I explained. 'You saw Lavinia. She didn't have time to kill Elizabeth and drop the stick in the bonfire before Una arrived, and if she'd been there at the same time as Una, Binny or Martha would have seen her. And Enid's not very big or strong. I don't think she could have carried everything *and* hit Elizabeth hard enough to kill her.'

'Very good!' said Daisy. 'I agree. By that argument, though, Una would have had time. She could have done exactly what we saw Lavinia demonstrate, and then come to the fire with her load of wood. That would perfectly fit with what we know – Una is certainly still a suspect. What about Florence?'

'She could have, while she was stoking the fire,' Kitty said. 'She's so strong. It would have been easy for her.

We thought that the murder must have happened at 7.45, but if Florence did it, then it could have happened earlier. Florence can hit things one-handed, I've seen her. She would have barely needed to pause, and she had time to drop the stick in the fire afterwards.'

'So we still have two suspects left,' said Daisy, nodding. 'Did anyone else have any deductions? I know I have another.'

'Yes,' I said slowly. 'There is one more thing. I realized when I saw Kitty and Lavinia picking up the stick and the rake. The murderer must have left them there beforehand. It wasn't a mistake, and they can't have been there by chance. So this murder must have been planned, from the moment the Five arrived at the sports pitch. It wasn't someone taking an opportunity. It was—'

'Purposeful!' said Daisy, beaming. 'Oh, EXACTLY, Hazel! This murderer knew what she was going to do, and waited for the right moment. This murderer is clever. I've always thought so, from the moment we found out the truth about the rake. This proves it. Yes, very good. Either Una or Florence has been very clever indeed, and very calculating.'

But Kitty's brow had furrowed. 'That's all very well, but which one of them was it?' she asked. 'We still don't know who has Binny. What if she's trapped somewhere? Or what if she's—'

She paused, and I looked at Daisy, concerned.

But Daisy had frozen, staring across the pitch. 'Just look!'

The match was still going on – there were five minutes left of the first half – and the ball was furiously in play. Clementine was chasing down a Fareham forward, who was coming dangerously close to shooting distance. Our goalkeeper was crouching, face tense. But of course, Daisy was not looking at the hockey. She was nodding at a man in a greatcoat. I knew who I would see even before I turned – it was Inspector Priestley again.

'Ooh! Inspector Priestley!' said Beanie. 'What is he doing here?'

'He's here to find Binny, of course!' said Daisy. 'The police were called in for Rose, and again when Binny went missing. You have to call the police for missing children. And if the Inspector is here for Binny—'

'We might be able to tell him about Elizabeth!' I said.

'We must have evidence, though,' said Daisy. 'And we don't have the stick.'

'We can get it!' I said.

I had been staring at the Inspector while I thought about this. I blinked and saw that he was looking at us all. His brow furrowed and his face broke into a crinkled smile. He raised his hand to wave, and the whistle blew time on the first half of the match. Girls swarmed the pitch – it was a most exciting score, with Deepdean one goal behind Fareham – and the Inspector threaded his way through them all, coming towards us.

'Oh, Lord!' gasped Beanie. 'He's coming over!'

'Of course he is. We must greet him,' said Daisy, tipping her chin up. Now that she is taller, she is almost up to the Inspector's shoulder, but as always, she is so confident that she could be looking him in the eye. 'And we must find out how much he knows about *our* case.'

She said *our* with a slight inflection on it, the way she says *our* school, and the way she might say *our* Inspector. Inspector Priestley was *hers*, just like Deepdean, and just like me.

Inspector Priestley approached, and I was glad to see that he was smiling.

'Ladies,' he said, and then, more quietly, 'Apologies, Miss Wells. *Detectives*. Only I can't say that out loud, under the circumstances. Are you well?'

'You're here for my sister,' said Kitty, face pale.

The Inspector stopped smiling. 'You're the other Miss Freebody!' he said. 'Of course. You have a look of her – the cheeks. My apologies. I didn't mean to make light of the situation. You are right, we are here to find your sister.'

'You all think she's run away,' said Kitty in a rush. 'But she didn't! She was taken, I know it.'

The Inspector raised his eyebrows. 'You think she was *taken*?' he asked.

'Yes! By—' Kitty stopped, and looked at Daisy.

I looked at her as well. What would she say? Would she pass on what we knew easily, or make the Inspector struggle for it?

'Does this have anything to do with the tragic accident that I have been told took place on Tuesday evening?' asked the Inspector. 'Your new Headmistress has told me all about it. But surely there is no mystery there. The culprit has been asked to leave the school.'

At that, Daisy went scarlet. 'Jones isn't the culprit!' she said. 'He was framed! And – oh bother, all right – it wasn't an accident. Elizabeth Hurst was murdered, and Binny's missing because she knew the murderer's motive, and was going to reveal it to the school. She's been taken, just like Kitty said.'

It sounded so unbelievable, when she said it. We had never had such a thin story to present to the Inspector. My heart sank.

The Inspector, as I knew he would, looked sceptical. 'Are you sure?' he asked. 'It is not always murder, you know. Sometimes accidents do happen.'

'Of course we're sure!' blazed Daisy. 'We are detectives! We have solved three cases so far!'

'But this doesn't have to be your fourth,' said the Inspector gently. 'The girl stepped on a rake, I gather. It was a mistake, a very sad one.'

'It wasn't the rake! It was a hockey stick! It was thrown onto the fire to burn, but it didn't take. It's still there.

We'll show you. When the match begins again, and they're all looking the other way.'

The Inspector looked worried. But he sighed. 'Very well,' he said. 'If you are able to give me evidence, I can reconsider. In the meantime, though, I suppose I ought to be enjoying the match.' He looked about him and cleared his throat. 'Er, up Deepdean!'

'You,' said Daisy crossly, 'have much to learn about the science of fitting in.'

6

The players lined up again, and the whistle blew. Florence darted forward to gather up the ball, and I noticed again how very pale she looked. Did she know she was one of the last two suspects? Was this her guilty conscience?

'Come on!' hissed Daisy. 'The bonfire—'

But then there was a gasp from the crowd as Florence tumbled forward across the pitch bonelessly. Her eyes were closed and her face was chalk-white. She had fainted before she even touched the grass. Several people screamed.

'Lord!' cried Kitty.

'Oh no!' gasped Beanie. 'Her heart! Oh, quick! What if she's dead too?'

'Wait,' said the Inspector, holding out a large hand to stop us moving.

I almost thought him cruel, but then I saw Miss Barnard rushing to Florence's side, kneeling on the ground, brushing a finger against her pulse. She looked up, and everyone stilled. She has that effect on people.

'Miss Hamersley has only fainted!' she said firmly. 'She needs help, quickly! Miss Talent! Help me, she must go to San immediately.'

Miss Talent knelt beside her, and then she hefted Florence up as though she was only a little shrimp, instead of tall and strong-shouldered.

'Come along then, you great lump of a girl,' she said to Florence, and it sounded oddly tender. 'Up you come.'

The Inspector was still holding us back, but he had no need to any longer. I could see that Florence was being looked after, but as soon as she got to San, Nurse Minn would examine her and discover her heart condition. Her secret would be out.

I stared around, and in the crowd I picked out the other members of the Five. Margaret looked sullen and half glad; Lettice was pale; Una was scornful and Enid pinched. None of them looked upset for Florence – they only looked lost. I felt sad for them again: they were tied together so tightly by the most horrible events, and yet they were still not friends in the slightest. Florence had been the closest thing they had to a new leader, after Elizabeth's death – and now she had fallen. But was she the murderer? And if she was, how would we ever find Binny now?

'Hurry,' said Daisy quietly. 'To the bonfire, while everyone's distracted!'

We rushed over to it.

'There, look, the stick – oh!' Daisy was staring down at the remains of the bonfire in utter confusion. 'It's gone!' she said. 'It's *gone!*'

We all stared. And it was true. There was nothing on the bonfire now but perfectly ordinary bits of wood. The hockey stick had vanished.

'Perhaps it's moved!' said Kitty. 'Look again!'

'No,' said Daisy slowly. 'It's gone. I know where it was lying. Someone's taken it.'

I drew away from her, ready to have her blame me – for it had been my fault that we had not been able to hide the stick in time before.

But Daisy did not turn on me at all. Instead, she reached out and seized my hand. We faced the Inspector together.

'It was here!' said Daisy. 'Hazel and I both saw it. It was the murder weapon, it had blood and hair on it, but now it's gone. The murderer must have come back for it!'

The Inspector looked very serious. 'Ladies,' he said. 'Despite what you say, if you cannot show me any evidence, I have to take Miss Barnard's word for what happened rather than yours.'

Daisy looked as though she was about to burst. 'Grown-ups!' she cried. 'You're just like the rest of them after all. You'll see. We'll keep working. We will! And you'll be sorry you doubted us.'

The Inspector wrinkled up his face. He looked as though he did not much like what he was having to say.

'You *will* be sorry you didn't listen to us,' Daisy insisted. 'After all, we've solved *three* murder cases now. We're professionals. Haven't you heard about the Orient Express?'

'I certainly have,' said the Inspector. 'Your most triumphant case yet, I think I heard it called. But that was then, and this is quite separate. When each case begins, it begins quite new. Surely you understand that?' He sighed. 'If you insist, I can speak to this Jones character, certainly. I believe I recall him from last year's case. I will see what he says about Tuesday's events.'

'You must!' Kitty broke in. 'Binny didn't run away, she's been kidnapped! I know her. She does run away quite often, but never for this long! She always gets bored, or hungry, and comes back. She hasn't any sticking power. I *know*.'

'*I* know you want your sister found,' said the Inspector, and he put a hand on Kitty's arm. Kitty drew a jerky breath and looked down at her feet. 'I promise that I will do my best to find her, wherever she is. I do promise that.'

When the Inspector gives a promise, it ought to be believed. But all the same . . . I wished he would take a leap of faith, and trust us that once again we had uncovered a murder.

I stared at him rather sadly.

'Now,' said the Inspector, 'I must get back to my work. I do have men to supervise, and a little girl to find.' With a swirl of his greatcoat he turned and walked away.

We all looked at each other, and I think we all felt very low. But we knew that we must keep on investigating. We had only two suspects left, after all. We had had a setback, but we could still solve the case and find Binny. And now there was no hope of help from the Inspector. He had said that he would not believe us until we had something concrete to show him. We would have to do it on our own.

Lavinia bent down, and kicked through the bonfire again.

'Oh, do leave it,' said Daisy. 'The stick isn't there. Don't you know that by now?'

7

We were still standing despondently in a group at the end of the match, which did not go well for Deepdean. 'We would have won it too, if Florence had been fit!' cried Clementine. 'I do call that unfair! That she could have hidden the fact that she didn't feel well – why, it cost us the match. It might cost us the inter-school cup!'

The inter-school cup was, of course, the thing that all the sporty girls had been talking about all term. Florence had been quite obsessed with it, making the team do extra training sessions, and runs and stretches and calisthenic exercises. And now she had jeopardized that by being ill, and hiding it. Deepdean had had to call on their reserve, who had panicked and lost us the match. Everyone was furiously angry, for it made Deepdean look weak, and that was all anyone talked of, all the way up to House.

Then reports began to filter in from San. Florence was not just ill, it was her heart. It was bad, very bad. She might never (I heard it whispered along corridors and as girls passed each other on the stairs) play again. She might be an invalid for life. She could not go to next summer's Games.

The secret that Florence had fought so hard to hide was out. I watched the remaining four prefects carefully as they came in for dinner. And I saw how afraid they were. Lettice flinched away from Una. Margaret could not look at Enid. And Una looked simply lost. I remembered her conversation with Florence – *we all fall, if one of us does* – and felt another pang. Only one of the Five had done it, but solving the case would mean that they were all affected.

Daisy was watching the prefects too, as were Kitty and Beanie, but Lavinia was hunched over her plate, fiddling with something in her hand.

'What have you got?' hissed Kitty, when she had nudged Lavinia twice without making her look up. 'Ugh, that's filthy! Put it down!'

'They're wood chips,' said Lavinia. 'They were on the floor, just inside the door into House. I picked them up.'

'Ugh! Why?' asked Kitty.

'Because I thought they might be important,' said Lavinia. 'Look at them! They're fresh!'

She held them out in her slightly grubby hand, and I saw that they *were* new – a bit smudged and warm from being in her pocket, but under that quite fresh and yellow, as though they had been new-made. And at the end of them was . . . varnish, and a few flecks of paint.

Suddenly I knew where those chips came from. *A hockey stick*. I could tell the others had recognized them too. Could they be . . . from the missing murder weapon? Daisy had pulled out her tiny magnifying glass and was examining them, eyebrows raised in excitement.

'The stick's gone,' said Lavinia. 'We know that. And so I began thinking about how I'd hide it, if I had to. It would be no good stuffing it in a book-bag, it's too long. Unless it was made shorter somehow – unless it was chopped up. That's what I'd do, anyway. It'd be easy, and awfully fun too. Then I could hide it properly.'

'You're odd,' said Kitty.

'But she's *right*,' said Daisy, looking up with the magnifying glass in her hand, and I could feel her prickling a little. Assistants are not supposed to find important clues. 'Look, these bits are from the outside, where the stick was varnished.'

'But what happened?' asked Beanie.

'I'll bet you anything that the murderer crept back up to the field while they were supposed to be hunting for Rose and Binny,' said Daisy, whispering so as not to be overheard by the rest of the table. 'They took the stick out of the fire, got one of those little axes from the tool room and chopped it up with that.'

'How did the chips get here, though?' asked Beanie, frowning.

I felt the hairs on my arm prickle. 'In the murderer's book bag,' I said. 'Just like Lavinia thought. What if it's still in there? Or – even if it isn't – what if there are still some more chips stuck at the bottom? We can look now! The prefects' bags are outside in the corridor – we can rule the last one of our suspects out!'

'Watson, you're a genius,' said Daisy. 'And you're perfectly right – we must look at once, while the prefects are still in dinner. But now they're watching – they'll never just let us walk out. Kitty, Beanie, Lavinia, cover us. We are about to be sent out in disgrace.'

Then she stood up, jabbed her finger so close to my eye that I jumped, and cried, 'Oh, how dare you! You – you beast!'

8

My ears rang. The whole of dinner stopped, and everyone turned to me. I felt eyes all around me, all sharply focused. Even after a year of being a detective, I have not lost all of my nervousness. I cannot perform for a crowd, the way Daisy can, but now, without warning, I had to try.

'I – I—' I gasped. 'What did I do?'

'You know what you did!' hissed Daisy. 'Sneaking about with a *boy*! Thinking I wouldn't notice! Oh, Hazel Wong, you cruel beast!'

I felt myself heat up. How could she use Alexander like that? Perhaps she had not really forgiven me. Perhaps our friendship was only pretending to be mended. Perhaps . . . but then I saw the glint in her eye, the raise of her eyebrow, and I knew that, as usual, Daisy did not mean a word she was saying.

I let out a gasp that I hoped sounded terribly upset. 'I wouldn't!' I wailed. 'I would never!'

Unlike Daisy, I do always say what I mean.

'He was mine!' cried Daisy dramatically. 'Mine!'

'Wells!' snapped Una, getting up. 'Wong! Be quiet, or I shall send you out.'

'No!' shouted Daisy. 'It isn't fair! You can't! She's the bad one, not me!'

Eyes were on me, once again. I was rather cross with Daisy. She was making me sound so dreadfully unpleasant. I could feel a rumour starting.

As Daisy knows perfectly well, if you tell someone not to do something, they will jump at the chance, so – 'Out! At once! Stand in the Hall, facing the wall, and NO TALKING!' bellowed Una, and we were banished.

We stood looking as shamed as possible, our backs against the wall. But as soon as the Dining-Room door swung closed behind us, Daisy leaped out of her position. 'Quick!' she hissed. 'The bags!'

Una and Enid's bags were in pride of place on the low table under the clock, with Florence's between them. The other two girls must have brought it up with them after she collapsed. With one eye on the Dining-Room door, we scrambled to open the buckles. First Una's: two school books, a hairbrush, a notebook (not the Scandal Book, alas, though Daisy froze for a moment with excitement), a little bottle of something that made my fingers oily, a hairpin, three pencils and an apple. Then Enid's, very neat and recently cleaned, with five school books, several scribbled-on exercise books, a ruler, pens, pencils, two bottles of ink in different colours and a rubber band.

Then we turned to Florence's. It opened, and out fell a chopped-up hockey stick. It had been wrapped in an old games jumper, the sort that is left lying about in the pavilion and never claimed, and wood chips and charcoaly bits were stuck to it horribly. The jumper, with the stick inside, had been shoved down amongst Florence's school books, which had all been bent out of shape.

Daisy and I both gasped. 'Watson!' Daisy cried. 'We have our murderer!'

It really did look as though that was the case. There was the stick, at last. Florence must have been carrying it about all day, looking for an opportunity to get rid of it, but, of course, the match and her collapse had happened before she could. It all fitted.

'We ought to tell the Inspector!' I said. 'He ought to know! Now we have the murder weapon again, we can prove that there really was a murder.'

'And how are we to do that?' asked Daisy. 'The telephone is in Matron's study, and she's in there at the moment. *And* dinner's nearly—'

There was a building roar, and the Dining-Room door swung open once again. Una was the first out, guiding the shrimps. I saw her see us, and the bag – and the hockey stick. She went pale, and then flushed. *She* knew what it meant, I could tell.

'Wells! Wong!' she stuttered. 'What are you doing out of your places?'

'We found something,' said Daisy, putting on her most injured and self-righteous voice. 'Something AWFUL. Florence has been destroying school property! Matron ought to be told. Matron! Matron!'

Matron came storming out of her office. 'What's this?' she snapped.

I could see Una struggling. 'Wells has found . . . there is a . . . Florence seems to have gone mad and chopped up a hockey stick,' she said at last. 'I think it's the one that's been missing. Miss Talent was looking for it *everywhere*.' Now Margaret had joined Una, and Lettice and Enid. Margaret looked puzzled, and then suddenly enlightened, Lettice horrified and Enid sharp and frightened. Did they realize what this meant? That Elizabeth's murderer had been found out at last?

'We ought to call the police!' Daisy went on, and the prefects twitched towards each other, as though the invisible string that bound them had contracted suddenly.

'For a stick, Wells?' said Una, her voice trembling. 'Don't be stupid.'

'Nonsense, Wells. Go up to your dorm immediately!' said Matron. 'Prefects, come here. Explain this to me.'

'Yes, Matron,' said Daisy as Una, Enid, Lettice and Margaret went up to Matron, 'Sorry, Matron,' and then she went marching towards the stairs. I followed her.

But if Florence was the murderer . . . where was Binny?

9

We had to go to Prep, then, but I was so worried about Binny that I could not concentrate on it. Florence was in San. How could we get her to tell us where Binny was? I knew Kitty was stewing over the same problem. I forced myself to write all this up, and I was still writing after Prep, when a shriek suddenly went up from the other fourth-form dorm.

Daisy was on her feet at once, scrambling for the door, and we rushed after her. My heart was leaping. The other dorm were all spilling out into the corridor themselves, gasping. I saw that Rose looked ill, as did Sophie, but Clementine was glowing with excitement, of a sort that I did not quite like. Her cheeks were flushed, as though she was feverish, and she was giggling. 'It must be true!' she said. 'It has to be! Can you believe it? Ugh!'

'What is it?' Kitty asked, and I felt a sort of cold flush going through me, like water along my arms and legs. Was this something to do with Binny?

'It's another secret!' cried Clementine.

'But I thought those were done!' said Daisy, sounding as bewildered as I was. The secrets were supposed to be over: Binny had the book, and so no more scandals could come out while she was missing.

'Not in the slightest!' said Clementine. 'There's a new one, and it's the best yet! When I unpacked my games bag, there it was at the bottom!'

'What does it say?' gasped Kitty.

'It's about Margaret!' said Clementine gleefully. '"Margaret Dolliswood has *unnatural feelings* for Astrid Frith." Isn't that shocking! It must be true too, I'm sure I've seen her looking oddly at Astrid sometimes. Ugh! Golly! Just think – we've had one of *those* as a prefect! All the times she touched us. How awful!'

'She didn't touch us, she *hit* us,' said Beanie, wrinkling her forehead.

'It's the same thing, to people like her,' said Clementine, in fits of giggles. I got a disgusted feeling as she said it. She was being so foul! It was not true, what she was saying, not at all. 'And the best part – we know who's been sending these secrets at last! It's got a name at the bottom. It was half torn off, but I could see it.'

'Who was it?' said Daisy sharply.

'Why, Florence! Imagine *Florence*, spreading all those secrets! Oh, gosh, what a wicked girl she is. Hiding her illness, chopping up school property, spreading secrets—'

'*Florence* put the secret in there?' cried Kitty, and there were gasps from all around us. Some of the fifth formers had come out to listen, and the third formers, so that the corridor was quite crowded.

'She must have done,' said Clementine. 'Odd. I was sure I dug down to the bottom of my bag after the end of the match. I was looking for that brooch I was wearing' – Clementine always wears contraband – 'and I had to go through almost everything. But, hah, I suppose I was distracted after what happened. Ugh! Margaret! And Astrid!'

Next to me, I could sense Daisy tensing up. I turned to her and saw the crinkle at the top of her nose. Something Clementine had said was spinning around Daisy's head, I could tell, and I thought I knew what it was.

'What's all this?' said a voice. We all looked up guiltily, and some of us gasped. It was Margaret herself.

'It's nothing,' said Clementine. 'We just know a secret, that's all. A very funny secret. About a girl with blonde hair, and about a prefect who likes her *far* too much to be safe.'

Margaret turned brick red. I thought she was angry, and then I saw that all of her, her whole body, was shaking. 'What do you mean?' she growled, and her voice shook too. I saw her glaring at Daisy and me. She must have thought that we had something to do with letting out the secret.

'Astrid Frith,' hissed Clementine. 'And *you*. I know what you think about her. It was written down!'

'Ooh!' someone squealed. 'Astrid's *here*!'

My heart sank even further, for Astrid Frith had appeared at the other end of the corridor. She looked about her, bemused, as girls fell back, giggling and rustling, and then she put her hands up to her hair automatically. But of course, it was much worse than that.

'What is it?' she asked. 'Stop it!'

'Astrid and Maaargaret,' hissed a third former. 'Sitting in a tree.'

Astrid looked up at Margaret and her face cleared and changed. I could see her understand. She spun on her heel, flushing, and rushed away.

'Wait!' cried Margaret, and she dashed after Astrid. Of course, the corridor erupted, and I heard more than one girl repeating the third former's words.

I felt rather sick. I know what it is like to be teased about being different, and I know I hate it. I do not think anyone else would hate it any less. I hoped Margaret had realized that we had nothing to do with what Clementine had said.

Daisy seized my arm, and I turned to look at her. She was pink-cheeked, and her nose was still wrinkled.

'What is it?' I asked. 'Margaret?'

'Oh, never mind that!' said Daisy, surprisingly forcefully. 'It's what Clementine said. About the secret! Much as I hate to admit it, Hazel, I have realized something. Florence could not have put the secret in Clementine's bag, and she did not put the stick in her own. *She is being framed*, and there is only one person left who could have done it. Una!'

10

We all rushed back into the dorm. Daisy had the look on her face that I knew meant another Detective Society meeting was on its way, and sure enough—

'Hazel, casebook!' she cried. 'Quickly!'

'Oh, what is it?' cried Beanie.

'It's Florence,' I said, getting out this casebook and making a new heading. 'The new secret.'

'She wrote it!' said Kitty. 'Her name was on it—'

'Goodness, don't you know that doesn't mean anything?' asked Daisy. 'Anyone might have written *Florence* on that bit of paper. But the important thing is that—'

'She couldn't have left it in Clementine's bag,' I finished for her.

'She couldn't?' gasped Beanie. 'But how do you know?'

'Because of what Clementine said, that she looked in her bag *after* Florence had already fainted, and didn't see

307

the secret there then. I think it wasn't put in until later. Florence couldn't have done it!'

'Ooh!' said Beanie, enlightened. 'I see!'

'And Clementine wouldn't have missed it?' asked Kitty, half questioningly.

'She isn't that idiotic,' said Lavinia. 'I mean, she is *quite* idiotic, but not that bad.'

'Florence is being framed!' said Daisy. 'And there is really only one person who it could be. Una!'

'We have to make her tell us where Binny is!' cried Kitty. 'Quickly!'

'She'll never do it,' said Daisy. 'No, we have to think! Now that we know it's Una, where would she hide someone, if she had kidnapped them? Not Oakeshott Woods, it's too dirty. Somewhere in school. But where have we seen Una going . . . Oh. Oh!'

'*The Hall!*' cried Kitty suddenly. 'She went that way at bunbreak, didn't she? What if—'

We all jumped to our feet. We knew exactly the place she meant. Daisy and I had discovered it last year during our first case. The tunnel.

'We have to go down to school!' said Kitty frantically. 'Now! At once!'

'But we can't just leave House!' said Beanie. 'We can't! Matron will catch us!'

'I'm going, and that's that,' said Kitty. 'I'll escape. I'll run away. You can come with me or not.'

I looked at Daisy.

'We can get into school easily,' she said, 'once we're out of House. Everything's been in chaos since Jones left. Things aren't locked up properly. The side door to Old Wing Entrance – you know, the little one – the gardener who's been locking up this week doesn't know that the lock doesn't catch properly. It'll give if we shove a bit, and then we'll be in.'

'But how do we leave House?' I asked.

Daisy grinned at me, and I could tell that I was about to not like her answer.

'Drainpipes work both ways, Hazel,' she said.

PART SEVEN

THE DETECTIVE SOCIETY SAVE THE DAY

1

The drainpipe was painful under my hands, and the brick of the wall scratched against my legs, and my arms felt as though they were being dragged out of their sockets.

'Buck up, Hazel!' panted Daisy, and she kicked out at me with her foot. I thought I would let go. I was sure I was about to. But I had to carry on. I could not let her down.

I came to the conclusion, as always, that things seemed much less difficult in books.

Below me, Beanie let out a small squeak and dropped into the bushes.

'Shh, Beans!' hissed Kitty. 'Quiet!' Then she was down as well, much more daintily.

Lavinia said something most unladylike and angry, and fell with a scuffle of leaves and a small crash.

'Assistant Temple!' hissed Daisy. 'Did you drop the torches?'

'Not far!' grumbled Lavinia. 'And they're supposed to rattle like that.'

'They are not!' said Daisy. 'And they are not supposed to be dropped.'

'Well, why did you give them to me, then?' asked Lavinia.

'Shh!' said Beanie nervously. 'Matron!'

'She's busy,' said Daisy. 'She and the prefects are all trying to get the shrimps in check. Betsy North is a good egg, isn't she?'

The younger years had been most agreeable when Daisy had asked them to help us. It really was us against the Big Girls now, open war. Half the shrimps were convinced, as we were, that Binny had been taken. It had not been difficult for Daisy to persuade them that it was one of the Five, and we needed their help to get her back. But all the same, I did worry. We were banking on Una being too busy to notice we were gone. But what if she did? Or what if Enid and Lettice saw that we were missing, and told Una? What if she put two and two together, and came looking for us? The dreadful thing about Big Girls is that they have almost as much licence to move about the world as grown-ups. They are hardly bound by bells and bedtimes; they are on their way to freedom, and that means that Una could quite easily make an excuse to go down to school at eight at night, while we had to creep and stall, and take twice the amount of time we really ought to.

My fingers scraped quite painfully on one of the pipe joins, and I said, 'Ow!'

I said it quite quietly, but of course Daisy heard.

'Oh, Hazel!' she said. 'You are not naturally suited to spy work, are you?'

'I don't see why I have to be!' I whispered back indignantly. 'I'm a detective, not a secret agent!'

'These days, the intelligent investigator may need to be both,' said Daisy, and I knew she had been reading spy stories again. I made a face.

'Don't make that face, Watson,' said Daisy. 'It's not nice.'

'You don't know what I was doing!' I said, blushing.

'I always know,' said Daisy. 'That will never change. Now stop blushing and *climb down*.'

I struggled on, aching and afraid but with a glad glow at my heart. Daisy and I were together, and we were on the case. Daisy might be dreadfully annoying, but she was my best friend.

And we were terribly close to the truth. We knew who and why, and when, and how. All we needed now was to find Binny. I felt dirt under my feet. I let go with a gasp and fell to the ground.

'Excellent!' said Daisy. She shone her torch about our group – at Lavinia, with twigs in her hair and mud on her skirt, at Kitty, brushing a bit of rust from her hands with a disgusted expression on her face, at Beanie, widening her eyes and shivering a little in her thin school pullover, and at me. I knew I was still red-faced from the climb, and one of my socks was torn. Daisy was quite trim and perfect. 'Now, Detective Society, you know what you must do. Our mission is this: to get down to school and liberate Binny Freebody from captivity.'

'Without the murderer finding us,' added Lavinia.

'Ohhhh!' whimpered Beanie. 'But . . . Una wouldn't do anything to us, would she?'

Daisy rolled her eyes, and I looked at Kitty. Her jaw was clenched, and for once she was not teasing Beanie. I felt then how terribly much this meant to her. It was not just another Detective Society mission, as it was to Daisy and even to me. This was family. If it all went wrong, or if we were too late, her life would quite simply alter for ever. Kitty looked as though she knew it, as though she was staring at two quite separate visions of her future.

'Not if we don't let her,' said Daisy. 'Which is why we must go quietly, and quickly, and not leave anything to chance. All right?'

'But what do we do if we meet Una?' asked Lavinia loudly.

'Scream,' said Daisy. 'Hit her. Goodness, Assistant Temple, use your ingenuity! Anyway, she is behind us, in House. We have nothing to worry about if we go *now*.'

I was not so sure, but I knew she was right that speed was of the essence. I gripped my torch tightly, and together we began the dark walk down to school.

2

The wind rushed around us, and all the trees rattled, and the hairs on the back of my neck and on my arms shivered. My hands felt very cold and clammy. We were walking without torches – we could not risk them just yet – and so I felt that we were swallowed up in darkness, lost in it. I could hear us all breathing, and walking, and Beanie whimpering gently from time to time. She was whispering something to herself, and at last I heard what it was: 'I'm brave, I'm brave, I'm brave.'

I wished I was so sure myself.

We stumbled and stepped, and at last, there was Old Wing Entrance in front of us.

Daisy went up to the little side door, and gave it a very careful shove with her hip in just the right place, and it swung open quite easily. Beanie clapped.

'Shh!' said Daisy. 'Remember, we're spies! Come on, in we go.'

She said it, as always, as though it was the easiest and most obvious thing in the world. I wonder sometimes whether Daisy knows how extraordinary she is, and how unusual her life really is – and I think that she does not. She never really pauses to wonder, which is the key to her. She simply is.

In we crept, stepping over a pile of tools and bits of pipe that had been left from some repair work that day. Without Jones, Deepdean was no longer the tidy place it usually was. Old Wing swam around us, very high and dark with shadows in the rafters. Its wooden floor echoed under our feet for our first few eager steps – and then we went much more slowly and quietly, only half breathing as we placed each foot in front of the other. Daisy switched on her torch, and the beam danced in front of us, making the shadows silkier and the space ahead of us blazingly bright.

'Where are we going?' whispered Beanie.

'To the Hall,' said Daisy, leading us past Old Wing cloakroom and then turning down Library corridor.

Of course, I knew where we were going. The tunnel really was the only place in Deepdean where a girl could be hidden. As I have explained in a previous casebook, there is an underground passage between the Hall and Old Wing. It was bricked up long ago, when Library corridor was built, and the little door leading in to it from the Hall is locked, but it has been used before, in Miss Bell's murder, and now it seemed likely that it was being used again.

On we went along Library Corridor, past the mistresses' common room, the Library itself, and the Reverend's study, and then we turned right at the end. My heart skipped. I felt creepy with déjà vu, as though this really was last year, and Daisy and I were once again on the hunt for Miss Bell's body.

But now there were five of us, and we were looking for not a body at all, but a real live girl. Or so we hoped.

We tiptoed past the Hall, the light from the torch shining upon the lumber of old desks and chairs.

'Oh,' said Kitty suddenly. 'Binny! Binny!' And she broke into a run down the corridor.

'Oh, bother,' muttered Daisy under her breath. 'Come back! Shh!' and she pelted after Kitty. It became an undignified rush: Beanie running after Kitty and Daisy, me after Beanie, and Lavinia lumping along behind, making loud, rude noises.

We really were all being terribly noisy, but I told myself it did not matter. There was no one to hear now, not like last year.

We went almost all the way down the corridor to the Gym when Daisy stopped and turned sharply right, to the door of the tunnel.

'It's locked,' said Lavinia. 'Padlocked. You'll never get in.'

'Hah!' said Daisy. 'Don't you know anything about spying? The best spies can open any lock in the world, and *I* have been practising.' She put her hand up to her hair and pulled out a pin, slipping it into the padlock. There was a breathless moment, and then a click. The lock sprang open.

'Una must have oiled it,' said Daisy. 'With that bottle, remember? And the pin.'

I remembered what we had found in Una's school bag: the hairpin, just like the one Daisy had used to pick the padlock just now, and the bottle of what looked like ink, although Una had had no pens. It must have been oil, of course, to grease the lock. Everything fitted.

'And now,' Daisy went on, like the ringmaster in a circus, 'we shall go in, and see what we shall see.'

3

Kitty pushed past her and stepped forward into the darkness. 'Binny!' she cried. 'Binny! Where are you?!'

There was a pause. I was holding my breath desperately, and then a voice spoke. 'Kitty? Whatever are you doing here? What's wrong?'

'Binny!' shrieked Kitty, as Binny stepped into the torchlight, rather dirty and with cobwebs in her hair, but seemingly unharmed. Kitty leaped at her, and threw her arms around her, and some of the dirt from Binny's collar got on Kitty's cheek. 'You idiot!' cried Kitty, stepping back and brushing at her face. 'You're *covered*. Look, I shall never be able to get it off!'

I saw something glisten in the torchlight, just beneath Kitty's eye, and on her hand, but did not say anything. Kitty would never forgive me, I knew. 'What happened? Why are you – why – oh, *Binny*!' cried Kitty. 'Trust you!'

'Trust you!' said Binny, snorting. 'Do stop worrying. I'm quite all right, only bored. And hungry. You don't happen to have a bun I could eat, do you?'

'But what did Una do to you?' I asked. Why was Binny so unharmed and unworried? We had just come to rescue her from a kidnapping. Why was she not more pleased?

'Locked me up, the beast,' said Binny. 'She pulled me over after school and told me she knew I was the one letting out the secrets, and then she dragged me in here.'

'Oh!' squealed Beanie.

'Oh, Binny!' said Kitty.

'But why didn't she kill you?' asked Daisy. Beanie gasped, and Kitty clutched at Binny. 'What?' asked Daisy. 'It's a logical question. Why aren't you dead?'

'Why should I be?' asked Binny, puzzled. 'Look, do you have any buns? Or a biscuit would do.'

Lavinia fumbled in her pocket and pulled out a rather fluffy square of chocolate. 'Here, have this,' she said gruffly.

'Because Una is the murderer!' I said.

'What?' said Binny through a mouthful of chocolate. 'No, she only locked me in because she was worried that the murderer might get to me if she didn't hide me. She pretended to check the tunnel, too, so that the police wouldn't find me. *Una*'s never murdered anyone. What are you talking about?'

And at that moment the door slammed to behind us.

4

Beanie screamed. I saw Kitty clutch at Binny, her torch flashing across the tunnel wall, spinning crazily to light up a grey Deepdean uniform and a prefect's tie. My heart was thudding and my hands were clenched in fists. I felt dizzy and the light from the torch gave me spots in my eyes. But then up went Daisy's torch. She is fearless, like Kipling's 'If' in the flesh, keeping her head where everyone else is losing theirs – and settled on, not Florence, but *Enid*. Her face looked set and determined, and in her hand was one of the bits of metal piping that had been lying in Old Wing.

'I've found you,' said Enid, to Binny.

I gasped in a breath of air and opened my fists. If Una was not the murderer, and Florence was not, and Lettice and Margaret could not be, then – it was Enid, after all.

But Enid could not be the murderer! We had ruled her out. There was not time, and she was too weak to carry everything and hit Elizabeth. Surely! But here we were.

My heart flew and plummeted like something dying. In all the cases Daisy and I have investigated, there have been awful moments, times when I have feared for us, but in that instant I knew that I had never really been afraid for my life before. Enid had cornered us, and she had a weapon. Every nerve in my body felt naked and every bone was water. But Daisy did not lower the torch. She held it up against Enid like a shield, and I felt her free hand brush against mine. I snatched at it, my life jacket. She was shaking.

'Did you kill Elizabeth?' asked Daisy, her voice not betraying her at all.

Enid blinked. 'I'm not about to tell you that,' she said. 'I'm not an idiot.' She shifted the bit of piping in her hand.

'You did, didn't you?' said Daisy. 'You were terrified that Elizabeth would let out your secret. You were stoking the fire at the beginning of the evening, when you saw the rake propped against the wall of the pavilion, and the hockey stick lying beside it. The stick was the perfect weapon, and the rake the perfect cover. You realized you could kill Elizabeth with the hockey stick, get rid of it on the fire and plant the rake beside her, and everyone would think it was an accident. You – oh! – you were still stoking the fire when the fireworks began going off, you made sure of that. You used your last journey to pick up the rake and the stick with some other bits of wood, then you walked up behind Elizabeth and you hit her with the stick. You put down the rake, pulled the Scandal Book out of her pocket, and went towards the fire to throw the book and the stick on it. But the book fell out of your hand, and you couldn't find it in the dark, and then the stick didn't burn properly – the fire had died down when Lettice didn't stoke it.'

I saw Enid twitch, and knew that it was most important that we did not stop talking, did not give her a moment's silence to gather herself and decide what to do.

'Is that how you found the book?' I asked Binny.

'I trod on it,' said Binny, 'just after the fireworks. I looked down and there it was. I picked it up and began to read through it, and then I realized what dynamite it was. Why, it was marvellous, spreading those secrets and seeing the Big Girls afraid for once!'

'You little beast,' said Kitty faintly. I knew she understood that I was stalling for time. Enid might be small, but she was older, and she had a weapon, while we were all defenceless. And if she had murdered Elizabeth, she must be less weak than she pretended.

'Did you know it was Binny letting out the secrets?' I asked Enid. 'Before now, I mean?'

'I had an idea,' said Enid. 'I thought it must be a third former. That's why I came back to House on Thursday, to search their dorm. But I never found the book, and then Binny vanished.'

I remembered meeting Enid in the main hallway and felt cold. We had been so close without knowing it!

'How did you manage to hit Elizabeth?' I asked, because I had been wondering about that as well. 'With the rake and the wood in your hands, how were you strong enough?'

'I put them down, of course,' said Enid, sneering. 'I hit her two-handed. But I never told you that. And I'm stronger than I look. You believed me when I said I was weak, didn't you? Everyone does.'

I felt myself fizz, and Daisy squeezed my hand.

'And you know why Enid did it, Binny?' I asked. 'You must, if you had the book. She's been cheating on tests, so she'll get into Oxford.'

'That's not true!' said Enid sharply, and I knew that had been the wrong thing to say. My stomach curled. 'You can't prove it!'

'What do you mean?' asked Binny. 'That secret's not in the book. None of the prefects' secrets are. It was terribly frustrating – I couldn't spread them! I wish I could have, I would have done them first. Do you know, I think that's what Una thought as well, that I was going to reveal her secret. I told her I didn't have it. It must have just been in Elizabeth's head.'

So Elizabeth, for all her faults, had, in her own strange way, kept her followers' secrets. She might have been going to tell them to Miss Barnard, but she had not written them down. It made me, just for a moment, feel kindly towards her.

Then I looked at Enid's face. It was horrified, enraged, confused – and then excited. I saw what she was thinking. If the secret was not written down, then only we knew it. And that meant that we were in terrible danger.

She stepped forward. 'You little beasts!' she said. 'I've been studying so hard. My parents won't know what to do if I don't get in. They've been coaching me for years. I'm their hope. They've saved and saved, and didn't send my little sister to a good school so that I had the best chance. And Elizabeth was going to ruin everything. I couldn't let her do it, and you won't either!'

'Wait!' said Daisy quickly. 'Don't be an idiot.'

'I think I'm being perfectly sensible,' snarled Enid, and she raised her arm.

With a yelp, something darted past me.

'NO!' shrieked Beanie, and before any of us could stop her, before any of us even knew what she was doing, she had hurled herself on Enid. 'YOU SHAN'T HURT MY FRIENDS!' she screamed, and Enid's hand came down.

I screamed too, and so did Kitty. Lavinia bellowed. Daisy dropped the torch, and there was a loud bang. I could not see what was happening – everything was rushing and confused, and my head was pounding. What would we do if Beanie was hurt? Someone was yelling, someone else was sobbing, and then light burst out again, in a long beam from a torch that swung around, catching all our faces. Enid was gone – no, she was on the floor, and someone was kneeling over her, pulling her arms behind her back. I knew that greatcoat, and that hat. It was the Inspector.

'Don't move!' he said fiercely to Enid. 'That's enough of that! Now, now, stop!'

But if the Inspector was here, who was holding the torch? And how had he known to come? How was he here to save us?

The torch dipped, and at last I saw who was behind it. It was Miss Barnard, and with her was a small figure I knew very well.

'Hello,' said Binny's friend, Martha, shyly. 'I found you!'

5

'Beanie!' cried Kitty, and I saw that Beanie was on the floor as well, in a little crumpled heap. My heart lurched as Kitty rushed to her. She rolled her over, and for a moment I felt dizzy again. Beanie was quite white, and she flopped in Kitty's arms.

Kitty shook her, and there was an endless, awful moment. Then Beanie let out a soft little sigh and blinked her eyes open.

'Oh,' she said. '*Oh*. What happened?'

'You're not dead, Beans?' said Kitty, gulping.

'Of course not!' said Beanie. '*Ow*, my head hurts. Why are you crying?'

We all piled on her, and for a moment everything else was forgotten.

'Girls!' said Miss Barnard sharply. 'Take care! Don't crowd her.'

'I'm all right!' said Beanie. 'Only . . . my head does hurt.'

The Inspector had Enid firmly in his grip now, handcuffed and pinned against the tunnel wall. He shared a glance with Miss Barnard, and then she turned to us. 'Miss Martineau may have concussion. Miss Freebody – both of you – you will accompany her to San at once. Tell Mrs Minn I sent you. Good grief, Binny Freebody, do you know you've had the whole school, and the police, looking for you?'

Binny smirked.

'Una locked her in to keep her safe,' I said. 'She couldn't get out!' I could hardly believe I was defending Binny, but then, I could hardly believe any of what had just happened.

'You have all behaved in a most shocking way,' said Miss Barnard. 'I shall have words with you tomorrow. Miss Freebody, take your sister and Miss Martineau and *go*! You others, you can go with them. I want you all out of this place at once.'

'Not us!' protested Daisy. 'Hazel and I need to speak to the Inspector!'

'Absolutely not,' snapped Miss Barnard.

'Miss Barnard,' said the Inspector, 'could they stay for a moment? I would like a brief word with them.'

I could see that Miss Barnard was scowling. 'Inspector!' she said unhappily.

'They were helpful to me before,' said the Inspector. 'I have reason to believe that they may be so again.'

Miss Barnard paused, and then she sighed. 'Oh, very well,' she said. Lavinia craned backwards hopefully. 'Not you, Temple! To San, immediately!'

Lavinia led Binny, Kitty, Martha and Beanie out of the tunnel, but although I knew that she was cross not to be staying with us, I had never seen her so proud of herself before. Perhaps detecting agreed with her after all.

Once the others were gone, the Inspector led me, Daisy, Enid and Miss Barnard out of the tunnel too, and into the deserted Hall. I stared up at the tiers of seats around us, the dim vaulted ceiling far above, and the panels painted with vague murals of enormous women who glared down at us as though we were slightly disappointing. When the Inspector spoke, the whole room echoed.

'So,' he said as Miss Barnard looked on. 'Explain yourselves, girls.'

6

Daisy explained our case, in a rush, and I put in all the bits that she forgot (as usual, Daisy gets excited about the end of a case, and forgets to be entirely scientific). We explained how Elizabeth's death had been a murder, not an accident, how Enid had killed her with the hockey stick, but left the rake next to her for cover. She had tried to destroy the stick later, but then, when it was discovered, tried to cover her tracks further by writing down Margaret's secret and signing it with Florence's name. The Inspector looked more and more serious, and Miss Barnard gasped in confusion and horror. She could not stop looking at Enid.

I tried not to. Enid had stopped struggling, and was sitting quite quietly on a chair, but she was looking at us with a despairing stare and it made my heart stumble. This is always the way of it – knowing who the murderer is does not make them a different person, but what they have done somehow overlays who they are, and turns them quite horrible. I had been wrong. I was not like Enid at all. I may not be a heroine, but I would never hurt one of my friends, not deliberately. Many things matter more to me than being good at lessons.

I imagined the moment: Enid raising the hockey stick in both hands and then bringing it crashing down on Elizabeth's head. She must have been horribly afraid, to plan such a thing and then carry it out. But then, that was what Elizabeth had done to everyone: trapped them, so they could not escape. It was awful that this was the only way Enid felt she could be free. And now her secret would be out anyway.

'Elizabeth was going to tell everyone she was a cheat,' I said to the Inspector. 'She wouldn't have been able to go to university, and her parents told her she had to.'

Daisy snorted. 'Imagine!' she said. 'Doing a murder for *that*!'

'It wasn't just that!' cried Enid suddenly. 'It was – it was everything. I had to get in, don't you see? Daddy would have never forgiven me. My life wouldn't have been worth anything.'

'Indeed,' said the Inspector. 'It certainly won't, now.'

I felt dreadful, all over again.

'In this case,' said Inspector Priestley to us, smiling rather, 'I must say I am rather glad that you honourably decided to break into school property in the dead of night. You recovered a missing person and revealed a murderer. As always, I must congratulate you, although as always, I must also point out that you have been fearfully foolish.'

'*Fearfully* foolish!' echoed Miss Barnard. 'Why did you not think to tell anyone where you were going?'

'We told the shrimps!' said Daisy. 'See? That's how you know.'

'We might not have done,' said the Inspector. 'I only happened to come into the house to speak to your Matron. I was accosted by young Miss Grey, who seemed desperate to talk to me. She told me that you had escaped House, and where you were going, and that she had seen Enid follow you. I telephoned Miss Barnard immediately, and rushed down to find you myself. You ought to congratulate Miss Grey. I believe she solved the case before any of you.'

'Huh!' said Daisy. 'Don't be ridiculous. We knew exactly what had happened.'

'Did you?' asked the Inspector. 'According to Miss Grey, you were sure that the culprit was Una Dichmann, but Miss Grey was terribly worried, because she could not work out why, if that was so, it was Enid Gaines who had crept out after you.'

'A lucky guess,' said Daisy airily. 'And we had everything in hand. Even if you had not appeared, we would have triumphed.'

'Daisy!' I said. 'That isn't true!'

'It's close enough!' said Daisy. 'Anyway, we've solved the case now.'

'Miss Martineau was hurt very severely,' said Miss Barnard sternly.

'I can't control the idiotic things my assistants do!' said Daisy crossly. 'I didn't ask her to throw herself on Enid like that!'

'I assume she thought she was helping you,' said Miss Barnard.

'She was trying to be brave,' I said. 'Will she be all right?'

'I'm sure she will,' said Inspector Priestley. 'From experience I'd say that she has very mild concussion, at worst. The blow glanced off her, it was not a direct hit. Nurse Minn will sort her out.'

'And will you bring back Jones?' Daisy asked Miss Barnard. 'He's innocent! It was murder, not an accident, so he can't have had anything to do with it.'

Miss Barnard sighed. 'I will,' she said. 'And I will give him my full apologies. Now, if you're ready, you need to go back up to House, if you please. I think your Matron will be missing you.'

'Where will I go?' asked Enid, and she sounded very frightened.

'To the station, with me,' said Inspector Priestley sadly. 'There is work to be done, and a trial to prepare for. Since you have confessed, things should be easy.'

Enid made a gulping noise. 'I'm sorry,' she said softly. 'I had to do it.'

'I'm not sure you did,' said the Inspector. 'Although the judge and jury may see things differently. Now,' he said, turning to us, 'you've been very successful detectives. I'm sorry I ever doubted you, but now it's time for you to be schoolgirls again. Think of it as an elaborate cover. Are you ready?'

Daisy nodded. She turned to me, and I could see she was grinning. 'All right, Hazel?' she asked. 'Let's go and pretend to be ordinary.'

7

Matron was quite furious, of course, and she could not understand what we had all been doing down at school – 'and in a dirty tunnel, too!' she cried. We both got rather stern slaps about the head, and were banished up to the dorm at once. But I think the Inspector and Miss Barnard must have spoken to her after that, because the next day we were given extra pudding at dinner, and Matron rather unexpectedly gave us a hug.

We went to see Beanie in San on Sunday afternoon. Kitty was there, by her bedside, and so were Binny, Lavinia and Martha. 'I'm all right,' said Beanie, blinking up at us from under a large white bandage wrapped around her head.

'She's got an awful bruise,' said Binny gleefully. 'It's lovely. All I've got are scratches from the tunnel, it's terribly dull. It was quite a boring kidnapping, really.

Una brought me food and drink, and I had a blanket to sleep on. It was just like camping!'

I remembered the apple in Una's bag. She really had been trying to look after Binny.

'You beast. Beanie nearly died!' said Kitty, who was able to be cross with Binny again, now she was safe.

'I didn't!' said Beanie.

'Whatever were you thinking?' Daisy said.

'I didn't think,' said Beanie, hanging her head. 'I'm sorry, Daisy. I only – I didn't want any of you hurt. You're my friends, and I couldn't bear it if something happened to any of you.'

'*Beans!*' said Kitty, and she threw her arms around her. Daisy grinned at me, and then we hurled ourselves on top of Kitty. Lavinia followed, and then Beanie was buried under all of us, squealing. I knew then that we could not be like the Five, not for anything. We were real friends, and whatever happened we would never turn against each other.

Enid was taken away to the police station, and from there on up to London, but of course it was all around the school by Monday morning. 'Enid killed Elizabeth!' went whispering all around the halls and corridors, and I heard some utterly awful stories about what exactly had happened, which were both less and more dreadful than the truth. I knew that Miss Barnard was tensed for the mothers and fathers to descend on her, and in fact a few girls were pulled out of the school that week. Deepdean seemed dangerous again, even more so now that girls had been bumping each other off, but the fact that Enid had already been caught saved us all, I think. The danger was gone before it was known, and so it was past, not present.

Jones was back, with no fuss, a week later. He was merely there one day, raking the winter beds. He raised a hand to us, and smiled crookedly at Daisy, and went back to his weeding. Daisy sighed contentedly, and I knew what she meant – that the school was as it should be again.

It was true that Deepdean felt different. The corridors were freer, I heard laughter again, and even the mistresses smiled. The remaining members of the Five were changed as well. I am not sure they were *friends*, even now, but they were together. What had happened had bent them into a new shape, and that mattered. They were not cruel to the younger years any more, they were careful, as though they knew what might happen to them. We still had the power as much as they did.

Our dorm really was closer than ever. Solving the case together had changed something between us, too. Daisy and I did not have to hide the detective side of ourselves at all, and it felt wonderful. Daisy looked at Beanie, Kitty and Lavinia in a new way – they had all finally proved themselves, and could truly be trusted. Kitty, who is quite clever with her hands, made us all Detective Society badges, which we wore pinned to the underside of our ties, and the Inspector sent us the most enormous parcel. When we unwrapped it, it was filled with a delicious spread: cakes and biscuits and five different sorts of jam. We had the most marvellous midnight feast – there was so much that we could even invite Charlotte, Binny, Betsy, Emily and Martha to join in. If this was the new Deepdean, I thought, as Lavinia and Binny tried to outdo each other in the number of bits of cake they could eat at once, and Beanie and Martha fed biscuit crumbs to Chutney the dormouse (he had made his way back to Beanie's tuck box a week after Elizabeth's murder, and had been living there very happily ever since), I liked it very much.

8

The outcome of the mystery for the Five was more mixed. What exactly Una had done in the tunnel was slightly blurry, but it was understood that she had tried to protect Binny, and for that she became Head Girl. She stopped ordering the younger girls about, and instead spent most of her time hovering about near the pigeonholes in the House hallway. There was word that her family had decided to come to England – they were on their way, but the journey out of Germany was difficult. I crossed my fingers for them.

Although Margaret knew that we had not been behind the spreading of her secret, she resigned as prefect. That was a nasty little after-effect of Elizabeth. For a while, in fact, we barely saw her. She kept herself to herself, and I knew that what had been discovered about her had damaged her. But one day, towards the end of term, I turned a corner at House quickly, and almost walked into her and Astrid together. My eye only caught the end of it, but I was sure I saw Margaret dropping Astrid's hand, and both of them turning away with blushes in their cheeks. I was glad.

'Margaret—' I said to Daisy later, and she said, 'Shush, Hazel! Ask no questions.' So Daisy knew – of course she did. We did not speak about it after that.

Florence did not come back to school. She was sent away to convalesce. Her dreams of the Games were quite over. Lettice, though, stayed. She withdrew, and became more quiet, but I saw that she had begun to eat a little more at meal times, and sometimes I even saw her smile. She would still be presented at Court in January, and her dress was nearly ready.

I had sent Alexander an explanation of everything that had happened, and how we had solved the case, and a week before the end of term I got a letter back.

Weston School, Thursday 28th November

Dear Hazel,

I am so glad you solved the case! I never guessed who it was. I thought it would be Florence. George says he did know it was Enid, but George sometimes doesn't know what he's talking about. Is Daisy happy now that it's all over?

Hazel, I've had an idea. George's brother goes to John's, in Cambridge, and he's going to stay with him this Christmas hols. Father wants me to go with him, so I can see what it is like (he was at Trinity, and he wants me to do the same), and I thought – Daisy's brother is at Maudlin, isn't he? Well, could she (and you of course) manage to go visit him at the same time? Would her parents allow it? If so, we could all be in Cambridge for Christmas! Wouldn't that be spiffing? Say you'll at least try – will you?

Write back as soon as you can,

Alexander

'Daisy,' I said, trying to stop my heart galloping inside my chest and my cheeks blushing. 'Alexander wants us to come to Cambridge this hols.'

Daisy frowned. 'He's very forward,' she said. 'Of course, he wants to see me.'

I bit the inside of my cheek so hard that my eyes stung.

'Not that he doesn't like you, Hazel,' Daisy went on. 'Of course he does! Well, let me think – oh! – I've got a great-aunt at St Lucy's who we could stay with. We don't talk about her much, she's awfully dull.'

'What about your parents?' I asked, and Daisy got the awful look on her face she always has when I mention them.

'I don't see how they'd be in a position to mind,' she said. 'No, the problem is you.'

'My father wouldn't mind either!' I said. 'Cambridge is all about learning. He'd be pleased, if we were chaperoned.'

'We could bring Hetty again,' said Daisy. 'Ooh, Hazel! This might be a rather good plan, now that I think of it!'

I sent off a telegram to my father, and the response came back:

```
YES  STOP  IF  CHAPERONED  STOP  BE
CAREFUL  STOP  NO  MURDERS
```

Daisy and I squealed when we saw it. We were going to Cambridge. We would see Alexander, and meet George, and have the most marvellous fun. It would be the perfect antidote to this term.

And with all of us there together, who knew what might happen?

Daisy's Guide to Deepdean

Hazel has once again asked me to write some explanations for the words she has used in this casebook. I think most of the words she has chosen are perfectly obvious — but, if you are not lucky enough to go to Deepdean, I suppose you might not understand them. If this is the case, I am sorry for you.

- **Big Girl** – the oldest girls in the school. They are very remote and important.

- **Bunbreak** – we have this every school morning at 11. We are given biscuits or buns and allowed to run about outside for ten minutes exactly. The best bunbreak is on Saturday, when we have squashed-fly biscuits.

- **Camaraderie** – this is a French word that means friendship. There is camaraderie between the Rest of the Detective Society, although Not me because I am President.

- **Chelsea bun** – a lovely sweet bun, with raisins and sticky syrup in it. It is an excellent bunbreak treat.

- **Chump** – an idiot. Someone who does not deserve to be in the Detective Society.

- **Coming out** – this is a party that is held at Court, with the King and Queen. You go if you are eighteen, and ready to be married. I shall go when I am eighteen, I suppose, although I do not intend to be married afterwards.

- **Contraband** – this is something, like a scarf or a bracelet, that you ought not to have by school rules, either because it is not part of the uniform, or because it is jewellery. Most of us wear contraband every day.

- **Corroborating** – this is a detective word that means 'agreeing with'.

- **Crocodile tears** – this means to cry even though you are not really sad.

- **Deportment** – a lesson where you are taught to move and sit and eat like a lady. I love it. Hazel is very bad at it.

- **Dorm** – the room in our boarding house where we live and sleep. Kitty, Beanie and Lavinia are in a dorm with Hazel and me.

- **Exeat** – a special weekend that you have in boarding schools, where your parents can come and take you away from House overnight.

- **Finishing School** – a special school for learning how to be a lady. It is really a whole school for Deportment.

- **House** – the place where we stay during school terms, since we cannot go home.

- **Major/Minor** – if there are two sisters in the same school, they cannot be simply called by their last name. So the older is Major, and the younger is Minor. It is quite obvious, really.

- **Matron** – the woman who is in charge of a boarding house, and looks after us. Our

Matron is quite unpleasant, but I suppose she could be worse.

- **Mistress** – our special Deepdean word for teacher.

- **Pash** – this is a word that means being in love with someone, but politely and not romantically. It is not all right to be in love with another girl, but perfectly acceptable to have a pash on her.

- **Pavilion** – the building on the sports pitch where we change and leave kit.

- **Pax** – this is a Latin word that means 'peace'. It is what you say when you want to be friends with someone again.

- **Pet** – this is another word for angry or bothered.

- **Prefect** – a Big Girl who is allowed to order younger girls about. She is a sort of deputy mistress.

- **San** – the place at school where we go when we are hurt, no matter how small or large the injury is. Our San is run by Mrs Minn, the nurse.

- **Semaphore** – a sign language with flags. You wave them about madly, and spell out the alphabet.

- **Scrimp** – a word for saving money, and being tight with it.

- **Shrimp** – the littlest girls in the school, almost babies, really.

- **Spanish Inquisition** – some rather unpleasant people in Spain who went about torturing their countrymen. It was quite a long time ago, though, so you should not worry about it happening now.

ACKNOWLEDGMENTS

This was a difficult book to get right. Enormous thanks, therefore, to the women who made it what it is: my editor Natalie Doherty and my agent Gemma Cooper. Your kindness and good sense have changed not only my words for the better, but somehow, along the way, myself as well.

Thanks to the others who gave much-needed advice and support during the process, including (but not limited to) Charlie Morris, Non Pratt, Rebecca Waiting, Katie Webber, Katy Watson and the whole loving Team Cooper group.

Thank you to Penguin Random House, my new publishing collective, for supporting my books so incredibly. I couldn't hope for a better author experience! I am so grateful to everyone who has played a part in *Jolly Foul Play*, especially Harriet Venn (publicist extraordinaire), Tom Rawlinson, Annie Moore, Sue Cook, Francesca Dow, Laura Bird, Nina Tara and Annie Eaton.

Thank you also to my wonderful colleagues at Egmont, who have been so supportive and understanding – Sarah, Stella, Hannah, Lins, Lucy, Ali and Lydia, I've loved being part of your team, and I wish it could have been for longer.

There has been one person who has lived *Jolly Foul Play* without ever reading a word of it: thank you to David Maybury for listening to me, believing in me and giving this book its title. And breakfast. Thank you for breakfast.

Daisy and Hazel have had four adventures now, quite a lot more than I was expecting when I first sat down to write *Murder Most Unladylike* four years ago. For that I owe everything to you, my readers. I can't say enough how much I appreciate what you have done, and continue to do, for my series. By talking about my books, and sharing them with your friends, you have made *Jolly Foul Play* possible. I'm quite sure that I have the most intelligent, passionate and interesting fans in the world – talking to you, meeting you, reading your emails and writing you letters has been the most unexpectedly marvellous part of this strange new life of mine. As far as I'm concerned, you're all worthy of being Detective Society members. Thank you.

And finally, thank you to the two people at the beginning of this book: my parents, Kathie Booth Stevens and Robert Stevens. I really was born lucky. I love you.

Robin Stevens
Thanksgiving 2015